A Lily Among Thorns
Janae Dewitt

Janae DeWitt

A Lily Among THORNS

Promises of Hope Series-2

Tate Publishing & *Enterprises*

 TATE PUBLISHING
& Enterprises

"A Lily Among Thorns" by Janae DeWitt
Copyright © 2006 by Janae DeWitt. All rights reserved.

No part of this publication may be reproduced, stored in a retrieval system or transmitted in any way by any means, electronic, mechanical, photocopy, recording or otherwise without the prior permission of the author except as provided by USA copyright law.

Scripture quotations marked "NIV" are taken from the Holy Bible, New International Version ®, Copyright © 1973, 1978, 1984 by International Bible Society. Used by permission of Zondervan Publishing House. All rights reserved.

This novel is a work of fiction. Names, descriptions, entities and incidents included in the story are products of the author's imagination. Any resemblance to actual persons, events and entities is entirely coincidental.

Book design copyright © 2006 by Tate Publishing, LLC. All rights reserved.
Cover design by Sommer Buss
Interiror design by Janae Glass
Author photo by Ray Ward

Published in the United States of America

ISBN: 1-5988670-9-1
06.08.04

Dedication

This is for Joe

"Like a lily among thorns is my darling among the maidens."
—Song of Solomon 2:2 NIV

Prologue

Scores of people filled the city streets. It is midday, contributing to the heightened flow of traffic. The train scheduled to leave from Chicago is ready for departure.

"You're all set to go, sir." The train attendant pivoted on his heel and strolled over to the passenger waiting next in the long, endless line. Blaine Jennings retrieved his ticket and tucked it into his breast pocket. He checked his pocket watch. There was just enough time to say good-bye to one of his most close and trusted friends.

"Well, this is it. The time has come for me to go . . ."

"You're doing the right thing." Jacob Pearce shook Blaine's hand, not oblivious to his trepidation.

"All aboard!"

The train whistle screeched.

"I do want to see my wife again." *My wife . . . Lacey . . .* The words fell off Blaine's tongue and sounded about as unnatural as inviting an Indian into his parlor did.

The line began to move much like herded cattle and Blaine was unwillingly being nudged forward. Rushing his thoughts, rushing his good-bye. This is happening too fast. Jacob held up his hand and waved. He, too, was inadvertently being pushed farther and farther from Blaine.

It was time.

One

It was time.

Sheriff Ed Randall locked up the jail and headed over to Lacey Jennings' restaurant. He'd taken special care of his grooming tonight, making certain that nothing she could do or say would make a difference in what he was planning. He would not think about Lacey's nonchalant and careless moods. It was hard, however, not to breathe a quick prayer on his way across the street. A prayer that she be in a pleasant frame of mind. Easier said than done.

Ed grinned as he spotted a new notice posted on the hostess podium of Lacey's fine establishment: *Wipe your feet or no service.* It was in that moment he heard the sharp tone of her scolding voice. Scolding some undeserved man, he was sure. Upholding his will to not be succumbed by his sudden downcast spirit, Ed ventured in.

"I'll thank you and your friend to leave. This instant!" She demanded.

The victim's friend defended with a jesting smile, "Hold on a minute. He was only being sociable."

"Sociable!" Lacey held a bowl of hot soup she was delivering to another table and poured it gingerly onto his lap. The spirit of jesting was replaced with anger and the man rose, grabbing Lacey by the arm.

"Let go of her."

He was unaware that Ed was standing in the background and complained, "You saw what she did, Sheriff!"

Ed's hand went to his gun. "Get your hand off the lady."

The man gestured to his burning groin, then to Lacey. "You call this wench a lady?"

In all defiance, Lacey stood there. Either complacent to what might have happened if Ed hadn't shown up, or she didn't care. Ed stepped forward, not wanting to exert his authority over the wronged men, but what else could he do? Although not intimidated, the men gathered their belongings. His partner took one last swig of his coffee, "I see how it is. Come on, too many witnesses to take on a man with a badge."

Ed held his stance firmly as they filed by. His eyes closed with shame as he overheard one say, "Got himself wrapped up in that wildcat's skirts for sure."

Lacey raised her chin proudly, or rebelliously, Ed couldn't tell which, and started clearing the table as if nothing happened. The remaining dinner guests resumed eating and all seemed right with the world. The nuisance and trouble was gone and out of sight.

"I don't usually allow men like that in here. You know that, Ed. It's just that I was feeling friendly tonight. My mistake."

He touched her hand, stopping her from picking up a plate. "Lacey . . ." His tone filled with care, worry lined his features.

"What would you have me do? They were saying derogatory things to me all night! And then he . . . he . . ." Her words alarmed him, causing defense for her to rise.

"He what?"

"Oh, never mind!"

"Did they hurt you?"

"No." Realizing she'd exaggerated the whole ordeal, Lacey wanted the discussion over. The man had merely padded her backside as she flirtatiously walked by. He had been taken care of, though, and she did not need the man standing beside her, defending her honor. She almost laughed, but instead whimpered. "Oh, thank goodness you came when you did." Lacey cupped the palm of her hand against his smooth cheek. "Lizette can finish serving. Let's go to Liam's for our nightcap." She caressed his arm down to his hand, and led the way across the foyer to Liam's Landing.

❧

Ed regarded Lacey's intake of sweet rum as normal. Too normal . . . but he would not bring himself to worry about it—yet. His eyes roamed as he admired her attire. Always dressed inappropriately in the sense of where she lived. She would have fit into the best of London societies if she weren't holed up in Lincoln County. Lacey caught his devoted look. She smiled wanly and toyed with her glass, "Tomorrow's the day."

Ah, so that's what she is in a mood over. "The Reverend and Cameron."

"I don't understand why they won't marry here. If they have to get married at all."

"Of course they have to marry. He's the Reverend, for heaven's sake! And I mean that literally."

With the dinner hour passing away, responsible families left town for their homesteads while the rowdy remained. Boisterous laughter and chairs scraping against the floor caused Ed and Lacey to speak louder in order to be heard. It didn't help their raw emotions when the piano keys were struck and Lacey declared haughtily, "Cameron's the dearest friend I have, and my own cousin has seen to it to take her away from me!"

"You know that's not true."

"It isn't, is it? Mark my words, Ed Randall, my cousin will *marry* her back east, then he'll bring her back and not let her see me. Look around! Do you really believe he's going to allow her to visit me in this sinful place? He'll make a preacher's wife out of her!"

Disheartened, Ed stated, "You say *marry* like it's a bad word."

Lacey rose from her seat right along with her temper. "Don't get me started." She bunched up her velvety black skirts and left him. Alone. Kimberly sashayed over to him with a fresh auburn colored drink, which Ed swished down in a gulp.

"I'm gonna need a bottle tonight."

Kimberly ran her silky hands across his shoulders and bent to whisper, her breath was sweet as was her scent. "That woman and her temper leaves you sittin' here by yourself a mighty lot, Sheriff." Her finger cupped his chin, "Care to take out any frustrations?"

His head began to swim a bit, and with glossy eyes he searched her beautiful, prostitute face, "Just . . . the bottle."

"Suit yourself, handsome."

He sulked at Liam's until things settled, what good he would have been as sheriff should the need arise—he did not know and he did not care, not tonight.

An hour later, he stumbled out into a brisk wind. The cool air was refreshing and somewhat sobering. Ed wasn't surprised the evening ended like it had. Tonight's scenario would only be tacked onto others like it. He cursed the ground as he headed home to his shack attached to the jail. It was where he often felt like the prisoner, not only from his physical dwellings, but also from the heartless beauty in plain view everyday. He would never be free from her. He never wanted to be.

The fall weather simmered by the time the sun rose. Maple and oak leaves were strewn about, tethered to this hitching post or that water trough. Lacey awoke with the brightness coming through her windows and with both pity and nausea—for Cameron's carefree life was going to be removed, practically doomed. Lacey took much time preparing herself this morning. As usual, her dress and her hair would be immaculate. Soon, Cameron would knock upon her door and she would do the inevitable, say good-bye. Life would be so dull without Cameron here to keep her company, to stay up late into the night as young girls, talking about life, hopes, and dreams. She was the only person in Lacey's life who loved her for who she was. Of course, the happiness of her friend followed into Lacey's line of thinking. But the apprehension gnawing at her would not comply to go away.

Reverend Andrew Jackson waited in the foyer long enough. If they didn't go to the train station soon, it would leave without them. His bride-to-be was trying his patience by lingering upstairs, crying her eyes out with his cousin. You would think Cameron preferred to stay here rather than go back east and marry him.

His unsure thought was dashed upon seeing Cameron's lovely face emerge at the top of the stairs. Even from the distance that separated them, he could see red blotches patched like raspberries on her forehead and chin—a given when she cried. He sighed in puzzlement; it was a temporary trip, for goodness sake!

"You look beautiful." Andrew stepped up a couple of stairs to intercept her. Lacey looked ready to call him out. "Really, Lacey. We'll be gone for two months, we'll come back and be with you for Christmas."

Lacey ignored him and heeded Cameron with a warning, "Don't mind my Aunt. Remember, do what *you* want, have the wedding that suits you . . ."

"I'll be fine. Andrew's mother will take good care of me. I wish you would come with us." Lacey's adamant refusal to join them was still a fresh hurt, and it showed on Cameron's face. But Lacey would have nothing to do with anyone in her family. With the exception of Andrew, and at times her feelings for him in the area of familial love seemed forced. Finally, Lacey had claimed the restaurant simply couldn't survive without her presence.

"I will miss you," Cameron whispered. "Take it easy on Andrew. I get to come back as Mrs. Jackson!" She stepped aside for them to say their farewells. Managing a tolerable smile, Andrew gave Lacey a peck on the cheek and told her to take care. Cameron wondered with a sigh how long Lacey would keep up her petulant behavior. It wasn't until their wagon was loaded up with luggage and the two were situated in the buckboard that

Lacey complained, "I don't like changes, everything is changing. Nothing is the same." Then she said what no one else would dare, "You won't even wait until Jake comes home."

It was a guard of protection around her heart, it was *their* fault these changes were occurring, and *their* fault that Jake Collins had been gone for so many months that caused her to speak so unfairly. But Lacey was also rebellious and uncompromising, and looked accusingly at both Andrew and Cameron. Andrew stared straight ahead. Lacey inwardly smiled at having set him off, she could tell by the firm setting of his jaw, his way of controlling himself. After all, he is the preacher and must always govern his conduct appropriately.

It was Cameron who answered, "We don't even know when Jake's coming home, if he's coming back. If he is home when we get here, we will do everything we can to have us all together again." She continued in tones a mother would use on a child, and Lacey could swear that Cameron was trying to reassure her own self just as much, "It won't feel as if anything has changed except my name, all right?"

The words rang empty in Lacey's spirit, they were simply untrue. Too much has happened the last year, nothing would ever be the same again; it was fact. Not with Jake and Andrew being childhood friends. Not with Cameron Engel choosing to be with the Reverend over the Bounty Hunter. Even though anyone with eyes knew it was a far better choice . . . a much safer choice. But to marry when Jake was gone? That was not satisfactory.

Lacey raised her chin and relented for the moment—for Cameron's sake, "Good-bye Andrew, have a safe journey and take care of her. I will miss you . . . both."

Andrew tipped his hat, "Stay out of trouble."

"Absolutely, Preacher!" The mischievous look she threw his way told him she would do anything but. He clucked the team and they were off, leaving an unsettled woman behind. Her teasing smile faded and she decided to see what Liam was doing.

She entered Liam's Landing, finding him as usual stacking glasses on the bar counter, preparing the place for a night of gambling and raucous behavior. Lacey knew that she would be in the very midst of it tonight.

Two

Jake Collins slept nearly two days, and he wasn't sorry for it. Four months on the trail, tracking down outlaws in the blistering heat had been no picnic. He owed himself a few slothful days. From his place on the bed, he looked around his room in the farmhouse until he felt its familiarity. He had yet to decide if he would stay—that depended on what the outcome of his trip to town would be. After bathing and putting on fresh clothes, Jake saddled up Hunter, heading first to O'Connors for a long overdue, clean shave and haircut.

His next stop would be something else he'd been deprived of for too long—good food. And the only place to get that was at Lacey's Restaurant. There was no way he would admit the other reason for going to Lacey's, not even to himself. Jake was setting himself up for austere disappointment, seeing how his other reason was on a train to Philadelphia, to marry his childhood friend.

From the corner of her eye, Lacey saw a tall man standing near the hostess podium waiting to be seated. Jake was as handsome as ever. She did not speak a greeting to him, but rather ran into the security of his arms and cried. At last, something the same, something solid and strong that she could tangibly touch.

"I missed you so. Don't you ever leave me again!"

He looked down into Lacey's black eyes, "Now don't start, I ain't promising you anything and you know it. Don't go ruining my supper or crying all over it either, I'm starving and want to eat." He set her back from him, dismissing her. For once, she would do what she was told; she would do anything for Jake.

Ed Randall came to dine and see Lacey, it was the usual hour he did so, and he found Jake sitting at a food-laden table—with his girl.

"Good to see you, Jake!" Ed smacked him hard on the back, "And in one piece at that."

Jake smirked modestly, "Albeit barely. I've had a close call or two."

"Seems to me you've been doing just fine. Even making a name for yourself."

Jake sombered, and his dark eyes roamed the restaurant.

Ed and Lacey exchanged glances, which quickly set off Jake's temper. Not able to wait another minute, he asked sharply, "Where's Cameron?"

Filled with sorrow, Lacey looked upon him, "She and Andrew went back east, to his mother's home in Philadelphia . . . to get married."

There was a moment of uncomfortable silence, then Jake readied to go. But before leaving, he asked contritely, "Isn't that how it should be?"

It wasn't really a question to be answered, but simply a statement for his own ears to hear and pay heed to. Jake headed across the foyer to Liam's saloon, where he planned to drown his feelings with a healthy bottle of strong whiskey. Mack Owens passed him by and was about to bid Jake a howdy, but the irritated scowl upon the bounty hunter's face warned him not to.

Mack turned into the restaurant to pick up his wife of almost a year. "You finished, Lizette? I got the buckboard ready."

Lizette flung an exasperated look Lacey's way, silently pleading if she could go for the evening. Lacey nodded, she would clean up the tables. She was rewarded with a beaming smile and wished she could reciprocate. Even with Ed next to her, the leering sense of foreboding started pulling on the strings of her soul once again—because the man that just walked away from them was a different man. Lacey couldn't place it yet, but something was going to happen, and it was going to affect them all.

❦

The morning was chilly and dew dripped from windowpanes. According to the sheriff, it seemed a bit early for frost to cling to the earthen soil, a sign of a bad winter to come in his opinion. He finished stoking the cook stove and began to percolate his morning coffee when he heard the front door to the jail open and close.

Jake rubbed the back of his neck, "I find myself anxious to get back on the trail." He sat down opposite of Ed's paper-scattered desk. "I'll take some of that coffee when it's brewed."

"You don't mean to go out in the winter do you? Stay on for a while, Lacey misses you."

"She'll get used to me being gone. She's got you, hasn't she?" Jake looked evenly at the sheriff. Before Ed entered Lacey's life, Jake alone took care of her emotional needs. She may be the strongest woman Jake's ever known, but she had needed someone to keep her afloat when her husband up and left her.

Ed replied with usual repetition, "Of course she does. But if she finds out that I'm the one supplying you with jobs that lead to your long absences, she just might wish to see the last of me! Have you ever considered the fact that if something happens to you, she'll never forgive me? You're like a brother to her."

Jake replied with sarcasm, "I'll try and save my skin so you can keep your girl."

"You know what I mean."

He leaned forward, "What's the next job?"

Not easily fooled, Ed raised an eyebrow. "I know it must be hard, seeing Cameron married to Andrew; but you'll need to settle with it sooner or later."

Irritation flashed through Jake's eyes; if Ed hadn't known him better he might have backed off.

"I don't want to talk about her," he said firmly. "And just so you know, it was over long before Andrew ever got involved."

Ed acquiesced and nodded; it might have been over, but Jake very much still cares for Cameron, she was the best thing that ever happened to him. Maybe it would do him good to be away when the newly wed couple returned home. Ed shuffled some papers around on his desk until he found a drawing of the latest wanted man.

"Here he is. Robbed two banks last month, one in Clearwater and the other in Hyndsdale, his name is Joseph Benton."

Jake took the rustled up sheet, immediately smoothing out the crinkled edges for a better view. After studying the crudely drawn image, he commented, "Looks young."

Ed agreed, "Folks say he's nineteen years old."

"He's either a fool, or he wants attention," Jake said regrettably, for he was just a kid.

"I think he's both. You up to giving him the attention he's seeking?"

Jake placed a rolled cigarette in his mouth, "When do I leave?"

"He's headed south, near enough that you shouldn't have to be gone all that long. If things go well," his voice held a hint of challenge.

"I will have everything under control, as usual." He lit his smoke, "I should be back before first snowfall. Before I leave, I'll be needing a decent meal. Comin'?"

"I'll be along shortly."

As Lacey wiped the few remaining tables, she glanced up every so often to see Mack, who was lingering around waiting for Lizette. The pleasure at seeing his wife that used to cross his face was no longer apparent; he was there simply out of the duty of husband. Lacey noticed all too well the signs—the signs of when a man feels like he's either suffocating or losing his rights as a free man. What did men think they could do once they got married anyway? She ferociously swiped at the tabletop till it squeaked.

What she regrettably saw in Mack's eyes was what she saw in her own husbands' once upon a time. Blaine leaving her was the most painful thing she'd ever endured. She'd wanted to die. Since then, however, Lacey rose up in her independence and relished in her own freedoms. Why couldn't there be a guarantee on love? There was nothing that said her love for Ed would eventually disappear, and nothing to say that he would not leave her as Blaine had. Why wouldn't her faithless husband sign the divorce petition and give her the real freedom she deserved? It was not fair. He was free to go and do as he pleased and with whom he pleased to do it with. Blaine has not changed, still as selfish and uncaring as always. She watched the unhappy couple depart. That girl loved Mack and had given him her heart, and he was just going to trample on it because he could. Because he was a man.

After witnessing Mack's boorish behavior, Lacey sat alone in the noisy saloon.

She had plenty of words to say to Mack Owens, but would not do so for Lizette's sake. Instead, she vented her frustrations out to poor Ed, who innocently enough decided to join her.

"I spend more of my time comforting Lizette than working! While that so called husband of hers gambles his life away!"

"I know, Lacey."

"Someone should say something to him. Someone should make him stay home with his wife!"

"I know, Lacey."

She eyed him rashly, "Don't patronize me. Not tonight." She swallowed the last drop of her drink and smacked her full lips together.

"There's nothing that can be done, they're married. It's their own business, not yours, and it's certainly not mine," Ed replied softly.

"See, that's what happens to married people. It's grand enough for a while, but then it starts to fit like an old shoe, it gets stale."

Ed sat forward, "It doesn't have to be like that." He pulled her fingers to his lips. "People go through hard times. The ones that make it get stronger and build families together. It takes work."

"How do you suppose to know that?" Seeing his wounded look, she retracted.

"I'm sorry. But you've never been married; the love fades, it always does."

"Is that why you don't let me talk about it? Why are you so cynical? You know I want you as my wife, stop treating me like a little boy. I know what I'm getting into and what I want. I'm man enough, responsible enough to know that I love you and never want to live a day without you."

"Stop it! You know I can't marry you, and even if I could, didn't you hear anything I just said? Maybe I like things the way they are."

"Did it ever occur to you that I don't? I'm not satisfied visiting your room a few times a week anymore, Lacey. I want more. I want all of it. A house, a baby or two, I *need* you." He wanted to remind her that at one time she had agreed to marry him, but after being with Lacey over the past two years, wisely knew his boundaries and would not push.

She sighed, being the patronizing one at the moment, "I couldn't marry you even if I wanted to."

Ed snatched his hand from hers, as if her cool demeanor burned him; he was hurt and angry. He tossed down his drink and stalked off, leaving Lacey feeling surprisingly vulnerable. In her bitterness over the unjust life she was destined to lead, her thoughts went to Mr. McAffey, the lawyer hired to find her husband. It's been months since receiving his report in regards to Blaine Jennings—who at the time of confrontation with Mr. McAffey said that he would "take divorcing her into consideration." What's to consider? Blaine was found in Chicago of all places, having the time of his life, while she had no choice but to remain in this dreary place to run a restaurant!

Why didn't he sign those papers? Why won't he give me my freedom? Her anger rose remembering the day she heard from the lawyer. When Mr. McAffey returned to check on Blaine's decision, he was gone—checked out of his hotel without a forwarding address. How she hated him!

Now Cameron was gone, Lacey missed her terribly, and even when she returned she wouldn't have her all to herself. In fact, Lacey would hardly see her, and Ed's pitching a fit, and Jake . . . gone again! Oh, how life is so unfair!

In haste Lacey ordered up another drink. No longer was her lover satisfied with the way things were, even that had to change; and Lizette, happy, loving Lizette would be affected by the ruins of marriage. Why was life so cruel?

It hadn't been but an hour when Sheriff Randall returned with a slight, beautiful woman on his arm. Lacey heard the slight jingle of bells above the door and went to help her customer. And her well-composed face faltered for one brief moment at the sight of Ed walking in with another woman. Easily putting on a cryptic smile, Lacey swished her elegant silk skirts toward the couple. Her full lips seemed to be smiling warmly at them, but Ed saw no warmth coming from her fiery eyes . . . eyes that could bewitch any man, any unlucky soul.

"Would you two like a table?" Lacey asked nonchalantly. She'd determined long ago that she would not let a man make a fool of her ever again. Her husband had been one too many. Lacey was slipping with Ed and realized that she needed to, she *must* form that cold, protective wall around her heart once more. This time, not Ed or anyone else would get through the door.

"This lady is in need of a place to stay."

Lacey looked upon "the lady" intently, and quickly surmised from experience that she might have been dealt an unfortunate blow or two in this lifetime.

"Of course, Ed, that's what I own—a hotel."

This woman went to the Sheriff for help; she had gone to *her* Sheriff. Lacey visualized the compassionate young man lending his ear to this sappy woman's problems, and it irritated her immensely.

"Has she any luggage?" Lacey asked impertinently. Ed recognized the coldness and eyed her tiredly. He loved this woman, but he was getting fed up with being treated like a nobody in her life.

"I'll bring what luggage she could gather over soon. I just wanted to make sure that Mrs. Hoffman got settled in."

Lacey looked him over coolly. "Well, she's settled," and with curt words, she dismissed him. After Ed's hesitant departure, Lacey introduced herself. "I'm Lacey Jennings, I own the restaurant and the hotel up there." She pointed out the obvious areas and obliged the woman for a short tour, "And over there is Liam's Landing, the best saloon in town."

"My name is Bethany Hoffman. I'd like to go to my room if it's at all possible."

Lacey saw tears forming in her guest's hurting eyes and almost felt regret for her rough course of action—almost.

"Right this way."

After dropping off Bethany's small carpetbag and suitcase, Ed questioned Lacey until he was confident that his charge was safely in her room. Lacey inquired as to what the circumstance was, and something in the sound of her words grated on Ed. His reply was, "It's nothing for you to be concerned about."

For some reason, he walked angrily out the door.

Three

Miserable solitude was a new feeling for the belle of Lincoln County, and to defy this unnatural circumstance, Lacey made her way throughout town as if she owned it. Three weeks was a long time for Lacey Jennings not to have a social outlet, a friend to visit, or any incoming letters. Doubting, but hoping just the same to receive something from Cameron, or anyone for that matter, she reached the crude post office. Lacey nearly burst with excitement after the postman handed her a small stack of mail. Flipping through the letters, she found one from her aunt, and more importantly, another from Cameron. She wanted to tear it open right there in the middle of the crowded boardwalk but governed her enthusiasm. She would make herself wait to read it thoroughly, privately, in her bedroom. Finally, she reached the hotel and haphazardly answered Lizette's question about the lunch menu and dashed up the stairs to her room, where she flung off her shawl and sat in the chaise lounge under the cool window.

    Dearest Lacey,
    I pray this letter finds you well. I have been introduced to a whole new world out here. But as busy and exciting as it has been, I have to admit I prefer the quiet of my home in Kansas. Your aunt is not at all "staunch and pious" (as you might say). She has been nothing but loving and pleasant to me.
    I wish you were here! Mother Grace, she insists on my calling her by that name, is planning the most elaborate wedding, and it makes me uncomfortable at times. I feel so undeserving. Too much attention has been drawn to me these past weeks, and you know I find such circumstances undesirable. Never the less, my purpose is to make Andrew happy, and he seems to be so much so here among his friends and family. We have had numerous social events to attend, which is where I see that Andrew has a lot of admirers, both male and female. I get the feeling by a few of the "ladies" that I'm not in the same class as their beloved bachelor. They are right, which is why I'm so fortunate that he has set his eyes on me. I do hope you're well, and remember to be kind to your Sheriff and to Lizette. Don't let your precious temper cause you any trouble. I miss you and will be home after Thanksgiving.
    With Love,
    Cameron Engel
    Post Script: Our wedding is to take place in just ten day's time . . . I wish you could see my dress, dear friend, it's ridiculously beautiful.

Lacey sighed, "'Mother Grace,' how shamefully absurd! Andrew Jackson, you'd best bring Cameron back home! I couldn't bear it if you took her away from me."

Lacey's complaints and mutterings increased and began to set her off in a strange mood lined with self-pity and resentment. She could not help but be happy for Cameron, even though her own life was so utterly desolate at the moment. Ed is being withdrawn. Lizette does nothing more than mope about, leaving Lacey to remind her employee to put on a pleasant face for her customers and, of course, Jake . . . Lacey buried her face in the pillow and took a long, melancholic, lazy, midday nap.

Ed was surprised to see Jake's horses tethered so soon in front of the jail. It had only been a couple of weeks since he left to find Joseph Benton. He leapt up the steps onto the boardwalk and opened his office door to find Jake sitting there ever so smugly, waiting for him. "I took the liberty of locking up the young fellow myself, seeing as how you weren't here."

Ed's mood was sullen and didn't match up to Jake's teasing tone.

"You're back soon. He gave you no trouble then?" Ed removed his gun belt and set it on his desk before sitting down behind it. He ran his hands briskly up and down the sides of his face. He looked tired.

"Not at all, in fact, I wish they were all as untroublesome as him. Joseph's young; I can see he feels bad. If he's directed right, I'm willing to bet he won't be robbing any more banks. In the near future at least." Jake smiled easy and sat back comfortably. "You'll find the bank's money in your top drawer there." He thrust his chin toward the desk. Ed opened the drawer and nodded his confirmation. "I'll wire Hyndsdale for your pay."

"Sounds good." Jake hadn't decided if he wanted to know or not, but gave in and asked anyway, "What's going on, Ed? You're not yourself tonight."

"A woman stumbled upon my doorstep. Her name's Bethany Hoffman. She was on a stagecoach recently that was attacked and robbed."

"She the only survivor?"

"She was . . . mishandled, a man shot and killed her husband as he went to save her. He witnessed his own wife being . . . I couldn't imagine! Out of five passengers and two drivers, yes, she's the only survivor."

Malevolent acts such as these were eating at Ed more than he thought possible, even though he knew men could be cruel and merciless. His thoughts turned to the wavering relationship he was having with

Lacey. It seemed as of late that this life affected him like a heavy weight—an anchor that was sinking fast. What *was* his purpose in life? No one man could stop all of the vile, evil things that transpired in this world. As sheriff, the only conceivable thought was to protect this town to the best of his ability. So why did he feel so inadequate? Jake's movement interrupted his wanderings, and he nodded as Jake told him to get some rest, and something to the effect of how haggard looking he was. When the front door closed, Ed went to the window. He could see the hotel clearly with lanterns lighting up every room. He thought about Lacey and what she was doing at the moment.

Her restaurant buzzed alive with people. At least Lacey could be content with her business; the revenue increased with the extended agreeable weather. It was cold for sure, but not enough to keep people contained in their cabins. There would be plenty of cabin fever once the snow fell. Lacey grabbed a pot of fresh brewed coffee, and with brief irritation, thought about Bethany Hoffman. She could only guess that she was grieving over something or someone. Lacey could not seem to reach out to her and was surprised to have been declined what she thought to be a generous offer. She asked Bethany to work for her and offered a more than satisfactory pay, not to mention room and board.

Lacey was not one to be shocked or taken aback easily, but this is exactly what she was when Bethany Hoffman, demure, young, beautiful Bethany, checked in her key, went straight across the foyer and asked *Liam* for a job. Liam! She would rather be a soiled dove than to work for Lacey Jennings. So be it! Lacey could have held onto the insult, but decided to spend her energy on people she actually cared about. A longing to make amends with Ed began to toil with Lacey's once resolute position. She reasoned she might accomplish this if only for gaining the upper hand again. She could hardly believe that her persistence of holding him at arm's length might actually bear out consequences against her. Lacey had not given him enough credit and assumed he would be like all of her past love struck lovers and come running. But then again, she was not as young as she used to be. Lacey and her determination would make him see that he needed her, that he still wanted her. She smiled with mild flirtation at a table surrounded by several cowboys and refilled their coffee. "How about some fresh apple pie?"

It was going to be a long night.

Liam Jamison arrived at his saloon with an armful of freshly cleaned linen. He thought he was alone as he made his way to deposit them behind the counter. As he bent down, his eye caught the slight figure sitting alone at the piano. Bethany was in a daze; Liam didn't even think she was aware of his presence until she said, "Morning, Liam."

He cleared his throat, "Morning. Is there anything I can get for you?"

She shook her head and continued touching the keys on the piano in a ghostly manner, barely touching each one with her fingertips. No notes escaped from them. Like herself, her body could be touched and used and displayed for its fine looks, but no one could touch the core of her, nor produce any feeling; she was what she was—empty.

Liam eyed her with curious concern; she must have been a fine lady at one time. He perceived this by the way she carried herself, holding her head high with subtlety. He didn't ask his ladies about their past, if they asked him for a job, and they had looks enough to entertain the men that poured through his place; it was theirs. He didn't need to be involved with them in any capacity other than handing over to them their share of money.

Bethany continued her eerie composure at the piano and asked, "It's Thanksgiving tomorrow, is it not?"

Liam pulled out a keg of beer from the backroom and heaved it without effort onto the counter, "It is. Don't worry, you girls don't work, we'll shut down. No wives worth anything would let their husbands come to gamble anyway. That includes my own wife." He smiled slightly, "She makes me go to her folks' house. Something I only do twice a year. Thanksgiving and Christmas."

Bethany gave him her attention for a moment; her green eyes met his, "I'm glad we're closed, it should be a day for families to gather and be . . . thankful." She closed the piano lid gently and walked sedately up the back stairs, stairs that took women to their rooms of "entertainment." Stairs that were not meant for Bethany Hoffman to set foot on. Liam watched her and compassion began to stir in his belly. He reminded himself he couldn't afford to care in this business and tied on his apron in haste. For some reason, he did not wish to be in the saloon at the moment and went to the cellar to take inventory.

Her spacious room was quiet. Solace was what Lacey was searching for this morning, and this was the only place she could find it. She walked over to her window that overlooked the main street of town. Although the autumn colored leaves were scarce, some found their way to and were scattered about the dirt road. Men and their sons loaded up wagons with food, household, and farm supplies to see them through winter, which was speculated to come hard and fast. Lacey watched people pass by. In her eyes everyone seemed happy, not a care in the world. Why did she feel as if her world was going to crumble? She wanted to shake the feelings of dread that crept up her spine every so often. Too often. She poured herself some brandy and sat in silence where her uncomfortable thoughts echoed from wall to wall. She was alone, and she missed Ed's presence. Soon she would need to swallow her pride and make things right between them. If it wasn't too late. She would make herself presentable, make herself look like she didn't feel, didn't care. Lacey chose the emerald green gown. With her raven black hair, she would appear elegant first, then confident and charming—in spite of herself.

When Jake entered the saloon later that afternoon, he took notice straight away of Lacey, looking out of place among the men surrounding her—with her exquisite gown and stylish hat. If a man was smart and he looked into her large, dark eyes, he would see things very differently. If anyone could get away with having two personalities, it was Lacey Jennings. A great big heart of gold when she wanted, or, if you were unfortunate enough to be an enemy, she turned like the flip of a coin into a cold viper that could poison you with words. When she saw Jake, she rose and rushed into his arms.

He held her at arm's length, "You'd better stop acting like a pining forsaken lover or you're gonna start the gossips." He smiled and kissed her cheek.

"You know I care not a fig of what people think of me, Jake Collins." The eyes of which he was just dwelling on cruised over him roughly and she said, "You look miserable!"

"Thanks, I always know where to come when I need a compliment."

Lacey frowned; he truly did look different. His broad shoulders were sunken, some of his masculine weight had fallen away, leaving him too thin. In her opinion, he used to be the most handsome man around. Now he just looked . . . beaten. Lacey hid her thoughts well and put on a charming smile. She slid her hand into his, "Let's start our own game of cards, shall we?"

The night wore on in the smoke filled room; bawdy piano playing and drinks were being carried from table to table by scantily clad dressed women. Jake knew Kimberly and Violet, and had even enjoyed their company in the past, but that was before Cameron. It was the new woman who caught his attention.

"Her name's Bethany, she's the one from the stage." Lacey followed his look. She snorted unbecomingly, "She prefers to prostitute herself instead of working in the restaurant."

A crooked smile spread across Jake's lips; not many people went against Lacey's suggestions, advice, or opinion. It would be good for Lacey if she's to have finally met her match. The evening was young in Lacey's eyes, and she collected winnings time and again. Jake looked at her and shook his head in mock disgust as she pulled more of his money toward her bosom.

She pursed her seductive lips together, "Well, you're not trying very hard, Jake. You and these two gentlemen here seem to have other things on your minds. Maybe I should find some new company?"

"Oh, no you don't! I'm not giving up that easily, deal those cards again, woman." One man retreated from his seat while the other said, "I'm still here, broke, but still here."

Jake laughed and took the offered shot of whiskey Kimberly held out to him. "Just put it on Lacey's tab." He winked at her. Kimberly let her gaze linger on him; her look was longing. Lacey rolled her eyes. Every woman in this place fancied herself in love with Jake Collins and counted it an honor to be chosen. But they had all given up when he took up with Cameron, and because they all adored her, it was easier to bear his absence. Now it was Cameron who was absent, and Kimberly decided to seize the moment. Jake looked away. Kimberly took the rebuff in stride and passed out the remaining drinks. She chatted with Lacey a few moments before Liam called to her. A gentleman was requesting her services for the night, and she had no choice but to accept. She linked her arm through his and said those false, flattering words that she was paid to say.

Mack came in just then without Lizette. There were three things for him to do in a saloon—gamble, drink, and be a good-for-nothing husband. Without realizing it, Lacey came to despise the man. Mack made his place at a table next to hers.

Conceit entered into the volume of Lacey's words, "I'm sorry, I know I owe you all a game, but I've lost my appetite for playing." With the grace of her petite body, Lacey excused herself from the table and went to her room.

The other fellow shrugged, "I guess it's for the best. My wife's gonna have words with me anyway. I best get home and get an earful of them now while I'm drunk."

He laughed and grabbed his coat from the rack by the door, and when he opened it, a cool rush of air bolstered in and snowflakes scattered across the entrance of the foyer. Jake remained alone at his table—then tossed back his drink and decided to see what was on Lacey's mind. Why did her mood change when she saw Mack? By the way, where was Ed? Jake took the stairs in two and halted in front of what used to be Cameron's door. He put out his hand to touch it, as if he could remember being there once upon a time. Loud laughter coming from downstairs brought him from his reverie, and he rapped on Lacey's door. She was in the middle of changing her clothes but opened the door anyway. "Lacey! Have you no shame?" She smiled and backed up so he could enter.

"You're just in time. I need help with these buttons."

"But you didn't even know who was knocking. What's the matter with you anyway?"

She ignored him and turned her back to him, lifting up her hair, exposing her slender neck. "I just don't care for how Mack is treating Lizette, that's all."

"Because he's playing cards?"

"Oh, you wouldn't understand!"

He struggled with her buttons, "These are pesky little things. How do you expect me to get these undone?"

Lacey turned her face slightly; he looked upon her perfect profile. "I thought you were an expert at these sorts of things, Jake Collins," she teased.

"Very funny." He swore, "I'm gonna tear them if you don't shut up."

Her laughter cut into the air as Ed opened the door.

"Perfect timing, Sheriff, *you* can do this." Jake gave up willfully. He sat down on a cushioned chair and kicked his booted feet onto the ottoman in front of it.

Ed paused for a moment, and Lacey said with irritation, "Come on, Ed, I don't want to be in this all night!" The three have always been close, spending many a night in this room playing cards in the peace and quiet. They ate together, drank together, and laughed together. As innocent as Ed knew this scenario was, there was just something not quite right about Jake seeing his woman change her clothes.

He couldn't help himself. "I'd like for you to leave while Lacey changes. And if you don't mind, I also want to be alone with her after that." Ed had never been jealous of them before and knew he had no right to be now. Still, he couldn't help but talk to Jake through clenched teeth as if he was just tolerating his presence.

Lacey spoke harshly, "Who do you think you are ordering Jake around?"

Jake stood up in a flash. "No, it's fine. You're right, I didn't think." He held out his hand for Ed to shake. Slightly embarrassed, Ed accepted and said, "I was out of line."

"Nothing to worry about. I'll see you two in the morning."

Lacey waited until he was gone then jerked away from Ed, "What was that all about? He was helping me with my buttons. You know just as well as he does that I would have finished changing in the other room!"

"I *don't* know that! I don't even know where we stand anymore! It seems you could care less about me and my life and what I'm doing. I was just at the Appleton's farm breaking up a fight between their boy and the Clarke's boy. I nearly got shot! It's a good thing Ronnie doesn't know how to shoot, or I might be dead for all you care! I come here and see Jake's hands all over your backside and you . . . forget it."

"And I what?"

"You don't even look at me like you used to. What exactly do I mean to you? I need to know—am I wasting my time?"

The hurt in his eyes actually touched her. She didn't know anything anymore. She was surprised to feel remorse, something she rarely felt. Lacey turned her face up and looked into Ed's eyes, something she had not done in a long while. It meant surrender to look into someone's eyes. He risked rejection and kissed her softly. When her hands came up and around his neck, he moaned a guttural sound of relief. He did not want to lose her, but he could only take so much hurt and pain. If she had not responded, he would not have come back to her.

The next evening appeared to everyone else eating at Lacey's to be a regular night of fine dining. The snow was not enough to keep patrons at home, most wanting to be out as long as possible before the dreaded cabin fever began. But agitation progressed throughout Lacey and she did not know why.

"Need some help tonight?"

Lacey whirled around, "Cameron!"

Andrew wisely stood out of harm's way while his wife and cousin nearly crashed into each other, hugging and unleashing cries of joy. He laughed out loud at the sight and said to Cameron, "And to think you were considered a lady just last week."

"Oh, you!" Lacey slapped his shoulder with the napkin she was folding.

"Looks like we made it back just in time. Starting to snow pretty good out there."

Andrew made himself comfortable at a table. "My mother sends her greetings to you," he said impishly, and he leaned back to observe her reply.

Lacey cocked her head to one side, "She did, did she? And did she try to keep you and Cameron there in the better, less sinful part of the world?"

Cameron pulled Lacey down with her to sit with Andrew. "It doesn't matter if she did. We're here, aren't we? This is our home."

Lacey clucked her tongue, "Our Cameron, always trying to make peace between everybody—that's what I love about you so much. It's good to have you back."

Cameron's eyes swept around the familiar restaurant. She would miss working here with Lacey. Her heart was filled with many memories, some she was fond of, others she would do well to forget. She hadn't realized her new husband was doing likewise, and he brought his gaze to Cameron's sweet face.

Lacey was asking her, "Did you find everything to your liking in your new home?"

She blushed, "Yes. It was kind of you to have everything ready for me at Andrew's."

Andrew laid his hand tenderly over hers; his touches sent furious shades of pink to creep up and down her neck, "It's *ours*, Cameron, not mine."

A sudden feeling came over Andrew that he could not justify and it bothered him. After contemplating a moment, he realized he did not want his wife in these surroundings. Lacey was a good woman but lacked certain convictions. This sudden revelation left him unsettled.

"I'll get some coffee," Lacey's joy was obvious. Without thinking, his voice stopped her; for some reason she was not surprised by his words.

"No need, cousin. We just wanted to stop by before the snow became too much for travel. I knew I wouldn't be able to keep Cameron away from here another moment."

Lacey looked sharply at him and did not miss his sly reference about keeping Cameron "from here." So she was right; this is how it will be. She was condemned from the start, no longer good enough for his wife's gracious company. Her face fell at this permanent blow, and Cameron looked apologetically at her. The visit had been absurdly brief. Mother Grace's voice flashed through Cameron's mind, recalling her lesson prior to marriage about honoring her husband. This was a new concept to say the least. *It is my own fault*, she thought. *It should be so easy, but I will not disagree with Andrew.*

Putting aside her will for the moment, she said softy, "I'll come by tomorrow for that coffee, Lacey."

Too quickly, Andrew said, "I have rounds to make on the congregation tomorrow. This town's been without a service for two months, Lord knows its condition. I need the people to know I am back should anyone need me for anything. Of course, they'll expect to see you by my side." He was reminding her of her new duties, and Cameron felt the hairs on Lacey's neck rise and saw her petite frame stiffen. Lacey tolerated Andrew because they were family and she loved him—but she would not tolerate his religion, nor understand the sacrifices one had to make in living with his faith ever.

"Well, Cameron. I suppose I'll see you when your husband finds the time for you." Lacey turned hurtfully away and left the two standing there to leave on their own accord. Cameron was silent. She wished Lacey had not caused a rift with Andrew. But it was also beyond her understanding why they came here in the first place if her husband meant for this reunion with her friend to be but mere minutes.

They passed by the rowdy saloon on their way out to the door as familiar sounds and smells emanated from the darkened room—and with it brought thoughts to Cameron. Thoughts of old longings that she didn't think she should have as a preacher's wife.

Four

He'd kept his wife to himself over the last several days as much as he could, and finally Andrew gave in to Cameron's pleas. They would go to Lacey's for dinner. With him at her side, what could possibly happen? They entered the restaurant for supper; both were weary, cold, and ready to warm limbs and bodies. In Cameron's opinion, she believed a look of concern passed across Lizette's face as she led them to a table. *Whatever was Lizette so nervous about?*

"Cook's got his best roast beef tonight. It's going fast, good thing you got here when ya' did," Lizette babbled.

Andrew retrieved Cameron's cloak and set it upon the coat rack, then he practically ran in to her solid stance. He, too, saw Jake. The silence was incredible. Lizette felt sudden tension radiate from him and waited. Cameron's heartbeat was erratic; she thought to have satisfactorily rehearsed what she would do once she found herself in this situation—face to face with Jake Collins. She had been wrong, her knees increased in weakness. She did not want things to be awkward. She wanted more than anything for friendship with the man she was once close to. Jake's eyes held only hers. He wanted to know what the condition of their relationships would be like—once and for all. He grew up with Andrew. He had no cause to regret seeing Cameron with a good man.

She righted herself and her thoughts. Cameron Jackson strode over to Jake who was caught standing ready for departure.

Extending her hand to him, she said, "Jake, it's so good to see you." She heard her voice, but it sounded as though it was coming from another direction entirely. Lacey let out her pent up breath.

"I can say the same." Jake released her hand, touching it as briefly as possible, and he left her. "Andrew, old buddy, glad you're home!"

"How are you doing?" Andrew thought he was done struggling with his wife's past. Trust and forgiveness, he told himself.

"Doing great. In fact, I was just on my way—I'm leaving town for a bit."

Jake made his voice even, wishing now that he'd left earlier. Better yet, he wished he had stayed the heck away from Lacey's altogether.

Cameron was alert to the fact that Jake baldly ignored her until he finally left. Well, the initial contact was over and done with; it wouldn't be so hard next time. Was she fooling herself?

"Won't you two get comfortable and have some dinner?" Lacey smiled weakly.

Why couldn't life be the way it was before?

It was Christmas and the Jacksons awoke to a glorious morning of white, white, white. The first holiday as a wife presented itself to Cameron, and she meant to make it memorable. Although a week has passed since she'd seen Jake, Cameron still felt as if she needed to make something up to Andrew. What—she did not know, but the feeling would not go away regardless. She would make him see that she has changed; that she loved him and only him. She would be the pleasant and loving wife of a preacher . . . of a good man. Cameron stood near the fire humming a Christmas carol when Andrew came from behind and wrapped his arms around her tiny waist. "Come," he stated and pulled her by the hand, insisting she close her eyes. Still shy to his romantic overtures, she never ceased to feel special around him.

"All right, now you can look." Andrew slowly, methodically placed gift after gift around a quilt as if to torture her with impatience. He smiled confidently. "Well? Sit down!"

"Andrew, what have you done?" She half fell onto her knees, surrounded in gifts large and small. She did not deserve this.

"They're not all from me. Mother has always been a bit indulgent when it comes to the holidays I'm afraid."

Cameron wrinkled her nose, "I suppose I did take away her one and only son." She broke through her shyness and hooked her hands behind his neck and kissed him.

Two of her many gifts impacted Cameron the most. Her eyes grew wide with surprise at the outrageous jeweled brooch Andrew bought her.

"Where on earth do you expect me to wear this?" She demanded in jest as he placed it upon the breast of her dress.

"I don't care, just wear it for me."

The other gift was a large box from Mother Grace, fully contained with baby clothes for both a boy and a girl. Neither knew how to respond at first, and Andrew didn't know if his wife would be offended or grateful.

"Andrew," she whispered, holding up the tiny outfits. "I do hope we will be able to use these. All of them."

"We will, Cameron. In time, we will."

He snuggled her against him and they enjoyed a lazy morning together, grateful for all they had. Cameron wondered how Lacey's day was, hoping she was with Ed, hoping for all things to go well in her friend's life. She watched the fire with her beloved until it fizzled out.

Lacey bid her few guests goodnight. It had been a quieter holiday meal than she was used to. Cameron and Andrew wanted to take dinner with themselves. "It's our first Christmas together. Please understand," Cameron had said.

Lacey told herself she understood, but she did not want to. She wondered skeptically how long the couple's undying adoration for each other would last. It was no secret that Lacey liked to surround herself with people, though tonight had been unusually somber. Ed brought with him Joseph Benton, who, once the money had been returned in full, miraculously got all charges dropped from his short stint as a bank robber. The nineteen-year-old was also indebted to work for a community, namely Lincoln County, under the watchful eye of the sheriff for six months. Jake was sullen but joined them having nothing else to do. Lacey balked at his attitude and demeanor; he'd brought no joy or conversation at all to the party. With the night over, she closed the door on the final two figures departing the uneventful occasion. Pity was never greater in her thoughts as it was tonight.

Ed walked Joseph back to his place behind the jail. He was sharing with him his tight quarters until he found more suitable lodging for the young man. Once the lad fell asleep, he assured Lacey he would be back.

Up in her chilled room, Lacey poured herself a glass of port and reclined onto her bed. Shortly after she'd settled in, she heard Ed's tapping on the door. She did not bother to put a wrap over her revealing nightdress and opened it wide. The last thing she heard was her drink crashing and spilling to the floor. She gasped. It took an earthquake to shake up Lacey Jennings, and she felt indeed the earth moving beneath her.

"Blaine." Her voice was hoarse, barely audible.

"Lacey." Blaine was at a loss for words. He could not remember what he had rehearsed and planned to say to her.

"May I come in?"

She stood mute. If he remembered right, he had better take his chance with her now before she caught her bearings. He stepped in cautiously. Blaine passed her by until he was securely away from the door. She turned and numbly closed it behind her.

"What are you doing here?" She breathed out the words, they echoed in her head.

"I wanted to come earlier . . ."

"You mean you wanted to come *three* years earlier!"

He flinched. He would get no better than he deserved tonight. She was visibly shaking, trembling.

She was getting her bearings.

"Lacey, I wanted to see you months ago . . . I ended up staying in a boardinghouse in Topeka until I got the courage to face you. After what I've done . . . it's Christmas, I wanted to come to you on Christmas. I saw you and your friends through the window and realized that you've moved on and have a life without me. You've done well for yourself."

"I've done well for myself?" She screeched and moved angrily around the room. "I've *had* to do well for myself you unfaithful . . . lying . . . deserting!" She picked up the crystal bottle of port and launched it at him. He shielded the blow with his arm—he heard his bone crack. Lacey was stunned for a moment, then, in her frenzied fury, started picking up anything and everything, hurling things over and over at him. She could not even see her mark any longer, she was blinded by tears. Tears of betrayal and hurt.

He rushed her as gently as he could, "I'm so sorry, I don't deserve even a moment in your presence, I'll ask for it though. Please—hear me out."

Exhaustion muddled her defense. She was weak, drained emotionally. She slid to the ground in defeat. Blaine paced her floor, ignoring the pain and bruises that were sure to come with her abuse. This was the least of his worries. She did not trust him. How could he ever make her see that he has changed? He looked down at her. She was still beautiful, that was what drew him to her in the first place. It wasn't until a year and a half ago that he was made whole, and God placed a renewed love in his heart for his wife. The wife he abandoned and left to the hands of God knows what . . . he couldn't think of that, not right now. It tormented him these past months, what he'd done to the priceless woman sitting hopelessly on the floor. He eased down to her level only maintaining some distance for her. He could only imagine how she must hate him; she must disdain his presence—his touch.

"When I got those papers . . . I almost signed them."

She looked at him, her eyes swollen and accusing. "Then why *didn't* you?"

"I don't know, it was so permanent. I wanted to see if there was a chance..."

"There isn't."

"Would you just let me explain?" That came out wrong, how could one explain abandonment, betrayal? The silence lingered.

"Well?" She asked smartly.

"I obviously can't explain, Lacey."

The response was a grunt from her. No doubt she wanted to see him struggle, no doubt she wanted to hurt him.

"I was selfish, I've changed..." She looked away in disbelief.

Regardless of her cold response, he surged forward. "I know that sounds insincere, but I'm not that man anymore, I've—grown up."

"So have I." She glared hard at him, contempt flowing out of her very being. "I've grown up to protect myself, to support myself. No thanks to you." She put on a look of defiance. "To be independent of you and to amuse myself with other... well, let's just say that I've had my share of men! Ones that don't betray! Ones that care for *me*!"

He closed his eyes tight. It was all his fault. *God, what am I to do?*

She shifted her body away from him. She wanted him to leave but found herself speechless. He conceded and lifted himself from the floor, "I'll leave you be, Lacey, for tonight. I'm not going anywhere though. I'm going to find a place to stay in town."

With all the words of courage he could muster he stated, "I'm going to fight for you, Lacey Jennings."

She waited until she heard the door click shut before allowing the gut-wrenching sobs to tear loose. What did he have to come back for? She had washed her hands clean of him. She hated him! Why did his words ring in her ear, words she'd once longed for? Dreamed of? She cursed him, and then with a pang of reality she let out a small cry, "Oh, Ed!"

Her premonitions of recent months were proving true. Something did happen to change the course of their lives. She had been seeking to change the wrong things; she had not once thought of Blaine. As far as she was concerned, he was dead and now she was helpless to stop the cloud of defeat that was intent on snuffing out her life.

She startled when the door burst open. Ed halted at the state of her then went to her. "I knew it." He swore. "I thought it was him. What did he want? What did he do to you?"

Lacey shook her head, her voice was muffled in his chest, he eased back to hear her shaky words. "He said... he... that... he was going to fight for me."

Ed felt as if a punch had been hurled into his stomach. Panic gripped him, then anger. Who did Blaine think he was? He looked down at the top of Lacey's silky black head. Did her husband have a chance? No. He couldn't. Lacey despised him. Still, he needed to hear it from her.

"Are you alright, my love? I'm here now. I will always be here." He squeezed her tightly.

"Do you promise?" She asked with uncertainty.

It was more than enough for him to hear, "I promise."

Blaine walked the familiar streets throughout town, desperate to get out of the cold. He'd expected this town to have added another hotel or two. It seems he expected too much. With great reluctance, he bundled his collar firmly around his neck and headed for the Half Moon. He hesitated before going in; apparently, it had *not* only changed, but had gotten worse over time. It was as dark and dingy as he remembered it being. He wished he could say that he had never patronized the place before—but he couldn't.

God, what is Your plan for me? Surely, You know what memories I have to fight coming here? It was late, and it was a holiday. He should be thankful for that he guessed. Nary a one was present except for Harry, uselessly wiping down the saloon with a dirty rag. Blaine set his leather suitcase on the murky floor, then decided it would be best if he held it. He cringed at what the beds must be like. Harry squinted at his customer; a haze of cigar smoke obscured his vision.

"It's me. Blaine Jennings. Do you have any vacancies?"

Harry laughed, the fat rolls in his neck bobbed up and down.

"Well, I'll be! Of course I got vacancies! Never thought you'd ever show your face in town again." He wheezed and coughed from the exertion of laughing and breathing. He turned serious, "I just sent the girls on to bed, slow night, ya' know. But I'm sure one of 'em wouldn't mind . . ."

Blaine held up his palm, he did not wish to hear those words. "Just a room, Harry."

"You got it. Take an empty one that suits your fancy." Harry shook his head as he watched the genteel man seek out each room before choosing the one he thought cleanest, which didn't say much. Harry thought of Lacey and her hot temper; no doubt she sent him packing. It was the only reason Blaine Jennings would actually sleep an entire night here.

"Sleep tight," Harry teased.

Blaine looked at him with what Harry thought was a brief twitch of panic or concern. *Funny,* he thought, *Blaine didn't seem to mind the unkempt place when the ladies were entertaining him not so long ago.* Harry shook his head in surprised thought one last time before thinking it safe to close up and lock the front door.

※

Ed stayed with Lacey in comfort. He woke up next to her and looked at the wrinkled clothes he slept in. He needed to get back to Joseph, but he did not want to leave her side. Fear of losing her, fear of giving her time to think and try to sort things out entered his mind more than once during his restless night. He never had complete security in her love, and this certainly did not help his case in claiming it. Knowing his devotion to her to be much stronger than hers for him he could live with. He'd *planned* to live with that. What he didn't plan on was interference from Blaine.

He did not want to give the man a chance alone with her again. In fact, he vowed to have a talk with the low-life snake. For once, he wished he were not a sheriff.

Five

Sheriff Randall stood between the feuding neighbors. This is not the place he expected to find himself today, especially in the freezing cold. Snow had been falling intermittently all morning, and he was reluctant to take the long ride up here.

"The best and only way to handle this, Mr. Zemke, is by the land office. They will determine where your land ends and Mr. Montgomery's begins."

After arriving and observing the tense situation, Ed was glad Clyde Montgomery sent a man to town after him. He kept his cautious eyes trained on Ian Zemke and the rifle he was gripping tightly in his hands. Each cattle baron was surrounded with foremen and ranch hands, ready in their loyalty to protect and preserve their boss's land and integrity. Even if it meant being killed in a gunfight, no one would *not* enter the fray—being called a coward was worse than dying.

"We're not going to get anything settled today, Ian. Not like this," Ed continued in a placating manner.

Ian Zemke glared at Clyde, but his words were directed toward the sheriff. "I'll let my shot gun do the talkin' from here on out. Always have before, have no plans now to change my ways." His voice was raspy with age and rough living. Clyde held tight his stubborn stance next to the rolled wires of barbed fencing. Both men were firm and set in their ways and each having ranched just outside of Lincoln County for years. Neither would relent their position on the matter.

Ed outstretched his cold hands in a futile attempt for compromise, at least for today if it was at all possible. "I'll send the land inspector out first thing tomorrow, gentlemen."

"There ain't no young pup around going to tell me what I already know." Clyde spoke, "This land is mine. I want none of his cattle roaming free grazing on *my* grasses. No more!" He stepped forward toward Ian, who held up his gun and aimed it at his rival's belly. "I'm sick of Clyde and his threats to put up that darned fence!" Ian's voice escalated, "The first post that goes up will be the last." There was no mistaking his words, but Clyde held his ground. "We'll see about that." He spit, as if to mark his territory. Ed waited until Ian left before trying to reason with Clyde.

"Clyde..."

"Ain't no use, Sheriff. You heard him—he speaks with a gun. Next time I'll be ready for him." With nothing else he could do for the two cattle barons or their disagreement, Ed went back to town to locate the unfortunate land surveyor.

The New Year was passing Lincoln County by uneventfully. Winter had not been harsh, adding worry and apprehension to Lacey's misgivings of what would be in store for the town. Surely something was going to happen. Nothing ever remained sedate or at peace for long. She knew—having lived here for years.

She replaced the calendar against the golden-toned wallpaper with a new one. Lacey's hand lingered on it a while, wondering what this year was to bring. She has not seen Blaine since last week at Christmas, leaving her to believe that the whole ordeal had been imagined.

What reminded her it was real was the constant nausea gnawing at her core, and Ed. His permanent presence told her that she had not imagined it. Cameron had been to see her immediately, coming every day. Lacey appreciated her support and friendship, but it did not matter. This was not something that would go away even if Blaine went away. The anger and pain was fresh and affected her despite her resistance to feel anything. It has been said that Blaine was asking townspeople if there was a home he could lease or buy. Lacey heard he was staying at the Half Moon and smiled in spite of herself. *Good, he should be quite at home and comfortable in a pig's pen.*

The candlestick Lizette was dusting clanged onto the table. "Goodness, I'm so clumsy!"

Lacey looked at her blankly and stepped from the calendar, which the days upon it seemed to hold her future. She gathered the soiled tablecloths and looked around her empty restaurant. It was Sunday morning, which meant church for most. It grated on Lacey to have her business wane week after week on this very day. Foul mood renewed, she snapped, "I'll be in my room!"

Lizette looked after with concern; she was used to Lacey's sudden shift in moods, but for the first time began to feel insecure in her role here. "And breakin' Lacey's fine things ain't helpin'!" She made a face at herself into the reflection of the candlestick, replaced it, and proceeded to the next one. "It's gonna be a long, long morning."

The congregation was small today. Few families risked traveling in the snow, even if it did look blissful and pleasant. No one dared challenge the deceptive calm that Mother Nature had them encompassed—not in Kansas.

Reverend Jackson greeted his few parishioners at the entrance of the small white church, saying "good morning" to each man, woman, and child. Cameron spent her beginning moments at church going over hymns that would be sung with the organ player, Mary Keiser. When she closed the hymnal and looked up, she took note of the gentleman with whom her husband was engaged. They must have been talking about her because at that moment, both men turned her way. The stranger could only be Blaine. What was he doing here? If the man knew anything about his wife at all, he should know that he would never see Lacey here . . . heaven forbid, at church.

The smile he gave her was not one of malice and it did not unsettle her, rather it was filled with humble benevolence, and he looked dispirited. She froze when he started walking the distance over to her, what could she say? Cameron could have kissed Andrew for his timing. He chose just then to take his place behind the pulpit, waiting patiently for their attention. Cameron quickly sat down in the nearest pew. The organ cords were struck, she heard words being sung, and she thought she even mouthed some of them, but did not remember. Blaine chose to sit directly behind her and she was irritated about that. She then remembered he was God's child, same as everyone else—only to see Lacey's swollen face from crying all night. She told herself she should not judge the motives of one's heart or actions. Then she would think about poor Ed Randall, what was he going to do? Everyone in the congregation was oblivious to the small battle raging inside the head of the preacher's wife, including the preacher, who would not have had to contemplate accepting all who came through those doors. The moment she truly dreaded had arrived, Andrew's sermon was over; there was no escape. Cameron rose and smoothed out her skirts hoping in vain someone would need her attention, anyone but Blaine.

"Mrs. Jackson."

She pasted on a smile and turned around clumsily. It would be highly disloyal of her to talk to this man. She did not want to hear his side, for he hurt her friend—deeply. Even though it happened before knowing Lacey, Cameron could feel the physical pain she was going through. "Yes?"

"I've heard a lot about you. I'm Blaine Jennings, finally nice to make your acquaintance."

I've heard a lot about you too. "Mr. Jennings, it's good of you to come today."

"Your husband invited me to dinner this evening, I hope you don't mind. I'm sure you know we're related."

If she had been eating, she would have choked.

"I . . . I'm delighted."

He was no fool, and she was a poor actress.

"We'll see about that." He smiled handsomely and proceeded to shake hands with former acquaintances. Most came up to him out of sheer curiosity, but the single women who came up to him came for other reasons entirely. Shameful.

⁂

Cameron was silent on the cold ride home. There was no fresh snow, but the wind bit at her face. A fire glowing in their quaint little home was a welcome vision in her mind.

"I saw that you met Blaine today."

"I did."

He raised an eyebrow, "Why so glum?"

"Did you ever consider Lacey in this?"

"Of course I have. But I also happen to like Blaine, I'm glad he's back. He says he's a changed man, and I intend to see that that's true, or at least help him along the way if necessary."

She grunted.

"Cameron, I hate to be bold with you, but you cannot judge him. We have all come from places of regret or shame. And some of us do change."

No doubt he's talking of me. Her attitude was wrong and she knew it. How was she supposed to get through an evening of entertaining an enemy? What would Lacey do when she found out?

"We need to be sensitive to Lacey, of course," her discerning husband announced. "But I've also come away from her manipulative ways. I wish you would as well."

"What's that supposed to mean?" Cameron was not happy to hear his words. Something in her disliked his superior attitude and uprightness, even if he was right.

"It means that you think too much of what she feels about you. You're so afraid you'll make her angry; you try to please her all the time. I want you to be able to speak the truth to her in love, and not cower to her moods."

"I don't cower to her moods, *Andrew.*" *Now we're fighting about Lacey, I thought this was about Blaine!*

Andrew wisely remained silent until they reached home and well enough after.

He later realized Cameron had moments where she did not let unpleasant things go easily. Especially as he sat there reading a book while she hastily prepared dinner. The dishes clanged a bit harder than necessary as she pulled down what she needed from shelves. He stopped himself from smiling at her fit. She was dedicated on letting him know of her disapproval in regards to his choice of dinner guest. Andrew had no doubt that she would ultimately be the good hostess he knew her to be capable of. He had no worries . . . should he?

Blaine arrived with his handsome smile and charming good looks and Cameron realized he was indeed the epitome of a man that Lacey would have once chosen for herself. Andrew retrieved his coat as Cameron excused herself to finish final preparations for dinner.

Blaine looked after her, "She doesn't like me much, does she?"

Andrew laughed softly, "Who she likes is Lacey."

Blaine got the point and figured he had his work cut out for him. In order to reach Lacey, he needed Cameron's alliance. He'd asked a lot of questions in town and quickly came to know that she was the best of friends with his wife.

When Andrew said a blessing over the food, Cameron dished the men's plates. She averted herself to keeping busy and out of their conversation as much as possible, all the while being polite, or so she'd hoped. After listening to the men for hours, the only problem she ended up having with Blaine Jennings was the fact that he was not dislikable. Could he have really changed? Or was he deceiving them all? Was he after something? But the question that burned in her tangled thoughts was did he still really love Lacey?

After shutting the door on Blaine's departure, Andrew said, "Thank you for the lovely dinner. I don't think he's eating all that well at the Half Moon." Andrew cringed, "Poor man."

Poor man! "He would not be in this situation if he had not left Lacey in the first place," Cameron replied in her smugness.

"Do you not think that God can work things out in such circumstances? Isn't He able to have good plans for people despite their bad choices?"

He took her hands in his, "Isn't He a redeeming God, Cameron?"

"Yes. He is," she whispered, ashamed of her doubt, of her attitude toward Andrew. "I'm sorry. I wish I were more like you." She allowed him to hold her.

"Don't try to be like me. Just be open to change—and to people."

She nodded, wishing she didn't feel like a child. She had so much to learn, she had to stop leaning on Andrew's faith and start building up her own.

Another week went by ever so swiftly, and Ed Randall was thankful in a distorted sense that he had been distracted and called out of town on more than one occasion to deal with the two seasoned cattle barons. These men handled issues and fought disagreements *their* own way and have for years. They gave orders, they did not receive them, and Ed wondered how far he could go at intervening peace and questioned himself constantly if he was up to the task. If feeling inadequate wasn't enough for him to deal with as sheriff, he was dealing with Lacey and their problem. He was furious with her.

She refused to let him confront Blaine and took it personally that she would protect the man who deserted her. "I am not protecting Blaine," she'd said. "I don't want you doing something to harm your status in the community."

Well, it was his choice, was it not? He would not step aside much longer in obscure waiting, not knowing if he was going to be put-off or not. Lacey was inconsistent and restless. He could not count on her to make a commitment. She had proven that time and time again, with or without Blaine's presence. The only thing going in Ed's favor was the fact that Blaine had not approached her again. And the man was only lucky that Ed had not seen him on the street somewhere. What was his game? To show up on Christmas, to stir things up . . . it didn't make sense.

Six

It was the beginning of February and Blaine was becoming a permanent fixture in church and the community. He placed his meager belongings one by one away into a rackety dresser. His new home was ice cold, he would have started a fire right off, but the chimney was full of grime and badly needed cleaning. He would tackle that chore next, if he didn't freeze first. The home he'd purchased was not much. Of course he could only imagine that anything was better than Harry's. He had tired of warding off the prostitutes that worked there and was surprised at how long it took him to find a home.

Blaine unloaded the crate of supplies from his used buggy and put the dish set for two onto the one and only shelf after wiping off cobwebs and half-inch layer of dust. He felt like a bachelor pure and simple. Though thoughts of Lacey never left him, he was thankful that he was this far. He was in a home and being irresistibly charming to Cameron.

He couldn't help but grin proudly. Blaine refused to feel guilty for applying at least one of his no good traits to earn his way into Lacey's heart once again—he'd started with Cameron's as practice. He said he would do whatever it took, and he would do just that. Cameron seemed to accept his overtures of kindness and his perfect behavior of being an utmost gentleman. Blaine had given Lacey ample time to contemplate his return, and now he would begin to . . . what? She'd loved him once, could he revive that? With God he believed he could, it was where his courage came from. This time, he would do things right; he was here to stay. He had to make her see that.

Cameron felt at home in the restaurant and sat herself. It was quiet. Lizette greeted her and poured a cup of coffee.

"Where's Lacey?" The shame she felt in regards to her newly acquired feelings toward Blaine was overwhelming.

"In her room, where she is most days. I'll tell her that you're here."

Lizette was hopeful that Cameron could rouse Lacey to her normal being. Even if it was reduced to orneriness, she'd have Lacey back.

Cameron fretted about and became discouraged. As hard as she fought it, she found herself liking Blaine nonetheless. She was sure Lacey would see through her disloyalty. A wooden toy fell from the only other occupied table. A baby screeched in laughter as his papa picked it up, waving it in front of the delighted little one. Cameron smiled to herself, thankful for the distraction.

Lacey joined her and set aside pride, "I've missed you so much."

"I've missed you. I wish traveling was easier, I would come more often if that were the case. As it is, Andrew does not know I'm here now. He wouldn't want me out in the snow, but I had to see you."

Lacey's eyes narrowed at the mention of Andrew. "You need to ask for permission to leave your own home?"

"He would only worry about me. There could be a snowstorm any moment."

"As if I don't know that," Lacey snapped.

"You've lost weight, Lacey, I worry about you."

"So worried that you have Blaine over for dinner almost every night?" Lacey's words were hard and confirmed her distressed thoughts on the matter.

"Andrew and he are close, yes. I don't know him that well." Cameron's nerves shook.

"But you don't mind him there?" Lacey accused, "Do you think he's handsome?"

This was too much for Cameron. Nothing could be farther from the truth.

"I cannot tell Andrew who he can or cannot have in his own home! I came here because I miss you. I want to help you through this. Please, don't shut me out."

Lacey sipped on her coffee and allowed bitter silence to permeate the atmosphere.

"Tell Andrew to stop speaking to Blaine. The man deserves nobody; he deserves to be miserable and alone."

Cameron looked downcast. "I can't do that. Andrew would not be unkind to anyone."

"Oh, I know that! He and his righteousness!"

Cameron got up to leave. "I can't have you talk of Andrew that way."

"I'll stop just—don't leave," Lacey's tone came close to pleading.

The two discussed trivial things until the tension loosed its hold.

Lacey looked at her over the rim of her delicate china cup, a gleam appeared in her dark eyes. "Have you seen Jake lately?"

Cameron's face flamed. She had no cause for it and she suspected it was because that was the response Lacey wanted.

"You know I wouldn't—er, haven't." She wanted to kick herself, getting all flustered over an innocent question, she broached a new topic. "Lizette seems quiet, she feeling alright?"

"Why should she be feeling alright? She's married isn't she?"

"I don't know what you want me to say. I'm so sorry about Blaine. I wish he never hurt you."

Lacey looked up in troubled thought, "Maybe if I hadn't lost our baby and we'd had a child, Blaine would've stayed."

Cameron reached over the table, squeezing her hand in comfort.

"Yet, if he loved me, I suppose that should've been enough, don't ya' think? Instead, he ran off with the first girl who captured his attention." Lacey held her chin regally.

The tender moment was gone. Lacey's hardness always overrode the softening of her heart. Instantly, she blinked her tears away and Cameron saw the wall go up. "Enough of this somber talk!"

This chatter was too close for comfort and Lacey wanted the opposite, she wanted the unwarranted attention shifted away from her. "This town needs a party! I can't wait until the Fourth of July Celebration. And nobody was in the mood for anything on New Years." She looked away from Cameron's concerned look and continued as if to herself. "So I will host a party! And no one may come unhappy, or I will boot them out. Will you help me?" Lacey locked her hands in front of her chest, anxiously waiting.

Cameron worried if she said no, she might lose their closeness forever; it was barely hanging on by a thread as it was. She knew that with or without her help, Lacey would do it anyway, and maybe this would be an opportune time to put things behind them. "You know I will."

"Splendid! Lizette! We're going to have a winter dance!"

Blaine came to dinner that night in Lacey's restaurant. It wasn't a very bold move, for he'd meant to see her while surrounded by people. She couldn't do anything brash in front of her customers—could she?

Lacey nearly dropped the plate she was placing in front of an older woman when she saw him. Fuming at the man's audacity to show himself, and her carelessness, she stalked up to him and hissed, "What do you think you're doing?"

"I'm hungry. I have no food at my place." He stated the obvious; then he secured himself a seat before she could make a scene. And he *really* was hungry.

"Well, I won't serve you! You don't belong here!"

"What will your customers say when I pronounce that you've refused me service?"

"I'm sure they'll understand when I tell them that *you* deserted *me* for another woman, after *we* lost the baby *I* was carrying!"

Seeing the horrified look on his face sent a shiver of elation throughout her being. Oh, how she felt better.

He hadn't prepared enough for her anger. She truly hated him. Who was he to think he could just waltz in here and . . .

"Lacey, what's going on?" Ed Randall asked, standing possessively behind her.

Blaine didn't miss the fire in his eyes.

"I don't want any trouble." Lacey looked around worriedly, she could not count on Ed to maintain a cool temperament. "Ed, please. Either go away or sit at another table. Far from him."

He looked irate and hurt. She felt sorry for him.

"I promise—it will be all right. I'll join you as soon as I can." She cajoled Ed, and after glaring at Blaine, he honored her request begrudgingly.

"Mr. Jennings, I don't want to hurt that man. He's been more faithful to me than you ever have. He's good to me. Why am I even telling you this? You don't deserve an explanation!"

"I know I don't. I was wrong, Lacey. I will be good to you . . . I will . . ."

She walked away.

Lizette served Blaine his meal. Lacey served nearly everyone else and kept her promise to sit with Ed. Blaine was at a loss. *Please God, is this really Your will?*

After an anxious and tense dinner hour, Lacey went to her room, uncaring of the mess left for Lizette to clean up. She sat on her chaise lounge and sipped her port—alone.

The candle flickered in the darkness. Her thoughts went unwanted to Blaine. It was not fair that he looked so good, that he did not look troubled. He might appear sad, remorseful—but he also had a different, unexplainable look in his deep brown eyes. She noticed how he'd aged slightly, only it was becoming. He was distinguished and mature now with the silver streaking above his ears; it was an attractive contrast against his sleek black hair.

She tossed down her drink bitterly and poured another, willing her mind and her heart toward Ed. His qualities far surpassed Blaine's. Ed was always there. He'd professed his love when she was unlovely, when she acted tired of him. He'd admitted with conviction that he could never live without her—which was more than Blaine ever said, in fact, his actions spoke quite the opposite. Lacey drank until the decanter was empty, until she didn't have to think. It felt better to have her mind clouded and unclear. She shivered against the coolness that penetrated the windowpane.

⁂

Across town and fields away, the same night air was crisp and clear, the remains of the fire maintained by hot coals. Cameron climbed into bed beside her husband. She felt the heat of her blush creep up her face and imagined herself red as a beet. She'd waited until three weeks had passed before telling him the news. She turned on her side to him. She could tell by his heavy breaths he was already asleep. To wake him up, she caressed his cheek. "Andrew." She said his name softly twice. He mumbled something and his eyes remained closed. She pecked his smooth cheek and said, "Andrew, you're going to be a good father." His eyes became miraculously alert and awake, he blinked hard a couple times as if to confirm himself up.

With Cameron's smile and light breath on his face, he smiled big. "Really?"

She nodded fervently, "It's true."

He sat up in bed, pulling her up with him and he kissed her long and hard. His palms grasped her cheeks. "That's wonderful!" He looked to where her gaze drifted and saw that she had set out their gift of baby clothes from his mother into little piles on the table. He laughed aloud, "We won't be needing those for a while!"

She joined in his laughter, "I know, but I couldn't help it. I'm so happy, Andrew."

"God is good, Cameron. I love you."

⁂

A snowstorm blasted its way through Lincoln County, leaving several feet of snow-covered ground in its terrible wake. Loneliness and isolation crippled those who were forced into solitude, those that needed to be around people. Those like Lacey, who was rescued from her reluctance of being alone when a dozen pending train passengers were snowed in and forced upon her hotel. The train would not depart until further notice of cleared tracks. Some of her new patrons were clearly unhappy about the delay, making it hard to please them. While others, tired from their journeys, welcomed the time in Lacey's environment. Liam took full pleasure in accommodating all that were stranded, offering an evening of free drinks in hopes that they would be willing to receive entertainment from his girls. The gaming tables had long been in place and were ready for use, having been dormant with business slow on both sides.

"Bring me a bottle of whatever, Liam." Lacey sat down at the table. "Boys, deal me in." Her demeanor changed when she was among others, she was safe from herself. Safe from her thoughts and wanderings. Safe from her fear of being alone, and safe from a husband's image that haunted her day in and day out.

It wasn't long before her two favorite men entered the foyer with Joseph Benton, dripping wet and covered in fresh snow. Lacey smiled seductively, it matched her dark and ambiguous mood. Her evening was now complete.

"It's not good traveling out there at all," Jake said with a shiver. "I'm afraid we're stuck here for the night." The trio stomped snow from their boots and shook their heads wildly in an attempt to speed the drying.

Lacey said, "I might have one room left."

Ed didn't waste a moment, "You mean for them two."

"I won't satisfy that comment with an answer." She turned on her heel; her silk skirts whipped his leg as she swept away from him.

"Way to go, Ed. Of course you're with her, she don't need to hear you say it every second. She means for us. Joseph, you'll take the floor." Jake grinned broadly. "I get the bed." They headed for an open gambling table, wading through strong smells of smoke and cheap perfume. Jake halted the young man, "One drink, no more. If Ed sees you, I had no idea on it." Joseph nodded, then rubbed his hands excitedly back and forth.

Liam's "girls" served drinks repeatedly. Liam took full opportunity of the crowd tonight seeking to please all. He escorted Bethany Hoffman down the stairs as if she were a prize. As much as he didn't wish upon it, she had his favor. Bethany did not portray herself as the same in terms of Kimberly and Violet, who cuddled up to men, vying for their attention. Jake watched the shy beauty ward off many attentions before giving anyone her time. She rarely smiled, and when she did, it was fragile and pathetic. Jake was beyond trying to figure her out. He knew she was devastated after losing her husband, but what an interesting way to mourn. Turning down a decent living to sell yourself.

Lacey had an unfortunate tendency to ramble on when alcohol loosened her tongue and mind. So when she announced that the Jackson's were expecting a child, Jake was gripped with something unspeakable for him in this situation—jealousy.

She giggled at her blunder, then shifted a challenging gaze toward Jake. He lifted his glass as a toast to Lacey and said, "I'll have to congratulate them when I see them."

Lacey's eyes were glazed from drink, something she was habitually doing as of late. Smacking her lips, she turned to Ed and said lazily, "We should have a baby too."

She wavered and almost fell off the chair. Ed swore, "You've had too much, Lacey. *Again*." He picked up her petite body and effortlessly carried her up the stairs to her room.

Jake's table began to empty, he said to Joseph, "Go on ahead." He complied readily as he witnessed Jake's good-natured mood turn desolate. Jake was left by himself, as he wished. His only company was a fresh bottle of whiskey that was all his own.

Seven

Blaine pulled up his collar against the biting morning air and waited nonchalantly between that of the mercantile and seed store, deep in the shadows—until Ed rode passed. No one could accuse him of being afraid of the sheriff; he just did not want to create a problem. He intended to fight for his wife all right, but he wouldn't have a chance to succeed if he was never alone with her. With Ed heading in the other direction, he needed to take advantage of the few moments he might have. Without malice, Blaine thought about how few moments alone Lacey received, that man was constantly hovering around Lacey like an old mother hen. When Blaine deemed it safe enough from confrontation, he ventured into the street and up the boardwalk to Lacey's.

"Good morning." His handsome face was not a welcome sight for her. "May I speak with you?"

"You have nothing to say worth listening to." Lacey responded warily. She was cleaning, doing menial chores, and doing such things made her grumpy. Blaine openly thought her adorable with a bandana over her hair. Dark ringlets escaped out the sides, making her look even younger than her thirty years. Her apron only managed to accentuate her small waist. She ignored him and his blatant observation as she loaded up the stove with more wood and pulled dry towels from the lines in the storage room. She was hot and cranky. Now she had to contend with him.

"Let me help you with that."

"I will not!"

He resigned his arms to his sides, helpless. She stalked past him and went upstairs to fold and put away linen.

He followed.

What could she do to get rid of him? To persuade him it was no use? She dumped the linen on a guest's bed and spun around, she hadn't realized how close he was upon her and he didn't know she was going to turn around. He was undone when he smelled her freshness; the familiar smell put an ache of regret into the pit of his stomach. Humbleness radiated from him. "Please forgive me."

His nearness caused her to be faint, the sensation had only happened once before and it, too, had been because of him—but that, she was quick to remind herself, had been a long time ago. She would not give in.

"No!" she cried out, louder than she'd intended, pushing him away from her. She turned on him firmly and with conviction, "I will never, ever forgive you! Did you really think that you could just come back and have my knees buckle at the sight of you?" Yet, that's exactly what was happening to her. Her voice was quivering, her stance against him was wavering, and he could see it.

"I do love you Lacey. I know it seems an outrageous concept. In the past, I've said those words without action to follow them up by. I want to have another chance with you." His large, humble brown eyes cut her deep.

She shook her head as if to shake out his face, his lingering presence. "Get out, please, just leave me alone."

She should have stopped him, she knew to stop him. But she did not and he put a calloused finger along her cheekbone, outlining her face as if he were a blind man. Blaine closed his eyes to remember the very creation and shape of her face, which relaxed beneath his touch. He opened his eyes slowly. Hers were closed as if in a trance and her lips were turned upward toward his own. Every ounce of discipline to be mustered up in Blaine's being was called to the surface. He wanted this so badly. In that brief moment, he recounted all the times he'd pictured Lacey in his arms, but not like this, it couldn't be. He would not allow a cheap moment of passion to ruin what he wanted to be a lifelong husband and wife relationship. The tip of his finger touched her silky bottom lip, and with an astounding force of controlled emotion, he backed away and out the door.

Confusion quickly escalated to anger. Lacey stood in the middle of the room and swore at his retreating back. "Don't set foot in my hotel again, Mr. Jennings, or I'll have you run out of town!" She fell against the wall and wept, body shakes enveloped her and she hated herself more than ever. Had she no shame?

※

Despite the feelings of confusion and ill will toward all men, Lacey forged ahead with her party. If she didn't attempt to create a sociable atmosphere and keep busy, she would go mad. Cameron helped with the preparations in between bouts of nausea and fatigue. Lacey remembered well those moments in her own pregnancy, only Blaine was not at her side as Andrew was at Cameron's. That took love and dedication, and her marriage lacked that. The saloon was turned into a dance hall. A small platform was built to accompany the stringed quartet Cameron managed to recruit.

Cameron's condition for coming was that no alcohol be served. Lacey reluctantly agreed and broke the news to Liam.

"What's more important, Lacey? Drinks, or me?" Cameron put guilt on her friend without remorse.

Lacey received her request lightheartedly; nothing would ruin this day that was supposed to be perfect. Maybe things were going to get better. Her friends were all back and nothing out of the ordinary had changed for quite a while. With Blaine's lack of honoring her request, he continued to frequent the restaurant. Too prideful to admit her lack of judgment and weakness, Lacey began to tolerate his presence without getting too upset. Only once she figured out to how handle him. If she treated him like a fixture around the place, she did not become agitated. If she allowed him to become near her in any way, shape, or form . . .

Of course he was not welcome at the party, and Lacey hardly imagined he was bold enough to come. She rounded up party favors and set a merry atmosphere. Kimberly and Violet took the blessed chance to dance and mix throughout a crowd that placed no expectations on them for anything else, and Bethany avoided coming down from her quarters. It was just as well she declined Lacey's invite. Who She could care less if the woman was present or not?. The stringed instruments brought on an elegance that fit Lacey's charm and grace, and she and Ed romanced each other mercilessly on the dance floor. Neither Cameron nor Andrew knew the sheriff could waltz.

"She must have given him lessons." Andrew smiled. He treated Cameron as if she would break, barely allowing her to do anything beyond making their meals. She scolded him numerous times.

"Andrew, women give birth all the time and are up on their feet working the very next day!"

"I don't care," he'd say. "I'm not married to them, I'm married to you."

Therefore, her dancing was as limited as it could get. The buffet table was lined with cold cuts, imported cheeses, sweet-glazed sliced ham, and an assortment of twisted breads and rolls. "Cook's Cook has really outdone himself, wouldn't you say?" Andrew stated and looked toward the dessert table where he saw Mack and Lizette stuffing their mouths with cookies.

Cameron laughed, "He most certainly did. It wouldn't matter if the food was bad, it wouldn't keep those two away from it."

A small group of rough looking men entered the saloon and Cameron's jaw dropped.

Her outlaw-fighting brother appeared in the doorway with his gang in tow. It had been months since she's seen him, and since he never stayed put, she began to wonder if she'd ever see him again. Would he never stay in one place?

"Thomas!"

His confused look sought the place of where his name was being called. Why wasn't the saloon open? He stayed in place when he saw her, no ounce of greeting was in his bones and she did not care. She walked up to him and grabbed him tightly, he raised his arms out of harm's way of embracing, unsure what to do with the emotions of his sister. Jesse, Lance, and Johnny stood awkwardly, they were expecting to play cards and receive entertainment, not encroach upon a tea party.

Cameron looked way up into Thomas's hardened face, undeterred, "It's alright to hug me back." She was used to his behavior. Finally, to her satisfaction she felt his arms come about her—albeit barely. It was enough.

Andrew greeted him, "It's good to see you back home."

Thomas acknowledged Andrew with a nod and Cameron pulled him toward their table. She tossed her head flittingly upon her favorite in her brother's gang, "Jesse . . . come join us."

Jesse, who would never be left out of a get-together replied, "I sure will!"

Thomas scowled at his jubilance, and yet, allowed at the same time for his sister to push him into conversation. "I hate to ask, will you be staying long?"

He adjusted his gun belt before situating himself into the chair she'd vigorously pulled out for him, "You know better than to ask me that."

Thomas looked around, "What's up with Liam's? He gone and opened up a dance hall?"

Lacey interjected, "Just having a party." She looked with accusation toward Cameron, "You can thank her for the lack of . . . spirits."

Thomas raised an eyebrow, "That so?"

She flushed and said with mock appall, "Well, certainly for one night!"

Kimberly was quick about pulling Jesse into a dance. Johnny had no taste for such displays and hit Lance in the arm, "Let's get out of here!"

Thomas cursed his luck for coming at all.

Ed nuzzled Lacey, she looked at Jesse and Kimberly, "It's good to see everyone enjoying themselves and getting on so."

Joseph brought some punch over to Violet, reminding Ed of something. "That boys come along way. Jake plans to ask him to take on his farm once his time is up with me."

"That's a perfect arrangement," Andrew observed, no longer threatened upon hearing Jake's name—or at seeing him for that matter. Time had a play in his resolved thoughts and the matter seemed to be settled, especially with his wife enlarging their family. "This has turned out to be a nice affair, Lacey. I believe the town needed a respite from this weather. A chance to come together."

"Thank you. I take that as a real compliment." Lacey was pleased she could show him that she wasn't as much of a "drunken loss" as he was sure to think her as. Andrew smiled kindly at her. He did love her, even with all her contention toward him and "his" religion.

"Reverend Andrew! Is Reverend Andrew here?" A small child's voice echoed in the foyer. His chair scraped across the floor as he rose.

"I'm here. What is it?"

The little boy said with panic in his voice, "Dr. Colvin tol' me to come and get ya,' my baby sister, she's real sick and . . ."

"No need to go on, Michael. Just lead the way." He looked back at Cameron.

"I'll be back later, stay here with Lacey."

"But I can come and help."

"No," he said firmly. She looked downcast, never feeling like she was a good helper to him and his ministry. She was more so than she knew, but now was not the time to let her prove it.

"It's too cold out and I'll be in a hurry and don't want to jostle you about in the buggy."

"He's right, Cameron," Lacey encouraged.

She complied with regret, "I'll wait here for you. Just be careful."

He put on his hat, hastily grabbed his long coat, and was gone with the child.

It was getting late, and the Reverend's departure reminded people they should be on their way just the same. Besides, if someone was sick enough to need the preacher, it couldn't be good, and no one could enjoy themselves any longer with that knowledge. Cameron said a silent prayer for the family and helped Lacey clean until she made her stop. She was definitely related to Andrew, and Cameron gave up trying to enforce her ability to do chores; they were a stubborn lot. So Cameron played cards with her old poker teacher, Liam. "Just like old times," she said as they gambled with dry beans. She was winning, and ever so often would ask him what time it was.

He checked his pocket watch for the umpteenth time. "Five minutes since you last asked. It's eleven forty-five," he said with patience.

Thomas inquired into her well-being and made sure she would be all right until Andrew came back. "I'll just go to bed upstairs if it gets much later." She assured him, welcoming the amount of attention she was getting, most of all from him. Lacey was in and out of the saloon with Lizette, the two worked back and forth, and before long the saloon soon appeared back to normal.

"Everyone had a wonderful time. We should do the same every year," Cameron said and realized with joy that next year at this time, she would have a new baby with her.

Lacey laughed, "I believe we will. I'll go upstairs and prepare your room."

"Thank you, I'm going to sit here a few minutes longer and wait for Andrew. I'll be up shortly if he's not back."

"Do you want some company?" Lacey asked.

"You're tired, go to bed. I'm fine, really."

Liam bid her goodnight shortly after, leaving a lantern at her table. Cameron rubbed her shoulders against the cold. The heat dissipated with everyone opening and closing the front door. She was just about to head upstairs when she heard the bells go off at the entrance. "Andrew? How is she?"

Jake sauntered into the saloon, "Where is everybody?" He asked, his voice hinted a slur. His dark eyes pinned down Cameron, "Where's Liam? I need a drink."

He flicked his temple as if to remember something. "I hear a toast is in order."

"Liam's gone home. Everybody has."

He drew closer to her, "Then why are you here all alone? Where's your preacher husband?"

He was drunk; she could smell his liquored breath from where he stood. "He's . . . I was just going to bed." She was sorry for him. He must have seen it in her eyes because his temper ticked—then flared. He circled her around a table. She was not afraid of Jake Collins, just afraid of what he would say.

"Sit down, Cameron."

"No."

"No? Not for an old friend?"

"I don't like to see you this way."

"Why should *you* care how I look?" He pulled out a chair for her, expecting her to take it. She took it, but only in hopes that she could reach out to him, put the painful past behind them once and for all. She did care for him, she wanted to see him whole and surrounded by the peace and comfort she now lived with. She sat. Andrew would not be happy with her if he came in. It was a chance she had to take.

"Lacey says you're drinking a lot. Looking at you, I'd have to say that I believe her. You're gaunt looking, pale, and thin."

"In other words, you're not attracted to me anymore!" He laughed at his ridiculous comment. "Congratulations for you and your baby." Suddenly his eyes became intent and deadly and serious. "I wish you all the happiness."

She wanted the truth, she must know. "Jake, am I the reason you're drinking so much and bounty hunting all the time?" She couldn't bear it if she was. She hit a nerve and he stood up angrily, knocking the chair to the floor. She jumped in her seat.

"Don't flatter yourself, Cameron. I couldn't be better. I'm just fine without you!"

She got up cautiously, no longer knowing this man. Cameron wanted him back the way he was. When had it come to this? How could she be so blindsided by his anger?

His face fell when he saw her hurt, "I'm . . . so . . . sorry."

With caution she looked at him, seeing a spark of the old Jake in his sobering eyes. He walked toward her, the brief tension gone, and replaced by an imploring, softer look. She allowed his nearness out of hopefulness.

"Cameron . . ." He held out his arms with an apologetic smile. She went into them. She went out of restoration, in desperation of repairing their broken friendship. He inhaled the sweet lavender scent that emanated from her golden head. He closed his eyes tight, memories rushed through his body . . . if he only had self-control.

"Cameron?"

She looked up to see his face, to answer his forthcoming question. He kissed her, as brief as it was, it shocked her senseless. As reality hit her like a bolt of lightening, she struggled from his tight grasp and squirmed relentlessly until she removed herself from his familiar hands.

"Jake!" She placed the back of her hand onto her tainted lips. It was all she could do. She could say nothing and backed away from him with panic-stricken eyes. She carried herself up the stairs in a flurry of anguish, appall, and outrage. All the while he could hear her wretched sobs. He cursed at himself, he only came for a drink, he had not expected to see Cameron sitting here in the moonlit darkness alone, of all things! He was cruel to have done that to her. She would never trust him again, and what of Andrew? He was blowing the long time friendship with him as sure as he was standing there.

Eight

When Andrew returned home the following day, he saw that Cameron was waiting restlessly for him. She was finished doing mundane things around their home to keep occupied. Trying in earnest to banish her fear of what could be happening with her husband, and in vain trying to steer her thoughts away from Jake and his unspeakable actions. What was she going to say to her husband? She looked into his insoluble and forlorn eyes, something worse than what happed to her last night occurred.

"Andrew?"

With his heavy, troubled heart, he searched her face, "It's scarlet fever."

He slept for just three hours before the doctor sent another person of a dying family member to fetch him. Andrew and the doctor made rounds on several homes throughout the evening past. Cameron prepared for him a cloth sack of biscuits and dried roast beef, and bid him a dreary farewell. Well into the afternoon, she paced their small living area, cleaned, organized, and paced more. She was having a terrible time sitting idly by, worthlessly doing nothing. She did not do well once the fear set in that her own precious husband was exposing himself to the sickness. Cameron kept coffee hot on the back of the iron cook stove, struggling between wanting to be there for him when he returned, and escaping from the tormenting silence of their home. A frantic knock drummed loudly against her door. Cameron opened it to Mary Keiser, hysterical. "It's Sarah! Something's wrong with her!"

"Calm down, Mary. Come in from the cold." Cameron gently wielded her in.

"No! You must come and be with her while I get Dr. Colvin!" She cried out in her frenzied state. Cameron placed her hands maternally onto her shoulders, "Mary, it's scarlet fever. The doctor and Andrew have been seeing many sick children." She looked past Mary vacantly, not wanting to be the bearer of the horrible outcomes of some.

"It's that bad? Is she going to be all right?" Mary backed away, shaking her head in disbelief. "She's going to be all right!"

"I don't know. This town has lost two children that I know of." Tears rolled down Cameron's face, for Mary's fear, for her little one, Sarah, and for the families devastated by such unnecessary loss.

<hr />

When they arrived at the Keiser's home, Mary ran up the stairs to Sarah. She let out a surprised laugh of relief mixed with hysteria. She hadn't realized she'd half expected to find the child dead until she saw her flushed rosy cheeks and heard her loud breathing. Cameron fought her nausea. *Now is not the time*, she scolded her protesting womb. She explored the vastly large kitchen until she found a metal bowl. She pumped icy cold water into it and snatched up a utility towel. She found the way up to her room from sound of Mary's crying. Cameron sponged Sarah's boiling temples, arms, and neck. Andrew had described the symptoms of scarlet fever on his way to falling into an exhausted sleep. Lifting Sarah's nightdress, Cameron saw tiny red bumps all over. It was a sign of the fever Andrew mentioned. They cruelly exposed themselves along the girl's chest and abdomen and they felt like sandpaper. Sarah chilled and moaned and Cameron replaced the heavy quilt. It seemed to her that she should be uncovered to expel the heat. But she recalled Dr. Colvin's words, "That is not how one treats fevers, it must be sweated out."

"Her mouth, in the back . . . it's awfully red, Cameron. She was throwing up all night, I thought that she was . . ."

"There's nothing you could have done different. We can only wait—and pray."

"Never have prayed much. Maybe you should do it, being preacher's wife and all," Mary stated, hopefully. Wiping away her tears, she kneeled at Sarah's bedside, taking over sponging her down with the cool water.

Cameron said, "I will pray, but it's never too late to start." She looked at the pale color around Sarah's lips; it was in stark contrast to her fiery complexion everywhere else. She wished Andrew were here by her side.

<hr />

Andrew was forced to go home by Dr. Colvin, there was nothing he could do except wait . . . and officiate funerals. *Four children, Lord, I don't understand. How do I explain to these loving mothers and fathers why their children are dying?*

Silence.

He stomped snow from his boots and opened the door to his cold home, the fire had gone out, and apparently so had his wife. He could only trust that she was all right and possibly helping a neighbor, a parishioner. He would sit in his wingback chair and wait. First, he stirred up the embers until an orange glow and warmth filled his home. It took Andrew only five minutes before succumbing to sleep and its beckon call. While he slept, a terrible wind picked up and made the powdery snow swirl around like ice dust, covering rooftops, barns, water troughs, and roads. And to add to the mass of white havoc, the weather deemed itself necessary to pour forth a fresh mountain of it upon the county, leaving the whole of it pure white. Wherever you were during those hours is where you remained if you valued your life. Andrew awoke with a start. With the exception of a slight tinge and glare of orange lining his fireplace, pitch black surrounded him. At the recognition of the time and that Cameron was not home, he rose and bundled himself up. When he opened the door, he stopped short in amazement. He could not even see their barn; he had no way to find their horses, not to ride them, not to check on them.

"Cameron, where are you?" Fear gnawed at him that she should be out in this wicked weather, wandering helplessly around. But something stronger than that fear overruled those dangling thoughts. Somehow, he knew she was safe somewhere. Where? He did not know. He exhaled powerlessly and slowly closed the door.

In town, Blaine Jennings carried a five-year-old to Lacey's door and kicked at it until she opened it. "What's going on?" she asked with immediate concern.

"I don't know, the little guy just fell down stone cold in the mercantile, his mother has a passel of kids with her. I told her I would take him to Doc's. He isn't there, and I don't know what else to do with him."

"Bring him up." The gentleness in which she spoke touched him. He brought the feverish boy to one of the hotel's rooms. "I'll go find Dr. Colvin."

"The boy belongs to Kate Reynolds, his name is Tyler. I'll take care of him, tell his mother where he is." She looked at Blaine, "Please."

Through the window in Lacey's restaurant, Blaine stared in awe at the fierce storm brewing before his eyes. On his own accord, he gathered all the lanterns he could find from the hotel and placed them along the boardwalks in case someone should be lost while looking for town. He was thankful to have intercepted the doctor before the storm. The poor old man was on his way home at the time, and with him were two small children. At nine months pregnant, their mother was incapable of taking care of them. She was sick herself and their father was a determined worker, absent from home often.

Just before the snow started falling, the siblings and mother of the Reynolds's boy made it to the hotel. It was just as well; he was in the vomiting stages of the fever.

Dr. Colvin simply could not go on a moment longer, and Lacey shuffled him off to bed. He was beyond the years expected for a doctor to work.

Blaine and Lacey found themselves without Lizette's helping hands . . . and Ed, well—thankfully the sheriff wasn't around just now. Lacey shuddered to think . . .

Blaine poured himself a cup of strong coffee and sat alone in the restaurant and prayed. He prayed for the children lying sick and dying upstairs, for the doctor to be strong enough to help them through this, and for Lacey—for their relationship to experience forgiveness and restoration.

There was no conversation as the three adults bathed several children in what they called now "the sick rooms." Beds were combined, moved into various positions. Blaine pulled cots from the storage area and gathered blankets from every empty room in the hotel. The mother of six was weary; all but two had fallen ill with sore throat, fevers, and rashes and she did not cease at nursing each and every one.

"Mrs. Reynolds . . ." Lacey assessed the older woman, they both looked a mess, hair loose and escaping from pins, soiled clothes from body emitments, and full out fatigue. "Kate, it's been several hours. The children are the same. Please get some rest. I'll stay with them."

Kate Reynolds looked at her questionably, as if seeking assurance that if she slept, would all of her darlings be here when she awoke? Her eyes were heavy, "You need sleep the same as me. Why don't you go?"

Lacey hesitated and said just above a whisper, "Because right now your children don't need you." She did not finish her thought, she did not need to. The Reynolds children would need her if . . . in the end.

Blaine stood in the doorway. He intended to relieve both women when he heard Lacey's plea to Kate. He agreed, "Mrs. Reynolds, I've readied a bed for you, it's this way." Blaine's voice was gentle, calming. She went unwillingly, out of necessity. Lacey turned to Alice Reynolds and held her sweltering hand in hers. Life was cruel, and these children did not deserve this. Kate was a loving, faithful mother and she did not deserve this. Maybe it wasn't life that was just cruel, but God himself? Keeping everyone in line, looking down, and when displeased, punished! Well, there were lots more people out in this world that needed punishing, needed to come face to face with His burning hand, and it was not these innocent children! She cursed at His mistake in this matter and blamed. Maybe He didn't seek those to punish; maybe He just showed his unjust power as He saw fit and didn't care! These unspoken, unwarranted thoughts were the closest Lacey has ever come to talking with God. She rested her head onto the bed next to little Alice and wept.

Blaine balanced himself between the two rooms, checking tenderly upon each child, adjusting pillows, bathing faces, spooning cool water into pale mouths. Lacey's emotions crawled with unease. She wanted to stay angry at the man who'd torn at her heart. She did not want to see this gentle, paternal side of him. It perverted her thoughts of him and her accusation that he had not changed, that he would never change.

He felt her gaze and turned toward her, smiling weakly. "May I get you anything?"

She averted her eyes and sat up stiffly. "No."

Blaine frowned when he felt Tyler Reynolds pulse. It was weak. He went to wake Dr. Colvin. The doctor returned doggedly, his silvery, thin hair stood sporadically upon his head, his eyes swollen in protest of being open again. After checking the wheezing boys pulse, he shook his head sadly. Lacey, with her tearstained cheeks went to arouse Kate. The same went for the two Hammond children. They would not live. J.C. Colvin could only pray that the wee one in their mother's womb would be born healthy and live a full life in place of its siblings that were not meant to. Kate held her son's face in her balmy hands and kissed his lips, she whispered pathetically words of love and adoration. It was too much for Lacey; she could not understand the death of a child. No loving God would do this, her cousin was wrong, misled, and she would tell him so.

At the end of three days, Kate Reynolds would say good-bye to half of her precious children, Tyler, Amanda Sue, and her sweet baby, Eliza.

Cameron helped Sarah sit up in bed and grinned at Mary's attempt to make her laugh. Her ma was making a funny, relieved face at her, utterly happy that her daughter appeared well. Sarah grimaced when she saw her peeling fingers and toes, an interesting sign of the departure of the illness from the body. Her throat croaked when she asked, "May I please have some water?"

Mary smiled as wide as she could at Cameron, then sprang into action, "Anything you want."

Cameron smiled and readied to go. Jake and his ill behavior forgotten, her only desire was to see her husband again.

Relief literally flooded Andrew as Cameron made her way home to him in the dead calm of the morning. She cried in her own mitigation when she saw smoke from the chimney and shadows dancing across the window from the lantern she knew to be on the kitchen table. "Andrew!"

He flung open the door before she was down from the buggy. He made a quick evaluation of her health before taking her into his arms. His hand went instinctively into her thick mass of hair and wound itself in it—he inhaled deeply before releasing her.

"Where did you run off to?" His bright eyes were not yet smoothed of concern.

"Mary Keiser needed me, Sarah fell sick." At seeing his look she assured him, "She's fine, Andrew."

"And you?" He took in the dark circles under her eyes and slouched shoulders. "Only tired, nothing sleep cannot fix."

<hr />

After much rest, Andrew prepared a light soup and ladled it into bowls for each of them. "Dr. Colvin said it must have spread throughout the school." He had Cameron bundled up cocoon-like in a chair beside the fireplace.

"How so?"

"As you must know by now, it's highly contagious. Someone needs only sneeze, or share a pencil. It's a terrible tragedy."

"I'm glad Sarah made it through. I don't know what Mary would have done to lose her. With her being a widow, I could only imagine the thought."

Andrew pulled up a tray to Cameron's side and placed a bowl of soup down. He pulled up his own chair in front of her. "Don't even think about feeding me!" she declared.

"I don't intend to. But it's hot, allow it to cool a few moments," he retorted, then added softly. "Sarah's older; it's the younger children who are susceptible to—"

Andrew looked into the fire, "They don't tolerate the illness as well." He blew on his teaspoon of soup and swallowed it. "After a bit, I need to head to town. I have some things to check into with Dr. Colvin." He knew what she was going to say before she said it, "And, no. You may not come," he said levelly.

"But I've already been exposed, you said so yourself, just know now, that it affects the youngest." She had a good argument. "Please. It's dreadful waiting here, alone, not knowing . . ."

He held up his hand in surrender, "Very well. You win. I'll take you straight to Lacey's and *then* you'll stay put."

She smiled, "And then I'll stay put."

❦

Blaine drove the wagon. Next to him sat the doctor and lying in the back were the Hammond's children. Both men's faces were frigid with cold and ruddy looking as they pulled into the Hammond farm. Blaine gingerly helped the older man down from his side of the wagon and walked him up the path toward the weatherworn house. He did not want to be present when Doctor Colvin broke news of death to awaiting parents, and so he left the doctor standing on the porch. Before descending the long strew of steps, Blaine heard Mrs. Hammond's terrible cries. His stomach tightened with grief, he prayed that the soon-to-be-newborn would bring some joy back into their hearts. He turned to check on Dr. Colvin and saw the father walking numbly toward him, his face was like stone and fixed to the back of the wagon where his children laid side by side, entombed in rough wool blankets.

Blaine stepped aside, wishing he were invisible. He looked away from the man toward the sky, surmising the weather. It did not appear ready to cease its assault.

And he was correct in this as day after day a torrent of gray snow layered onto the ground. Animals died from lack of water and care from their owners who were unable to access their barns. Farmers and ranchers couldn't see five feet in front of them against the endless white world. No shipments of food came for the townspeople; it was up to them to have been prepared for a harsh winter or make due with what they had if they weren't. The train remained stilled on the iron tracks, no passengers coming or going.

Andrew wept quietly as he wiped Cameron's sweat laden brow. It had has been three days since the merciless fever latched itself to her. She was barely conscious, the slight moans that escaped her lips twisted his stomach; she was in pain and he could do nothing about it. Andrew came just short of forcing fluids down her throat. He kept her dry, cracking lips moist as best he could. He blamed himself. He should have never taken her with him to town earlier in the week.

"Darn her protests!" he said in frustration, throwing the damp rag to the floor. He raked his shaky hand through his mussed up hair and stared hard at his wife's bleak, still face. Dark circles under her eyes gave her a bruised appearance, and her breathing . . . it did not sound right. He stalked around the room; there was no way to get the doctor in the wretched weather. Somehow, he knew that Dr. Colvin would only do what he had been doing all along, bathing, feeding, and the worst . . . waiting.

Andrew read against the dim light of the lantern for hours between nodding off and checking on Cameron's status. The gray dawn slowly began to creep through his window, reminding him that it was a new day. He got up tiredly and went to the kitchen and rationed out some food for breakfast. There would be no coffee today, when he wanted it most, for no for the water must to be saved for Cameron. He scooped a ceramic cup throughout the bucket and filled it half full of cold water and brought it to his wife's lips.

"Cameron." His voice was soothing, hopeful. "I'm going to give you a drink now." He tilted back her head and poured a slight stream of water into her mouth. She swallowed. He realized, as he placed his hand on her cheek, that she was no longer hot. He closed his eyes and gave his thanks in prayer. Her countenance was different. She was no longer struggling for health, but simply sleeping. He peered outside. The snow appeared to have succumbed to the silent pleas from humans and came to a standstill. Andrew could only hope it came to an end entirely, and did not care to see a winter like this ever again. He lay down with Cameron and slept beside her.

Nine

Not one to give into idleness, frail health or not, Cameron was giving her all in hand-sewing a blanket for the baby. The material was light blue with a cream colored pattern of baby toys woven throughout it. "I've never been much of a seamstress," she commented offhandedly.

"It's going to be beautiful. Anything you put your hands to will do well." She eyed her husband. She knew him, and he needed to get out, he needed to tend to others, not sit with her and falsely compliment her sewing talent. Cameron could see clearly his torment upon leaving her alone and seeking out the needs of the people in and around town. He placed a thick piece of bread that Mary brought over this morning and some thinly sliced beef before her. His eyes thankful and patient and kind.

"Go."

"I want to stay here with you," he said, and she believed him.

"I know. But you're needed elsewhere. I'm fine. You've taken good well care of me. I'm just weak because of the baby; he drains any energy I have."

"He?"

"Of course, *he*." Cameron sat up a little higher, proud of their son. He grabbed her hand and gently squeezed it. "I love you, Mrs. Jackson." She smiled to herself and hummed a lullaby to her son.

For those unaffected by scarlet fever and for those who did not lose family due to lack of provision from terrible weather, life was normal. Snow fell in light intervals from time to time after the brutal storm, and then ceased altogether with the end of March upon them. Cameron struggled with her lack of strength on a day-to-day basis, despite her many hours of rest and doing nothing. It was true that she had not seen many women expecting a baby when she was younger, but hardly thought that this absolute weakness was normal. Whenever she read Dr. Colvin's concerned face during his visits to her and after examinations, she knew it was not. Andrew did everything. He ran the church, saw to everyone's needs but his own. He visited families upon their requests and often when he felt led to. He cooked and cleaned at home and took care of his incompetent wife. And Cameron resented it—every moment. This was not how ones first year of marriage ought to be. What kind of a wife could not fulfill her duties? Duties as simple as cooking and taking care of her husband? As going to church with him, remaining at his side while he greeted the town's citizens? She looked upon Dr. Colvin as he was preparing to leave.

"When am I going to regain my strength?"

He closed his aged and worn medical bag before standing. He heard in her voice fear of being inept, desperate to return to life as she knew it before. He saw in her worry-creased brow concern for her baby and slowly shook his head. "I should think that you would be better by now." He spoke the truth. "I sense nothing wrong with your baby, but the fever should not have had this affect on you for so long. I don't know, my dear, we'll just need to wait."

She was tired of sitting in bed, tired of staring at the walls of their lonely home. She couldn't stand to see Andrew come home, wary after a day of meetings, or traveling only to prepare dinner for her. His smile always gracious and his tone always polite, she wondered how long he could stand it as well.

"I'm sick of waiting!" she said passionately, exasperated.

Cameron wished she weren't so testy, especially after Dr. Colvin traveled to her home week after week. He was tired and old, but he came out of reassurance for her and at Andrew's behest, she was sure. "I'm sorry, Dr. Colvin. I can't take this *waiting* as you put it." She picked at the quilt on her lap; she was on the baby's second blanket. *At this rate*, she thought wryly, *her son would have a heap of blankets by the time he was born.*

"No need to apologize, child. No one thinks ill of you for being bedridden, it happens."

She looked up at him hopefully, "It does?"

"Well, not often, but I've kept a few expectant mothers detained to their beds a few times in my career. I have to say that they responded just as you. But we must not forget, the important thing is your baby. If your body is too weak to be up and about, it's best to keep you resting. If you come to find that you have a burst of energy, feel free to act on it. If you feel tired, rest. Obey what your body is telling you. It will be best for Junior in there." He stated this mini-lecture with a spark in his eye. "I'll be by next week. Maybe you'll feel more like yourself then." He slid his arm slowly through the sleeve of his coat and bid her good-bye.

Knowing Andrew would be home soon, Cameron began to brush

her tangled hair and willed her state of being to be less impatient and less cross.

❧

Blaine anguished as he watched the sheriff needlessly aid a strong-willed Lacey out of the mercantile. Ed had the palm of his hand resting on the small of her back, steering her throughout the people on the boardwalk to their wagon parked near the entrance. A trainload of goods arrived the day before and townspeople scrambled throughout Lincoln County to stock up on much needed food and supplies. Lacey, with her well-respected status in the county, had first pickings at the mercantile. After all, her account was always in good standing and the proprietor would not have been wise to allow for her to pursue business elsewhere. She sat perched in the buggy seat of the wagon as the sheriff and clerk loaded up her many supplies. She caught Blaine's eye as he watched her and an unexplained tingling sensation happened beneath her corset. He was too far for her to see the lines in his face—but she could picture his deep brown eyes nonetheless. It was not a picture she wanted in her head, and when she realized that Ed was waiting for her to answer his question, she scowled at Blaine and smiled sweetly at the man she loved. Still, as completely aware as she was of Blaine standing there at the edge of the boardwalk, she paid Ed more attention than was necessary. Her husband wasn't lurking; he stood there bold as the day. *Was this his tactic? Torture me with his unwanted prowling? Insolent man.*

Blaine never came near her when Ed was around, which was often. But it was as if he knew the exact moment when the sheriff was called out to duty somewhere. Because every time that happened, the man who claimed to be her husband appeared magically. With his sweet words and unforgettable good looks, it was getting harder and harder for Lacey Jennings to put him from her mind.

"What would you like to do this evening, Lacey?" Ed asked again. He tapped the reins and lurched forward the wagonload of food, fancy new dishes, and clothing through the heavy traffic of the snow.

She sighed, "Oh, I don't suppose there's much to do but play cards." Lacey spoke passively, her words lacked the meaning that should have been behind them. The forever-present knot in Ed's gut pulled tighter. She was trying too hard. She should not have to *try* to listen to him, *try* to be happy when she saw him, *try* to pretend that she liked being around him. Ed was sure she loved him in her own way; he just didn't have the energy anymore spending all his time securing that love. He wanted all of her, all of the time. Ed once thought he would take whatever she gave, but when his heart became overwhelmed with feeling, he could no longer accept being second. Second to what? That was the problem. From the start of their relationship, he'd always been second best in her life, and that was even before Blaine came back. The competition he'd face where her husband was concerned had has not quite surfaced yet. Ed barely saw the man. But for whatever reason, he sensed, as he always could, Lacey's withdrawal from committing to him. It didn't take long for his heart to become fragile—he could no longer protect it from being broken and hurt. For some unexplainable reason, he could not be the one to let her go, he would never let her go. But she would leave him, and when she did, this unknown insanity and warring within his heart and soul, at long last—would come to an end.

"Cards it is," he said simply, and clucked the horses on toward the hotel.

The sheer volume of noise and business was very welcome to Liam and Lacey. They did not see the crowded saloon as a burden, with its raucous patrons and shortage of working girls. The restaurant and saloon had been too long in slumber and was ready to waken up. It came alive as more and more men filed into the saloon after supping at Lacey's, where Lizette was dizzy with busyness. The promise of spring did this—brought people out of their homes—one would call it cabin fever. Whatever it was called, Lacey didn't care, it was good to be surrounded by people. She didn't mind that for once she was losing in cards badly to Jake. Lacey's spirits were high and drink made them even higher. After an initial horror-filled appraisal of Jake and his rough, miserable appearance, she was determined to work on him. It would not do to have her friend waste away in loneliness and be without hope of finding someone to love again. Her eyes soared over Ed and his handsome features, considering herself lucky to have him in her life.

"Blast it!" Ed said in mock anger. He threw down his losing hand, causing Lacey to laugh; it was light and airy, and very feminine. To Jake, Ed complained, "You're not even trying very hard. You don't even look like you are enjoying yourself. Yet you're winning every hand!"

Jake half-smiled, "It's just the luck of the draw. That, and skill." He sat up from his slouched, disinterested position and scooped up his winnings for the fourth time.

A curt nod and phony pretense of flattery acknowledged Jake's lust-filled smile of thanks when Bethany brought over a tray of newly ordered drinks. Bethany wouldn't have even acknowledged Jake at all if she hadn't seen Liam watching her.

Lacey's face faltered. At one time, Jake could barely give a woman, *any* woman a glance and make her melt with desire. She thought he could easily have that affect again if he didn't look so dangerous and lethal. When had his appearance gotten so ill-kept? She took note of his deerskin jacket, stained with water spots and sweat. He'd let his hair grow, and it was pulled back and tied with leather. His eyes were darker than usual, appearing hard and edgy. He now wore a knife sheathed at his side, as if he might need it in any given moment. Lacey realized that the weaponry and guns he carried had increased . . . had she been that distraught over Blaine to not notice her friends changing? She always knew deep down that this year brought with it unwanted change. No matter how hard she fought it and tried in vain to hold on to what was—it still seemed to slip away. She became desperate to spend time alone with Jake. Lacey was losing him. He didn't care about anything anymore. She had only seen him like this once before in his life, it was when his sister died. This time, she feared, he looked wild, ruthless, and worse—unpredictable. The trio found themselves alone at a round table. Others, tired of losing money to Jake, went in pursuit of the other distractions Liam's saloon provided.

Whiskey filled Jake's belly and Ed, too, was relaxed. Lacey was not quite the epitome of soberness either, but was determined to ensue her assault on Jake's profession.

"Well? How is it that you are always gone?" she demanded hotly.

"You might as well tell her the truth, Jake. She isn't going to let up," Ed insisted.

"I'm a bounty hunter, you know that." Jake's voice was husky, "And, I like what I'm doing."

"You mean you like keeping your mind off of certain people." She sat back, her lips protruded into a pout. Jake rolled a cigarette and ignored her peevish mood. She ought to know by now that that didn't work on him.

"Think what you want." His dark eyes squinted as he lit his smoke. He didn't care, and what he preferred most right now, more than anything else, was to be on the trail.

Lacey glared at Ed, "So you've been in on this? How could you?"

Jake intercepted her childish questioning. "Knock it off, Lacey. You're not going to take this out on anyone. Because it's none of your business. I'm your friend, I'm not your lover, your brother, or your husband." From the look on her face, he knew he'd succeeded in putting her in her place. "By the way, how's Blaine these days?" Jake was merciless, and he did not care. Not anymore, it wasn't just Cameron and Andrew any longer, he was what he was, and it differed very much from the Jake of last year. It was time for Lacey to see that firsthand.

"How can you speak to me this way?" Lacey always had the upper hand on things, especially men. Her petulance might not work. Well, she needn't pretend to be hurt and confused with this unnatural turn of events. Panic beat against her heart, control slipped further from her.

"Don't ask such a stupid question. I can speak to you any way I see fit."

Jake's voice held a threat that had never been used on her before. "And leave Ed out of this. I aim to make a living bounty hunting, and he provides me with the names of wanted men. This is the last discussion we'll have on the matter, and if you so much as punish him with your little manipulative ways, you'll hear from me. As you can tell, I'm not very tolerant of such behavior."

Lacey's face flamed and Jake took comfort in the thought of seeing her real self rise above her feigned look of shock. She pulled her petite self to a stand, glared at both men, and walked coolly out of the room.

Ed Randall exhaled heavily. "Man, I'll be sure to pay for this!"

"No," Jake said levelly. "You need to take charge of whatever it is between you two. If you don't, you'll lose her for good."

After a moment of thought, Ed mumbled to himself, "If I haven't lost her already."

Ten

Andrew paid the lumber mill for his purchases that this morning and Blaine accompanied him home. His plans were finally beginning to unfold, and now they could build an add-on to the house. "Might as well add two rooms, Blaine. I don't plan on stopping after one youngin.'" Andrew mounted up on the lead horse and Blaine followed with a flat wagon bed of freshly cut wood. With them was ten-year-old Sarah Keiser. Andrew thought to surprise Cameron, who enjoyed the girl's chatter during the long days that he was gone. He also purchased another package of material fit for an infant for the two to work on together as he and Blaine worked outside.

Blaine hollered ahead, "This is perfect weather we're having today. It'll make working outside a bit pleasant." He winked at Sarah; she blushed and looked away. Sarah held a fondness in her heart for Cameron. The bonding started the moment she'd heard heartfelt prayers whispered from Cameron's lips while she laid with delirious fever. It was Saturday, not the usual day for Sarah to come over, but she had pestered Andrew through and through to spend the afternoon with Cameron. She fled Mary's side as she saw the men drive by while they did some shopping in town. Mary had frowned, "I suppose it's fine with me, if Reverend Jackson doesn't mind."

Seeing Sarah's determination caused Andrew to oblige her. The repercussions of Cameron's recent illness and weakened health were beginning to wear on him. Andrew was thrilled to be having a baby, to see his family grow. He recalled Cameron's beaming face when she announced the fluttery feeling their baby presented in her womb. That had been a good day; if those days would only last. He did not like seeing her helpless, not because he had more work to do, but because he could see plainly the affect of being still was having on her. She was irritable when he tried to distract her from loneliness and then sorry and tearful when she mistreated him. Sarah would be a blessing for his wife today. It would allow him to work guilt free on things he'd neglected and needed his attention. Sometimes, he wondered if Cameron faired better emotionally when he wasn't present anyway.

They cut through the Jackson's property and Andrew announced his homecoming. "I've someone come home with me to visit you, Cameron."

Sarah bounded inside the warm home and knocked on Cameron's bedroom door.

"The coffee's still warm, Blaine. Help yourself," Andrew said.

Sarah disappeared inside Andrew's room and came out immediately, and what she said was barely an audible squeak. "Reverend Andrew . . . Miss Cameron . . . blood." She burst into tears. He rushed past her and Blaine hurried behind. Cameron was white as the melting snow outside and all around the middle of the bed was a haunting, bright red pool of blood. Cameron's lips were gray and she was lying unconscious. Andrew was paralyzed with fear, prompting Blaine to step into gear.

Andrew heard Blaine's faraway voice. "Cameron! Cameron! Can you hear me?"

She moaned, it was a sign of life at least. Blaine shook Andrew by the shoulders, "I'm going for the doctor, I don't know if she should be moved or not. Andrew? Do you want me to move her?"

Andrew shook his head and came to his senses, "No!" He scooped Cameron away from her blood. "Hurry, Blaine!"

He needn't look away from Cameron to know that Blaine was already gone. Andrew wept, why had he left her alone? Couldn't he do anything right? She was his responsibility under God, and he continued to fail time and time again. Sarah stood shakily in the doorway, "Mr. Jennings told me to help."

Andrew forgot about her as he held Cameron. His head jerked toward the sheets on the bed, "Clean sheets. I don't want her lying on those." Cameron moaned again.

Hoping she could hear him, he said, "I'm here for you. I'm so sorry I left you. I shouldn't have . . ." He could not lose control. If she'd she ever needed him by her side, it was now. He cradled her like a baby until Blaine came back with Dr. Colvin. By then, Sarah had new sheets on the bed and hot water boiling on the stove. Andrew replaced his thin bride in the clean softness of their bed and kneeled in prayer at her bedside. After several minutes of Dr. Colvin's administrations, he spoke to Andrew. "I've been reading up on her symptoms, Reverend. I've also been in contact with some of my colleagues back east. They are more current in the field."

The older man paused and waited until he had Andrew's attention. "I believe what she has is called anemia."

Panic stretched across Andrew's face; the diagnosis he'd just spoken over his wife did not sound good.

"That is why she's so weak. That is why her body rejected the baby."

He let his words sink in, the silence vibrated throughout Andrew's ears and all he heard was *rejected the baby . . . my baby*. Dr. Colvin did not have the luxury of time or to wait for Cameron's husband to digest the news, he continued. "Losing blood has made it worse. I'm going to need to treat her, or we *will* lose her."

A numbing sensation overtook Andrew; he was not hearing this, he was not the receiver of these words of death spoken by his old friend.

Blaine's voice cut in, "What do we need to do?"

Dr. Colvin looked at Blaine square in the eye, "I need Thomas, now! I need to transfuse his blood into her body."

Blaine blanched and saw the task was not a welcome one to the doctor, but a necessary one. He nodded and left.

It was the crude looking instrument that settled the men into uneasiness; with the exception of Dr. Colvin. Thomas looked toward the crease in his arm as soon as he felt the stinging pressure, then looked away from the copper metal tool invading his flesh. He gripped tightly the arm of his chair, the unfamiliar sensation making him queasy. Dr. Colvin's hands were steady as he slowly pulled back what could only be called the trigger on this tube, draining blood out of him. Blaine stared at the whole process in awe, and when the doctor slowly pulled the long, ugly needle from Thomas's arm, he cringed.

Dr. Colvin walked with easy care toward Cameron, needle upright. He wiped the blood oozing from the sharp point with a cloth and gently pulled Cameron's limp arm into position to receive her deposit of blood. The only sound heard was Andrew's soft prayers as he knelt at his wife's bedside, out of the doctor's way. The foreign process to all of them was repeated not once, but two more times. No one dared utter the unasked question to the minister of medicine—*will she be all right?*

Thomas looked almost as pale as his sister did. The doctor sternly shook his head when he tried to rise from the chair. "Sit down, Thomas!" He said tersely. "Blaine, get him something to eat or drink." He spoke to Thomas in a calmer tone, "You can get up after you get something into your body. I don't have the energy to be working on you should you have a spell and fall. You're going to be weak for a short while." The doctor's intolerant tone snapped Andrew out of his reverie of prayers and he took note of the fatigue in the old man's eyes. This doctor of theirs, faithful and sound, was not going to be able to carry on his administrations much longer. He felt a conviction of ungratefulness to him—and here he had done all he could to save Cameron.

"Dr. Colvin, please sit at the table and rest, eat, whatever you need to do. I don't have words enough to say thank you, but *I am* very thankful to you."

"I know you are." He stopped on his way out of the silent bedroom, filled with uncertainty and much hope, and looked at Thomas. "You are a good person, young man, despite what you think of yourself or what anyone else thinks or says of you. If she lives, it's because of you and the good Lord above."

Thomas shifted uneasily, he might have done a decent thing today, but that sure didn't atone for all of his miserable dealings in the past. He was hardly a good man.

Sarah was dismissed from Cameron's side when Thomas entered with Blaine. She had no desire to be present anyway. She kept herself busy instead. Common sense told her to prepare food for the family. She did as her mama taught her, chicken was frying in the iron pan on the cook-stove, and bread was baking inside of it. Both coffee and hot water were available for the men at all times. Blaine and the doctor emerged together from the room, and she looked questionably toward them.

"We won't know for several hours, child." Dr. Colvin took a welcome seat in the small kitchen. Sarah placed black coffee in front of him, and Blaine and went with hesitation into the bedroom. She proceeded to scoop up the soiled blankets when Andrew said firmly, "No!" The unexpected act of his brashness startled her to tears. She only wanted to help. Andrew stared at the sheets. Somewhere in them was his baby, his son or his daughter. He could not let go. This would was not real, it would not sink in—ever. "I'm . . . I'm sorry," she stammered and backed away. Andrew had never spoken so to her.

Thomas opened his eyes lazily, "Just leave that be a little while longer, all right?"

Sarah nodded obediently. She was confused, why would the reverend want those bloody blankets lying in a heap next to him? She checked on the supper fixings and served the household. Everyone ate except the man and woman who lived there.

Winter darkness was still over the land, even though it was early morning. Andrew nodded off in the chair and woke to the sound of retching. Cameron was spewing vomit over the bedside and he rushed to her aide.

"Darling . . ." He stood helplessly over her, pulling her soiled hair out of the way from bile. He stroked her gently and laid her back once she was done. She lay there a while, and suddenly, her hands clutched her abdomen, opening her eyes wide. She focused on her husband and said in a croaked voice, "My baby?"

Fresh tears formed in his eyes—it was answer enough for her. Cameron turned away from him and stared blankly at the wall. She did not answer him when he talked soothingly to her, as if she could be comforted. She closed her eyes and willed for him to go away and leave her alone.

Lacey came as soon as light came to the day with a fit of jealousy toward the messenger. Why did Blaine know about Cameron over her? Why was he always around anyway? This was her life, she did not wish to share her family with him. More importantly, she should have known how ill Cameron was. She should have been there yesterday. Instead, she'd slept until noon, hazy from the prior evening's bout of drinking. She pulled the string outside the reverend's door. No answer. She walked in after knocking lightly.

"Cousin." Andrew's eyelids were heavy and swollen, he sat, unmoving in front of the burned out fireplace. Lacey headed toward their bedroom.

"She won't see anyone. She will ignore you, or if you're lucky, she will speak to you and tell you to go away."

With hesitation she said, "That doesn't sound like Cameron."

"It doesn't, but she's not herself. Please, don't go in there just now. I've only just come out and . . . she needs to rest."

"Alright, for now." She reluctantly heeded his warning and advice and went in silence to the kitchen, poured out cold and stale coffee, and began to percolate some a fresh.

Eleven

After seeing the doctor and Sarah home safely, Blaine finally made it to his own. He looked upon his shack in wonderment, if one could call this home. A twinge of sadness beheld him as he walked up the path—alone. Steam curled from his breath as he opened the door. It was dark and very cold inside. He lit a lantern and fixed his eyes upon the bed in the corner; a mouse scrambled off and away. Was he really living in a fine hotel, only months ago? Getting room service, receiving acknowledgement from his peers because he was a successful businessman? What was he doing? Wasting his time, that's what. Lacey's stubbornness and coldness toward him was working and finally taking its toll. He didn't have a chance. He bellowed out an insane laugh that was not his own and blew out the light, for no for the thought that he'd ever had a chance struck him funny. Blaine crawled into bed, no longer caring and too tired to try. The emotional turmoil he'd just experienced with Andrew, then coming home to this hole in the earth, was beginning to weary him. It was the first in over a year that Blaine Jennings forgot to pray before going to bed.

❦

"She won't see anybody, and she won't eat," Andrew complained to Dr. Colvin. The reverend looked dejected and helpless. "That doesn't surprise me. She's lost not only a child, Andrew, but gained a feeling of failure. It was her body that lost a baby, *your* baby; that sense of loss affects one's ability to rationalize natural circumstance. Cameron was really sick, but no but she'll get better, and you two will have lots of babies to fill your home."

Dr. Colvin could see Andrew contemplating the advice and encouragement he'd attempted to give. "I don't know. It's almost as if she blames me. I love her so much. I want to reach her and don't know how."

"Walk with me, Reverend."

Andrew's red-rimmed eyes noticed he'd stopped the old man in the street. He flushed and fell in step beside him.

"I'm on my way to the telegraph office," Dr. Colvin volunteered. "Do you know why?"

"No, sir, I don't."

"I'm advertising for a new doctor."

Understanding registered on Andrew's face, "I guess it's time for that."

J.C. Colvin snorted and laughed, "Been more than time for that! Should of done this years ago—but I love what I do so much I kept this town all to myself. Time to spread the wealth, you could say." His eyes took on a mischievous twinkle. "I've been holding out on some young fellow, making someone miss out on sewing up stab wounds, pulling out bullets, setting broken bones, and yes . . . delivering babies. She'll come around. You have an advantage over most of us, you have faith, hope, and love. Folks think that preachers need to do all the praying, but I'll be doing some praying for you."

They reached the telegraph office together. Andrew blinked back the moisture in his eyes, "We appreciate you and your kindness." He looked at the message in his friend's wrinkled hands; it contained the end of his life as he knew it.

"And I'll be praying for someone to take your place, if they can be only half as good as you, we'll be getting us a fine doctor."

"Go on home to your wife, Reverend, and give her time—time to mourn, and as unnecessary as it is, to forgive herself."

Andrew sat in his darkened living room with Cameron, as usual, in the back bedroom. All was quiet with the exception of sputtering and crackling sounds coming from the fireplace. With elbows balanced on knees, Andrew tucked his face into his hands. He needed a few moments—to think, to pray, to ponder.

There was simply nothing else he could do for his wife's state of mind. Nothing except give it up to the One who is beyond able to comfort and care for her—for their marriage. Several moments of silence and waiting passed before Andrew felt a peace settle over him, removing anxiousness, doubt, and fear of not being enough for his hurting bride. Yes, he was her husband and had a role to play, but it had been played out. He was doing and handling all things. "Forgive me, Lord. I've taken responsibilities beyond myself. I give this situation, Cameron, our . . . baby up to you. I ask that You make a way for things to be right, touch her heart as you've been so faithful to touch mine."

Release and ease came. Andrew looked toward the door that was always shut, the door his wife used to separate him from her, unconsciously using it to shut out hurt and pain. Andrew stood, no longer torn between duty to his wife and the church. He was not abandoning her or her needs. She had to know deep down that he was always there for her. He was just done pushing and pleading for her to accept the situation and him and the way things were. It was his baby, too, and the pain of it all had blown him away, but he did not understand Cameron's lack of hope, and he did not understand her depression and not being able to rise above this. He was ready to step aside and allow God to work in her life. It was time for him to leave, to go to the church, prepare a sermon for Sunday. Newly filled with hope and peace, Andrew whispered to the closed door, "Bless you, Cameron Jackson."

She heard the door click and was torn between relief at being alone and anger at him for leaving her. As her feelings warred with one another, she curled herself up and laid on her side. Cameron was letting herself go, having no desire to do anything but lie in the safety of her bed—alone—eating only out of necessity and seeing no one. She did not care about anything, for no for nothing was worse than losing her baby. And Andrew, how could he move on so quickly? Did he not care? With an abundant amount of time alone, Cameron began to think about her childhood. Her drunken father's rages. She spent many hours as a child crawling up into a ball in a corner of the house, pulling her dirtied apron over her head so she couldn't see. Shoving her palms against her ears so she couldn't hear. To sit and wait for the moment her mama would cautiously, so as not to scare her, tug at her apron. When she did, it meant it was over. Her pa would be asleep somewhere or gone again. Her mama would then hold her tightly, and Cameron would see fresh wounds on her arms and face as she held and sang to her, usually for hours. And she remembered her mama dying of pneumonia, and on her deathbed, ordering her seventeen-year-old daughter to go and find Thomas, the brother who'd been forced to leave while Cameron was in her mama's womb. She remembered being rejected by this new brother. He was supposed to be family, and he'd rejected her time and time again before finally coming around and accepting her. Finally, in Cameron's more recent memories, she saw Jake Collins's face before her. She had given herself to him, not knowing it wasn't right, not knowing he was not meant to be her husband. She remembered the time she was alone at Spillman's Creek; it was the time she went in search of the God Andrew always spoke of, and she'd found Him. She had been full of His love, full of His peace, and full of contentment that day and from then on. Until now.

Cameron turned and laid on her back, placing her hand on her empty womb, she cried aloud, "Don't you see, God. I've been through all of those things. I could go through them all again if needed. But this . . . anything but this . . ." Bitter tears slid down her cheeks. "This is not fair, this baby was a part of me. You should not have let him die . . . after all I've been through." She did not give Him a chance to respond, to comfort, or to settle her spirit. She did not want to remember anymore.

※

Lacey was obliged to work at the restaurant with the beautiful spring weather bringing in customers. It narrowed the time she could spend tending to Cameron, who, by way of isolating herself, had hurt Lacey deeply. Quite frankly, Cameron was not easy to be around; she was either withdrawn in an eerie manner or looked as though she despised you. Andrew was right; she was not the same. If this can happen to a preacher's family, then there truly was no hope for the rest of them. But Lacey knew this all along; she only needed prove her point to her fanatic cousin. What else will it take for them to see that they are wrong to believe what they do?

A week of rest and refreshing of the mind brought Blaine into the restaurant that afternoon. It was as if he hadn't ever had a seed of doubt where Lacey was concerned.

Blaine made his way to Lizette, "It's a fine afternoon, wouldn't you say?"

She nodded mutely, as though speaking to him would land her in trouble. Lizette led him to a prime table by the window where he could observe the town's goings on while he dined. Only he wouldn't be looking at the town today, he had eyes only for the woman with black raven hair. When Lacey took notice of the new arrival, she scowled her usual scowl. He received it with a grin; nothing she could do today would shake him. Blaine had resolved in his mind again that he was here to stay and to fight, however long it took. He unnerved her; he could see it in her mannerisms. She looked radiant to him with her hair all pinned up and over-fine dress. Blaine's annoying gaze faltered; she turned to see why. Ed Randall was waiting for her attentions, oblivious to Blaine. Lacey wasn't oblivious and took this opportunity to forget about him and his unreasonable, discomfiting presence. Coquettishly, Lacey reached up and laced her slender fingers around Ed's neck.

She was glad for a distraction and needed to fight the impulse of appreciating her husband's handsome features. "Come and have a drink with me in my room, Lizette can finish up here."

Ed hesitated; the wall he was trying to put up never seemed to make it past the first layer. He acquiesced and allowed himself to be led up the stairs, never having much discipline in his life, and certainly had none where Lacey Jennings was concerned.

Blaine drained his coffee. His stomach twisted as he watched them leave together. So much for unwavering resolve. Why was he putting himself through this? How much more could a man take? Rejected over and over again. He paid his bill and left—confusion teased him. He thought he was doing what God wanted, restoring what had been lost. Could he have been wrong? Maybe he was reaping the consequences of his past actions. But somehow, he couldn't get himself to imagine God forgiving him, guiding him, only to punish him. Blaine wanted more than anything absolute answers and concrete direction; when was he ever going to get that?

***

Lacey sat on her settee and reflected on her last trip out to Andrew's, only to leave once again hurt and disheartened. What was happening? She, of all people was being shut out of Cameron's life. All was lost now. No one had ever not needed Lacey Jennings. Cameron wanted to live in pathetic misery, fine. Jake wanted to succumb to a horrible life of killing for money and being aloof, alone, and mean. Andrew, sweet Andrew, even set boundaries on their relationship; apparently he thought she was too controlling.

Ed pulled his vest on and adjusted the Silver Star. "I need to pay a visit to Clyde Montgomery today. Joseph said his foreman stopped by. I hope to settle this mess soon." He tugged on a boot. "Lacey?"

"Hmm?"

A flash of anger scourged through him. "Nothin.' Nothin' at all."

She heard her bedroom door close abruptly, looked back, and saw that Ed was gone. Shrugging her shawl closer about her shoulders, Lacey poured herself another drink and continued to gaze out the window. Was her purpose in life just to be here? Run a restaurant day after day? She snorted aloud; she would be an old, ugly spinster who nobody wanted. How come everyone was finding that they could function without her, or worse, wanted to function without her? There had to be someone who needed help. Someone destitute, unhappy, scared.

If only she looked into a mirror, she would find that someone. Lacey looked down onto the street and saw Lizette and her light frame struggling beneath a heavy sack of flour. Suddenly, strong hands removed it from her as if it were a small sack of rice.

"Blaine. Thank you." She looked toward the buggy loaded with supplies, "I . . . can manage the rest."

He laughed at her and her attempt to keep his distance away from her boss. He brushed past her, deposited the flour into the kitchen, and returned to finish unloading. Before long, Blaine, his kindness, and his humor was contagious, and Lizette was relaxed and enjoying his company. She was laughing with him on their last trip to the kitchen . . . and this is how Lacey purposely came upon them.

Lacey's gaze burned at Lizette and her act of disloyalty. Blaine smiled sheepishly at Lizette, "Good day, Lacey, wouldn't you say?"

A smile was in his eyes as he spoke to her and in no way reflected her mood. "Lizette, I assume the tables are set for the next meal?" Lacey inquired haughtily, baldly ignoring her handsome, handsome, husband.

Lizette stifled a nervous giggle, "Yes, ma'am. But I do have other things I can tend to."

Lacey's rudeness backfired, now she would be left alone with . . . him. "As do I," she spoke to Lizette's retreating back and proceeded to follow her.

"Not so fast, Lacey Jennings."

She stiffened. "Do not use that name!" she shrieked without turning around.

Blaine watched her stalk off with nothing other than a warm smile upon his lips. He'd had his moments of giving up, but always after seeing his wife and seeking and praying, he'd find hope again. He couldn't help but hope they had made progress together when ministering to the needs of those families affected by scarlet fever.

A scuffle was heard down the street, and Blaine went along with others to the site.

"I'm telling you, *Sheriff*, stop interfering with Mr. Zemke's business." As he spoke, Byron Slate gained their attention. Distinguishing himself as Ian Zemke's right hand man, namely, his hired gun.

"Are you threatening me?"

Byron peeled off his black Stetson, ran a finger along its rim, and replaced it. He looked up toward the gray sky as if contemplating how to answer such a stupid question. Looking smartly into Ed Randall's eyes, he said, "I am."

Seeing as how this would not or ever would be settled in the lawful way, not with guns being hired on and the like, Ed resigned. "I will arrest the first man who disobeys the law. I will not be intimidated."

Two of Byron's cronies stepped up alongside him. They had been watching, waiting for action from the boardwalk, choosing now to display their presence as they felt it was needed. Ed placed his hand on the butt of his gun; he was surrounded, but meant what he said. He would not shirk into cowardice.

"Don't do it, Sheriff." Byron's hand, too, went to his gun. Blaine watched the scene unfolding in the middle of the street. No one seemed to care that it was broad daylight. He stepped down from the entrance to Lacey's. Obviously unarmed, but he would help the sheriff in any way he could if it came to that, despite his feelings toward the man.

"Mr. Zemke wants to handle this himself, or else . . ."

"Or else what?" Ed's sweaty palm now had a firm grip on the familiar handle.

"There's gonna be a range war. One way or another."

"I said I would arrest the first . . ."

"Yeah, yeah, yeah, we all heard what you said." Byron stepped aside, as if it was beneath him to do what needed doing. "Boys."

Ed looked angrily at Ronnie Appleton. He'd dealt with the boy one time too many. Clearly, he hadn't made an impression on the young man as having any authority. *I'm too lenient.* Ed's thoughts were resentful.

Garrett unholstered his gun and aimed it at Ed and Byron said, "Let's try this without guns." He folded his arms and kept an amused look on his face. Ronnie grabbed the sheriff's gun and tossed it away with his own. Garrett threw his aside and both men began to circle the lone man with a star of insignificance on his vest. Ed's arms were raised in a defensive position, trying to follow each man, his eyes shifting this way and that. But he lost sight of Garrett. Knowing there was no use, he plunged on ahead and struck first. His blow snapped Ronnie's head back. Ed did not back down while he had the advantage, the unction, the temper. He swung violently, throwing as many punches as he could, hitting one man after the other. He'd never fought so in his life. He'd been pelted around, sure enough, but never fought thinking he might win. Ronnie's face was bloodied, but Garrett had successfully ducked out on most of the blows. Garrett turned the sheriff's body toward his away from Ronnie, who was staggering with dizziness. Blaine watched with caution, surprised at the vehemence in which Ed fought. Ed was weakening, though, his arms tiring. He shook his head to focus on his fully charged and not very wounded target. Garrett swung; the left side of Ed's jaw cracked. He rubbed it, opened, and reopened it, testing its flexibility. The other side of his face near his eye was being battered. The sheriff held his stance, swinging whenever he could, sometimes hitting his mark, sometimes not. When Ronnie regained momentum and picked the gun up from the dirt, Blaine stepped into the fray.

"Butt out, Mister."

To Byron he said, "You said no guns. This isn't a fair fight."

Byron stood to his full height and weighed his opponent's protest. Upon Ed falling to the ground under Garrett's persistent jabbing, Byron announced it was over. Turning his threatening eyes to Blaine, he said, "I think the *sheriff* has learned his lesson for the day."

Blaine looked down at Ed's lifeless body. A deep cut oozed thick, sticky blood above his eyebrow. One eye was almost sealed tight from the bruising impacts and immediate swelling. He was just about to offer his help when Ed moaned, "Get out of here, Blaine. I never asked for your help!"

Without extending his hand fully, Blaine walked away and said to one of the onlookers in a tone void of much emotion, "Your Sheriff needs some help."

Twelve

Thomas Engel was not known to be a man of compassion, least of all a comforter to women. But what was he supposed to do when the Doc demanded he go see his sister? The cranky old doctor threatened to not treat the gang next time they needed it if Thomas did not bid his "request." Seeing the fierce look in the graying man, Thomas believed him and agreed to one visit. But he made it clear, "I don't guarantee nothing. If she don't wanna see me, I will not push my way where I'm not wanted!"

There was no answer after knocking on the door. Thomas paced uncomfortably across the patio and ran his calloused hand through his hair. "Let's get this over with," he mumbled. He entered inside cautiously, not wanting to startle Cameron. The place was dark because no curtains had been opened yet. Thomas saw a healthy fire and bread slices on the table waiting to be spread with the jar of berry jam next to it. He surmised that Andrew had laid out his wife's breakfast. Thomas contemplated taking off his coat; it would mean a commitment to stay longer than he wanted to—but how would it look going into her room with it on? He cursed in indecision, a bad habit of his that Cameron had scolded him about often. Thomas crept toward her bedroom. His last time there was when the doctor took his blood and gave it to her, still amazed at that, he said aloud, "Crazy Doc."

"Andrew?"

Thomas took off his coat and opened her door, not waiting for the invite he was sure he would not receive. He took a seat in the chair under the window. Cameron was sitting up in bed reading a book by the light of a lantern, even though she only needed to open a curtain to have light.

"Kinda depressing in here, don't ya' think?"

She laid down her book and looked at him, the brother she'd fought so hard to win his favor, his love. He looked back at her with their mother's hazel eyes. He was concerned and it touched her heart.

"I hadn't noticed."

"I can see that, Cameron. You're looking well."

She looked away from him. His attempt at humor had not moved her. In truth, she wondered what she really did look like. She knew how she felt though. "Did Andrew tell you to come?"

"No." A half-truth. Let her think he was here on his own accord. "Would it matter if he did?"

Unable to keep to herself another moment, she blurted, "Everything was fine, Thomas! I have you, I have Andrew. I was going to have a baby!"

Thomas had to search for words, "Can you only be happy if you have a baby?"

She looked sharply at him. "You have no idea."

"Of course I don't! But I know that we have to pick ourselves up, for Pete's sake!" He hadn't meant for his tone to rise, but seeing her like this, his once radiant, enduring sister. "You, of all the people I know have persevered and kept going, no matter what."

"Maybe I can't anymore, Thomas. I just can't."

Whatever tears she thought were long gone and dried up surged forth and spilled down her wan cheekbones. He cursed softly, he did not like tears.

"Stop swearing."

Should he go to her? He removed his gunbelt and sat on the edge of the bed with her, as close as he felt he could get without having to touch and physically console her. "You blame Andrew?"

Looking straight ahead, she replied, "I guess I did . . . I do." It sounded absurd even as she said it. Of course it wasn't Andrew's fault. She hadn't blamed him for the loss itself, it just didn't seem as if it bothered him the way she thought it should. "I don't know what to think! I've been so awful to him. The kinder he is to me, the more horrible I am to him!" If the tears weren't coming before, they were now. Shaken by her abhorrent behavior, Cameron dwelt on Andrew. It only took an outsider to show her, to speak the truth to her.

"I don't know what to tell you about that. Somehow, I don't think you could do anything to make him not love you."

She nodded pathetically, swiping at her tears. "I'm sure I know that." Cameron turned her eyes on him. He stiffened, feeling that a hug was forthcoming. "Thank you for saving my life that day, Thomas." She laced her thin arms around his strong shoulders and stayed in that spot longer than he thought was necessary. He patted her bony back awkwardly. "I think first things first—you need to get some meat on your bones."

She would never forget her son, just like she would never forget her mama, but she knew somehow her life would come back and she would know it as before. Her brother's presence had been a gift although she was sure he would never know it.

When Andrew came home that evening, prepared to cook dinner for himself to sit in solace well into the night, praying for his wife and their marriage, he had surely been surprised. Cameron, still very pale from lack of sunlight, nutrition, and life, had the table set for two, and he could smell the scent of fried chicken wafting throughout his warm home. He stood at the door waiting, wondering if it all meant that she was his again, wholly and completely, and knew it was so as she humbly walked into his open arms.

Thirteen

The man was judgmental, conceded, and reproached those beneath him without tact or remorse. Charles Grover was the new physician for Lincoln County and made his way through the defiled town toward the residence of Dr. J.C. Colvin. The seasoned, older doctor opened the door and received his visitor warmly, "Dr. Grover, is it?"

His guest took in Dr. Colvin's hunched physique, his eyes rested upon the doctor's slightly shaky, age spotted hands. "I presume you are Dr. Colvin?" The man talked down his nose, his eyes roaming Dr Colvin's residence. Regrettably, Dr. Colvin closed the door. It was a bittersweet sensation to be able to retire, knowing you've done your best to help those in need, to heal and to deliver life. But to see this upcoming, obviously intelligent young easterner come to take his place ... would he care for the people? Would he serve the community? Both men spoke proper greetings to one another; Dr. Colvin offered tea or coffee.

"Thank you, no. I just came to meet the famous Dr. Colvin and obtain some knowledge about this, ah, town." They covertly appraised the other during their short time together; neither was fooled by their prospective dislike. Dr. Grover thought sourly that the man before him should have retired long before now; why, the man could barely pour himself a cup of coffee. It's a wonder he could still doctor, then again, that's why *he* was here—because he couldn't! Dr. Colvin looked upon the dour face of the man in his living room; he would not do for the people. He could feel it in his old bones, but there was nothing to be done about it. He'd hired him, and unless Dr. Grover quit, the town was stuck with him. The new graduate had surgery skills that were fresh and innovative, and he supposed that was more important than character. While they sat chatting, Dr. Grover received his first patient.

"You know where to put him," Dr. Colvin announced, moving out of the way for Ed to stumble in with one of Ian's henchmen, who was barely conscious.

"What have we got here?" Dr. Grover snapped. After laying the injured cowboy onto a patient's bed, Ed stood.

Exertion showed in his reddened face and looked questionably at Dr. Colvin. "Who's this?" Before the familiar doctor could answer, Dr.

Grover said with curt authority, "*I* am the new doctor. Tell me exactly what happened."

Dr. Colvin shrugged his shoulders helplessly to Ed, permitting him to answer.

Stating the obvious, Ed said, "He's been shot."

Dr. Grover watched the sheriff's retreating back as he left Ian's man in their care. "Whatever in the world . . ." The patient moaned, placing the irritated doctor's attention where it belonged. Always prepared, Dr. Colvin held a chloroform scented sterile cloth over to Dr. Grover and waited to see the man's medical gifts and abilities.

"This man's in extremis!"

The word was not quite one that Dr. Colvin would have used being a simple country doctor, but he agreed, "Yes, he is near death."

"Where is your surgical tray?"

"Here."

Dr. Grover looked at it with dissatisfaction. "I suppose it will have to do for now."

Joseph Benton was nearly finished with his tenure of consequence under watch and care of Ed Randall, and he was now in training to serve as his deputy. Joseph had proved himself over the last several months and gained Ed's trust. The young man was fiercely loyal, not only to Ed, but also to Jake, and he would serve the town well. He followed the sheriff around, asking questions, seeking answers. He surprised Ed in his tenaciousness to be like him. Ed Randall was sure there were better mentors out there for Joseph and tried to tell him as much, but the young man closed his ears to it all. He'd found his true calling; someday, he would become the sheriff of a town all his own. Blood pumped through his veins hot and fast as anxiousness for the sure to come range war loomed ahead of them all. Joseph thought of the recent shooting and asked, "The trouble settle down with the baron's?"

Ed shook his head somberly, "For the moment."

"What exactly happened?" Joseph picked up a stick in the street in a boyish way and broke it into little pieces as Ed explained, "Ian's man picked a fight with Clyde while he ordered up some fencing for his property. Clyde's man didn't take too kindly to it and shot him, plain and simple."

They were within a few steps of the jail and Joseph inquired, "But we haven't arrested anybody."

"That's because it was self-defense."

"But it wasn't."

"And don't we all know it. Listen, we don't move hasty like in these situations, we wait until the whole thing erupts, otherwise they'll use ya'—each side will just use ya.' We'll take it slow and see what happens; it's all we can do."

The very thought that crossed Joseph's deputy training mind was that the sheriff said "we," which meant he was included and his day was made. Ed realized that his experience with Byron Slate was just the beginning. All the taunting, disputing, and threatening had been done with the purpose of building up hostilities and placing people on either the side of Ian Zemke or Clyde Montgomery.

The fifth month of the year arrived, supplying Lincoln County with an abundance of rain. Lacey drank in solitude in the saloon, attempting to drown away her loneliness. Never in her life has she felt herself so alone, not surrounded by friends or even regular people for that matter. Lizette came, worked, and went home to Mack.

It was not yet noon and Liam cast wry glances Lacey's way, not sure if he should tell her she was on her way to drinking too much. He'd never done a thing like that before with her and didn't relish in starting to now. Of course, he'd never been worried about her state of mind before now either. Lacey mistook Liam's attitude toward her as judgmental and not concern. She roused herself up in bad temper and shot him a glare and tossed back her drink as a man would have. She grabbed her shawl and slammed the door behind her. Liam shook his head and proceeded to set up for the evening. Lacey wandered over to the livery and ordered up a buggy to be prepared, despite Mr. Donovan's warning of "terrible roads to be traveling on." Lacey whipped the reins on the backs of her team and left town. She'd had no plans other than to get away . . . from what? Herself? Her shawl and hat whisked around with the heavy breeze and unwise pace. A feeling of drunken euphoria enveloped her, and before realizing it, she urged her horses to move faster. The route she chose to take out of town was not one she was familiar with and was unsure for a moment why she chose it. She remembered a pond in the area from an eternity ago and decided to find it. It wasn't really a pond, but a large indentation in the ground that filled up with spring waters—and come upon it she did, right in the thick of it. Lost in her thoughts of self-pity and acrimonious attitude toward her supposed friends, she did not see it ahead of her, beyond a hedge of stout weeds. She cursed in disbelief and found herself stranded in the buggy, her horse's knees deep in mud! Looking around for a possible passageway out for her, she saw none. Lacey clucked her tongue and gently coaxed the animals, pleading for them to pull out. It was useless.

To top off her horrible, incomparably worst day ever, raindrops fell lightly onto her porcelain cheeks. "To blazes with it all!" she shrieked. Looking in the back of the buggy, she found an old, smelly blanket, which she did not deem herself ready for, and tools to fix a broken wheel. But what she wanted right now was what she brought. Lifting a bottle of sweet rum and opening it easily, she looked around to confirm she was indeed by herself and drank straight from the bottle. Now what? Clouded by enough drink to fog her rational thinking, she stepped from the buggy with her treasured bottle tucked under one arm. Her free hand lifted her satin skirts to avoid getting them dirty, she took a step . . . and fell. Red-faced and swearing like a mad man, she fell repeatedly, getting sucked in the mud time and time again, never gaining solid footage. She responded to her absurd circumstances and laughed loud and hard, tears rolled down her face at the drunken mess she was in; the horses looked at her curiously, alert to their insecure situation. Lacey decided it was time to go for help. She crawled in her sodden state to the edge of the cursed "pond" and stood on shaky legs. That was when she saw the rider, not caring what she looked like, if she had been sober, she surely would have . . . she called out to the man.

Blaine Jennings stared stupefied at his wife. His elegant creature of a wife was covered head to toe in mud and drunker than a skunk. "Oh, Lord!"

Lacey scrambled herself up and took notice of her rescuer. Rolling her eyes heavenward, she declared to the skies above, "You must *really* hate me!"

Blaine, with utmost caution, dismounted and tried desperately hard not to laugh, for that, he knew, would only add to the fire in his wife's eyes.

"You," she said before stumbling, "can just get on your horse and go back to wherever it was that you came from!" It was a humorous sight to see her adjusting her attire and hairstyle with a filthy hand and holding onto a bottle of alcohol in the other.

"If that's what you want," he replied. Blaine wondered how far she would let him go without humbling herself. There was simply no one around for miles that would be able to offer his or her *better* assistance. Her pride lasted longer than he thought possible, he barely heard her call out to him. He turned, nonchalantly around on his horse, cupped his hand over his ear, "Yes?"

"Ugh!" She began stomping toward him with her coveted bottle. The rain picked up, drenching her silky black hair as she walked toward him. Blaine stayed still, high on his horse. If he appeared too anxious, she might feel as if she had the upper hand; if he appeared like he was, aloof and uncaring, *he'd* have it. As lightening began to crackle overhead, he realized that neither one had time for games. He snatched her protesting self upon his horse and cantered back to the buggy, shielded somewhat by an uncommon area of dense trees. Blaine plucked her down from him, soothed the startled horses, and pulled their calves out of the mud. He unhitched the buggy and flipped it upside down.

"*What* are you doing?" she snapped haughtily.

"Making a shelter for us. Unless you'd rather stand out in the rain, you think you're above getting struck by lightening?" He sat underneath the overturned buggy; the leather seat touched the tip of his head. She looked around as if she was debating what would be better, lightning, or climbing into that intimate space with . . . Blaine. The thunderous sounds above decided for her, but not before daring a long swig of her bottle, her comfort. She climbed in with him. Both were silent in each other's presence and nearness, as if speaking would break loose the hedge of protection set up around both hearts. An agonizingly long hour passed and the rain had only increased in strength, all the while, she stubbornly ignored him. Blaine's legs were soaked. In order for Lacey to be fully submerged underneath the wagon, he'd had to stretch out his legs. He was nearly beside himself when she collapsed from drink and exhaustion. The top half of her body eased across his lap. He lifted his arms, as if guilty of touching her in any way. Before he knew it, he was adjusting her position to what he considered would be more comfortable for her. Not knowing exactly what to do with himself, he placed his arms at his sides, keeping them idle. Lacey moaned in her "sleep" and started weeping slightly; his stomach clenched and his heart ached at the renewed love he had for her. Unable to restrain, Blaine began stroking her face, clearing the dried, muddy hair away from her cheeks and eyelashes. He set his gaze on her beautiful features, and that's where he remained until he fell asleep. It was barely light out when they stirred and woke several hours later. Sobered, Lacey looked at him in abrupt anger as if it were his fault they were in this predicament.

In an accusing voice, she said, "*I'm* leaving!" singling herself out in case he thought to follow her.

He sat back relaxed, even placed his hands up behind his head. *Fine, let her see the conditions out there.*

Off his look, she snorted and mumbled, "Arrogant!" Lifting the flap Blaine must have arranged with the old blanket, she gasped. They were entrenched in mud. Blaine's horse stood somewhat dry underneath some trees, feeding on weeds, and Mr. Donovan's team wasn't far away, doing the same. Lacey began to tremble and look sickly.

"Oh, no!" He blurted. Lacey vomited the contents of her stomach all over the area. Helpless, Blaine watched, sad for her, knowing he could make her life better, happier. If only she would forgive him and allow him back in her life.

"Land sakes, Lacey. I couldn't begin to drink as much as you did!"

She looked at him with brazen amusement, "No, I don't suppose you could."

"Well, you messed up our shelter. Despite the rain, we're leaving. It's stopped thundering so it's safe enough, I expect."

"Where do you intend on taking me?" she asked coyly, seeming to feel better, more like herself. Blaine gathered the horses. His was the only saddled one, "My place."

He smiled to himself—*now that shut her up.*

"I will not go to your place!"

He mounted with ease. "Suit yourself." Blaine watched stubbornness work with confusion, and, after giving her a moment, he held his hand down to her and was both happy and surprised that she accepted it. Lacey braced herself as he pulled her up, sitting in front of her husband almost made her swoon, and she would have if she hadn't conjured up memories of betrayal and pain. He felt her body stiffen against him and although he would cherish this moment for what it was, a desperate situation, he knew his work was still cut out for him.

Unwilling to venture into his domain, Lacey stood proudly and very near the front door. She looked around his unrefined cabin, wanting to find something she could criticize; she found nothing. Blaine always had fine, if not exquisite tastes and she took note that he'd done his best with what he had. A violent shiver overcame her as Blaine was reviving and rebuilding a fire in the cook stove. She'd done her perusing of his place while his back was to her and was glad he did not see her brief countenance of approval.

He wordlessly disappeared. When he returned with a bundle of clothing for her, he watched a while as she stood near the source of heat. Her palms reached toward the warmth of it; he found that he could soak in the sight of her for a very long time. She felt his presence near but did not turn around for fear of him seeing the anguish that was surely showing on her face. The whirlwind of emotions stirring inside of her frightened her to the core.

"Lacey."

Her name on his lips came out in a hoarse whisper; clearing his throat, he said, "Please put these on. They'll be plenty big on you, but at least they're dry."

She turned to him, forcing herself to look stern. Her gaze followed down to the clothing in his familiar hands and her haughty gaze softened. She accepted his offering and her hand brushed against his, causing feelings provoked to rise and fall in the pit of his stomach. She carried her petite frame to where he came, knowing it must be his bedroom, and she momentarily hesitated at his door before setting down her pride and entering.

Lacey changed. Her husband's clothes hung comically on her despite many tucks and rolls. She could not help it. Instead of not caring about what she looked like for the man she disdained most in this world, she went to the small mirror on his dresser and made haste to fix her horrid appearance.

Ed Randall was in the saloon and witnessed the late hour Lacey entered the foyer. He looked at her in disgust and watched her climb the stairs in man's clothing. He heard a buggy driving off and stepped outside. A jog down the boardwalk showed him who dropped her off. Panic gripped his middle, and not long after, hatred and loathing followed. But it was not solely directed at the figure of Blaine as he drove off, but toward himself, he was an idiot and a fool.

Fourteen

It had long been routine for Blaine to join the Jackson's every Sunday for dinner, and this particular Sunday, Cameron took note of his excitable demeanor.

"Cameron, you've out done yourself! This is the best ham I've tasted in a long while," Blaine praised, before placing a forkful of it into his mouth, his grinning eyes glancing back and forth between them before slicing off another piece. Andrew cocked an eyebrow at his wife. It was good, but ham was ham, wasn't it? Cameron smiled circumspectly, waiting for Blaine to share what was really on his mind. News of the eccentric doctor and his abrupt manner and intolerance of "plain" folk had infiltrated the town and beyond. Without gossiping, Andrew shared his concern and decided to pay a much needed visit to Dr. Grover. "I agree, before something else happens like the incident with Mr. Hanover," Blaine concurred.

"What happened with Mr. Hanover?" Cameron asked innocently. Both men laughed before Andrew composed himself enough to explain, "Mind you this is just what we heard..."

"Dr. Grover had the audacity to inform Mr. Hanover and his wife, who had just given birth to their fourth child, that they should be done increasing their family. It looked to him as if they couldn't afford anymore children, and so he suggested that the man *abstain* from his wife."

Blaine sat up and finished the telling, "So, Mr. Hanover, fuming mad, I'm sure, retrieved his shot gun from the mantel and chased the doctor out of hearth and home. He even fired off a few shots to prove his anger. The doctor ran for his dear life, I'm afraid."

Cameron stifled a giggle, picturing the stiff-bodied doctor running scared. "Dr. Colvin seems to be liking his retirement, been at Lacey's for breakfast most every day, I've been told." Cameron wisely set the conversation in the direction to where she really wanted to go, to Lacey.

Blaine grinned broadly, "I hear that too."

The door was open and the opportunity had arisen for him to talk about the ordeal with Lacey. Cameron listened in both concern and elation.

"So," Blaine held their attention with hope in his eyes, "We ate a light supper together. Mind you, she kept cautious of me, but for the first time, I did not feel as though she wanted to poison me or something rather."

Andrew smiled at his jest, but was pleased, "We've been praying for her, Blaine, for the both of you."

"Thank you, and please, whatever you do, don't stop."

"May I come in?" Cameron asked.

Their relationship was strained and rightly so since she'd rejected Lacey's visits. But it was time now to make things right. Lacey stared at the door, surprised to hear Cameron's voice on the other side of it. Instantly recalling that she had recently been abandoned by the very one knocking, Lacey said casually, "If you must."

It only took a moment after entering that the two found themselves crying in one another's embrace. Sobbing apologies and regrets into each other's shoulders, Cameron held Lacey's reddened wet cheeks between her hands, "I've missed you so. I've been a terrible friend!"

Lacey nodded her agreement.

A laugh escaped her lips and Cameron sighed, "Well, what do we do now?"

Lacey sighed and wiped her cheeks and chest daintily with a lace handkerchief, "I'll just be a moment." She opened her door and stepped out.

Cameron was left alone for how long she didn't know. She made herself comfortable at a round table, upon it were photographs scattered about. Picking one up to admire, she saw that it had been a wedding picture of the Jennings. The delicate face of her beautiful friend with the blackest hair she'd ever seen stared back at her, Cameron blinked back tears. Lacey was clearly happy, young and in love, standing next to an equally handsome young man. Lacey arrived with a tray of bread and cheese, some cookies, coffee, and tea.

"I didn't know what you felt like eating." Her voice was solemn; she wanted to make up for all of the conversations over coffee she had missed.

"Lacey..."

"That photo is ten years old." She set down the tray and sat still with her hands in her lap. "I hated him, Cameron. I have tried so hard to hate him still, but I just can't. Not after spending time with him. I can't explain it, but I do believe he might have changed after all." Lacey began to relay pieces of the chance meeting between them in the rain, and although Cameron had already heard it, she listened intently to Lacey's side.

"He was so gentle, so aware. He made sure my needs were met that night, something he would have never done before."

It was not up to Cameron to talk of Blaine's transformation; Lacey would need to see it for herself. God had a plan and timing for everything under the sun, and Cameron was not about to mess with His plans.

"I'm so glad for you. That you were able to see Blaine and how he is now, that it's not an act." Cameron poured tea for the both of them and pushed a small plate of cookies toward Lacey, who would do well to eat something.

"It's been some year hasn't it, Cameron?"

"I suppose I have learned that hurt, pain, happiness . . ." Looking pointedly at Lacey, she continued, "Relationships help us grow, change, and become the people we are—which can be good or bad. I want to live a life worth talking about. I don't ever want to live in regret or bitterness; it's too hard to do, it takes too much work."

Always needed and never the one to need, Lacey resented her situation. She needed Cameron, she needed whatever it was that she was just then talking about . . . but couldn't quite reach out and embrace it. Not yet.

Fifteen

Byron Slate watched the train workers unload cargo from the iron beast, still huffing and grinding in its cool down phase. He placed the butt of his cigarette into the dirt and ground it out with the heel of his boot, his spurs rattled. With great pleasure, he waited until Clyde Montgomery's wagons were filled with the fencing he not only threatened, but promised to put up across his land. *Finally, I'm going to see some action.*

He lazily kicked himself off the fence post and pulled himself onto his horse. He couldn't wait to get news to Ian. It wouldn't be long now. Having since learned that Thomas and his gang hired on with Clyde made Byron's blood boil with excitement. At least they provided a respectable challenge, knowing it would be profitable to have a victory over the town's longstanding, most notable idols. He set his sights to travel straight to Ian's ranch.

It wasn't long before Thomas hailed those wagons toward the direction of a large barn on Clyde's many acres. He worked alongside Clyde's top hand, Travis Dayton.

Thomas cursed, noting a wagon train of seven steering its way up the dirt path. "Well, this is just grand. This ridiculous sideshow is advertising Clyde's fencing abilities to the whole town!"

Travis laughed in agreement, "That would be his way, that's for sure." He streamlined a spit of tobacco juice next to his own boot, not caring if he hit it or not. "Well, let's get the men to unload, then I want full guard on that barn twenty-four hours a day with your best men. If I were with Ian's men, I'd burn it to the ground."

He turned to Travis, judging him to not be as stupid as he looked, "Course, we aim to not let that happen."

"I'll get right on it, Boss."

Joseph Benton looked at the new shiny star on his black leather vest. Pride couldn't have shown brighter on his face. He'd just been sworn in by Sheriff Ed Randall as an official deputy of Lincoln County.

"Now for even better news," Ed said with outright alleviation. "Jake's given you some property to live on and take care of."

Joseph didn't miss Ed's relief, "I know, Sheriff. You've been saddled with me a long time, and finally, you get the place to yourself."

"Go see to your new property, Jake's waiting at the farm to take ya' there."

"Sheriff Randall?"

"Yes?"

"I just want to, well, I never had much of a home anyhow, so, thank ya'—for everything."

"Go on now. Don't keep a bounty hunter waiting, Jake gets meaner everyday."

If Joseph hadn't proved himself capable and changed so much since their first meeting, there would have been no way Ed would have succumbed to the boys pleading about being deputized. Ed just hoped he didn't make a wrong choice. Especially when it came time to deal with the powerful cattle barons, whenever they decided it was time to face off. He went back to work, but not before wishing desperately for the feelings for Lacey to go far from him—it hurt too much.

Lacey had been standing at her armoire for much too long. She felt as though she should forever wear black with her disconsolate and morose moods. What had happened to the spirited, not one to give up, beautiful woman? She glanced with shame at herself in the full-length mirror, feeling out of control of her emotions. Well, she would attempt one last endeavor toward pride and put on the old Lacey's face, even if it did not match her true internal self. One last chance to see where her miserable life was going, and if it spiraled downward, well, she would worry about that if and when the time came. She had outdone herself and did so on purpose. She pulled open her parasol to shield the sun's warmth and glare from her face. Everything would be just fine if Ed was only in his office. The whistles of appreciation that came from ogling cowboys boosted her confidence—she had to admit, she did look gorgeous this day. Lacey tapped on the door to the jail lightly and entered. Ed and another man were looking intently at a map spread out on his desk, clearing her throat she said,

"Hello, Ed." Both men looked toward their interruption; the stranger dropped the cigar from his mouth as he took her in. She smiled demurely at the two before sitting ever so delicately into a chair, as if she had business for the sheriff to attend to. "Uh, Royce, would you mind giving us a minute?"

"You bet ya'! Be right outside." Ed did not watch the man leave, nor did he address Lacey. He kept unseeing eyes to the map at hand. Giving himself a moment, he attempted to swallow the lump forming in his throat.

"Ed, I . . . you make me come down here to see you?"

Anger stirred with confusion. He looked at her then, silently complimenting her and her strategy, looking humble, distressed. Only he was not so foolish and gullible any more and that was her mistake. He stared at her from head to toe. She took it as admiration, for either love or lust, she did not care. He did admire her, he was a man, but it wasn't for love. Black ringlets hung down her sculptured collarbone, teasing the curves and roundness of her breasts. The scarlet red gown she adequately chose came to a low "V" in just that area. Her matching red lips were formed into a pout, asking to be kissed.

"I did come to see you, a few days ago."

She raised her eyebrows. "Well? I never saw you, and why haven't you bothered to come since?"

He could not believe his ears. Shaking his head, he said through clenched teeth, "You weren't there! In fact, I waited several hours, it was late. I saw you come in. You are right, you didn't see me."

"Ed, stop playing games! Why didn't you just come up to my room? You are acting a stranger to me. It isn't funny, if you're trying to teach me a lesson, fine! It's working!"

The gall this woman had. "I did not come to *your* room because I did not want any leftovers, thank you!"

She placed her hand over her chest, as if to halt increasing heart palpitations. "How could you say such a thing to me? Just a few months ago you wanted to marry me." She had failed. Not only had she lost Ed, but the beauty that once caught him. If she could not get him back looking the way she did, then her life was over. She would have nothing ever again. Seeing genuine remorse finally befall her face, his heart softened.

"I saw you come in wearing a man's clothes, Lacey. I looked outside and saw Blaine driving away. What am I supposed to think of that?" She was adamantly shaking her head in denial, but he would not let her speak, he would no longer listen to foolish words. "I thought you hated him. The Lacey I knew would not have given him a moment of her time. If you truly despised him . . . you would not have been with him, no matter what the circumstance."

"Ed . . ."

"No, Lacey."

Joseph Benton burst through the door, "Clyde's puttin' up his fence, Sheriff! Ian and his men are riding over, there's gonna be trouble!"

His nervous excitement filtered throughout the office. "Get my horse, Joseph."

"Yes, sir!"

Ed adjusted his gun belt and grabbed his hat. He stood at the door a moment—at least this was it, this would be the final good-bye, no more wondering.

Lacey stood abruptly, "Don't leave me like this, Ed. I have to explain!" She was reduced to begging? She would despise herself after this night, she knew that, but wasn't ready to let go of the present. The past was painful and the future was too uncertain. She must have Ed, her life depended on it. He secured his hat on his head and turned around toward the most beautiful woman in the world. She had been his at one time, if not with heart, then with body and soul.

With obvious emotional pain, he said, "It's over. It might have been over even if you didn't come to see me . . . there's a war about to start." He put on a brighter tone to his voice, "So you see? I might be out of your life forever, and you needn't worry about us at all. If you're lucky, I might not make it and may never come back."

To add to the sting of his words and for closure once and for all, he said, "Good day, *Mrs. Jennings.*"

Reverend Jackson concluded his sermon, "We must pray for peace in this territory. Good men are getting ready to fight, each one based on principal and pride. Good men will probably die." He looked toward his wife, "We must pray also for their souls, Amen?"

"Amen!"

The first church potluck for the beginning of summer had been cancelled, and people's nerves were tight and on edge. Men had been bought and, therefore, obligated to take sides. Cameron stood next to her husband as he said good-bye to each parishioner filing out of the church.

Andrew touched Cameron's hand after the last person descended down the steps, "Thomas can watch for himself." He encouraged, "He's smart; he won't be going into anything without a plan."

She could only nod, her thoughts and words were not as positive as her husbands. She needed to find hope and peace and was determined to seek God later and pray, as instructed by the Reverend, for her brother's soul and safety. If she'd had any strength to spare, she would go herself in protest of Thomas's involvement. As baseless as the attempt might be, no matter how Thomas conducted his life, she was never free of worrying about every breath he took and hoped that the dire circumstance before them all would not provide him with his last.

Blaine Jennings arrived later that afternoon for Sunday supper; the conversation surrounding the meal was at a low point. Somehow, it seemed unnatural to enjoy a family dinner when such division and hatred was going on around them.

"Good Word today, Andrew." Blaine lathered a thick sliced of bread with butter and scooped up the last of his creamed corn.

"I spoke what I felt to speak. I don't agree with either Clyde or Ian. Both are stubborn! Why can't people work things out amicably? Instead, they've called upon men who are farmers, small time ranchers, and merchants to fight for something that doesn't involve them. To fight for cattle barons who have everything they could possibly want!"

"It's the warrior in us," Blaine said this without sarcasm. He spoke truth and put it simply.

"Well, you're right, I suppose."

Cameron poured fresh cups of coffee and said, "I just want it all to be over."

"We all do."

"Well, I hate to eat and leave. I have business to attend to in town." Blaine pushed back an empty plate.

"On a Sunday?" Cameron's eyes sparkled mischievously.

Blaine stood. "Hotel's not closed on Sunday."

"In that case, I don't mind you being rude and not staying for dessert."

He pecked his hostess's cheek, "Thank you for the lovely meal, Mrs. Jackson."

✦

Blaine tethered his horse in front of the hotel and noticed a small and curious crowd following behind Jake Collins as he rode down the middle of the street. A packhorse with a dead body slung over it trailed behind. Jake was unrecognizable. Although his physique had filled out and built up, his hair was long. A full beard covered his hardened face and his eyes held no compassion whatsoever. Jake caught Blaine's eyes and barely nodded a greeting.

Blaine tipped his hat and coolly said, "Jake."

People stood in awe as they watched him fling an apparently wanted dead man's body onto the boardwalk of the jail. After adjusting himself, he ventured into the empty jail and office.

"Jake?" He spun around, hand immediately on the butt of his gun. Joseph flinched.

Jake released his tension. "Don't ever sneak up on a man like that. Not if ya' wanna live to see tomorrow!"

"Sorry . . . sorry. I wasn't sneakin' though. I saw you coming and wanted to tell you that the sheriff is gone." His eyes wandered over to the stiff body, a bullet hole targeted the middle of his forehead.

Jake snaked his hand impatiently throughout his hair, "When will he be back?" He wanted to claim his money. He had another job to do.

"He's up in cattle territory . . . Ian and Clyde . . ." Joseph waited for his words to ring a meaning to Jake; surely he was not that out of touch with the happenings of town.

"Yeah, right. *A range war*," he stated sarcastically.

"It's true, Jake! Men lining up all over to get the lowdown on their duties. I just came back to town for more supplies. Sheriff Randall expects we'll be gone a while."

Joseph lit up as if he had a bright idea. "Are ya' gonna help fight?" He liked Jake, most of the time, and knew if anyone could help the sheriff, it was him.

"I got a job to do."

"You mean someone else to kill? Ain't you ever gonna bring a man in alive?"

Jake cursed, "You sound like a woman!"

Joseph looked down. Jake used to be nice.

"What do you think they're gonna do out there? Men are going to die, *Joseph*. What's the difference if I bounty hunt or get myself involved with something I could care less about?"

"Ain't no difference!" Joseph spun around and went to the mercantile. Jake angrily swiped out a piece of parchment from Ed's desk and wrote a hasty note. Locking up the dead man so he could later claim his reward, he stalked out.

His horse needed a rest and a good feed, and he needed a long overdue visit to Liam's.

⁂

The Clarke family and the Appleton family had long been in feud with one another, being into its second generation now, though nobody really remembered why. They just knew that they disliked the other more than anything.

Naturally, upon hearing that the Appleton's were riding with Ian Zemke, it did not take much encouragement to persuade the Clarke's to hook up with the Montgomery outfit. It all seemed a legitimate excuse to vent their hatred and superiority over one another. Mrs. Clarke handed her husband, Duffy, a sack of food stores and a full canteen. Her eldest son, Brandon, accepted another set of the same from her.

"Now, you both go get 'em and come back home to me in one piece, ya' hear?"

Both knew she wasn't referring to Ian's men, but to the Appleton's. The matron of that family had been the one to up her last and she's been in an avenging mood since.

"Will do, darlin.'" To his other children, Duffy said good-bye. "Bye, Mama." Brandon's three youngest siblings wrapped themselves into their mama's skirts. "Be good for Mama," he ordered. Her men mounted their horses, and she wiped her hands on her apron and shielded the sun from her eyes. "Dirty, uppity, Appletons! Your day has come!"

Clyde Montgomery's bunkhouse was filling with men arriving from all parts of the county, his own small army much larger than Ian's. Travis Dayton stood in the middle of the sleeping quarters; men sat on beds, chairs, and the floor.

"Listen up! Mr. Montgomery has some words for us all." He turned toward the rich man and gestured that the floor was now his. "Mr. Montgomery."

"All right, boys, first of all, allow me to thank you for coming. I paid you all twenty dollars for just arriving, and those that stay until the end will receive another hundred, *cash*." The men groaned and murmured their excitement.

Continuing over the noise, he added, "*But* you *must* stay until the end."

"We didn't come only to crawl back home with our tails 'tween our legs, Clyde."

"Ain't planning on letting no man tell us what we can or can't do with our own land!"

"Who does Ian Zemke think he is? He wadn't even born here!" Man after man shouted their agreement and reasons for being here. It was exactly what Clyde wanted, each man to feel as though they were fighting for their own. Royce Armstrong reined his horse up to the bunkhouse and tore open the front door.

Clyde looked at him, "What the . . ." His scout looked him square

in the eye. "They've started it. They're bustin' up our fence sure as you all sit in here havin' your little meeting with all due respect."
"Where's Thomas?"
"He's there with Jesse and some others. I heard the gunfire start on my way back here."
"Mount up!" Clyde swore names and words that went unheard during the chaotic rustling of boots, chairs scraping against the floor, and voices of anticipation as they all made haste to their horses and guns. Clyde Montgomery did not want one man to die for his cause. But more than that, he did not want Ian Zemke and his cattle roaming around on his land. The old times were over; his stock was richer and fatter than Ian's, his land primer, lusher, and fuller. And by God . . . he was done sharing it.

He had done well to hire Thomas Engel. He marveled at the set up he'd had, welcoming the forty-two men who decided, some with the enticement of money, to ride with him. Others came to make a stand against one man telling another what he can or cannot do with his own property. Clyde wasn't the only man who'd built up a homestead or farm or ranch from nothing but sweat, hard times, and hard labor. Clyde, like many surrounding him, aimed to be his own boss, always and forever. What was soon to be a battle site was land that slightly swooped downward. Clyde was building his fence along the bottom of that slope. Half the fence now torn down and chopped to pieces by Ian's men. Thomas provided cover for men by wisely hitching up wagons—one behind the other and a few scattered here and there. Ian had a couple of trees for his shelter, certainly not enough for all of his men. Blue grass and Buffalo grass covered the area and swayed in the slight breeze, patches of clover spotted the grazing fields.

***

No one expected Sheriff Randall to come riding up in between both sides, along the fence. The fence that stood for separation, stubbornness, and divisive action.
"Ian Zemke! Clyde Montgomery!"
First Clyde, then Ian made their presence known, each stepping in front of their band of men, regulars and gunslingers. "Come down here, just you two. Let's talk about this!"
Ian, being closer to Ed, did not have to shout, "Too late for talk, Sheriff, ain't got nothing to say."
Clyde walked down the hill, "Well, I got something to say! You *will* pay me back for my fencing if it's the last thing you do on this earth!"
Ian grinned, his gruff appearance contrasted against his opponent's

polished look, giving Clyde an aura of superiority. Ian spit out his chewed up cigar, "I'll give you nary a dime. The fence ain't goin' up."

"Gentlemen, if I may still call you that, this isn't worth it. Killing isn't worth a fence, Clyde." Ed tried to reason with the more rational man.

"Isn't my doing. But I will not tolerate a man causing destruction on my land any more than you would allow someone to break out of your jail." Thomas stepped down the hill a bit; he swore to protect Clyde and noticed some trigger-happy men on the other side. Just for good measure, Byron Slate did the same, edging closer to Ian—tensions were running high. A shot rang out, spiraling through the air, and sent Ed reeling from his horse.

Thomas swore along with many others, "Hold your fire! Hold your fire! We are not going to waste bullets, get behind the wagons!" He grabbed a man that was aimlessly shooting off his gun by the collar of his neck and proceeded to drag him along. "I said now!"

The firing stopped. No one but the perpetrator knew who shot first, other than it came from Ian's side and somehow, between bullets flying without any purpose other than anxiousness, Joseph had managed to get Ed off of the field.

"You're hit!" Joseph adjusted him upright at the base of a tree trunk.

"Isn't the first time, Joseph. Although I reckon I'm fine." Looking at his wound, he knew it was not fatal. *Unless*, he thought grimly, *lead poisoning set in*. Which would be just his luck the way his life was going, maybe what he'd spoke to Lacey earlier might come true after all. Was he going to be killed this time around? Would he, in fact, never return home? Joseph bandaged up the area around his mentor's shoulders the best he could with his scarf. "I oughta go get the Doc." He scrambled up, "Can you ride?"

"Of course I can ride! But I ain't leaving, I'm gonna witness and account for every act these idiots do!" Then he laughed unbelievingly, "As if that Doc of ours would come traipsing down here in the line of fire . . . ruthless bunch that we all are." He held up his forefinger, "Now, Doc Colvin, he'd be here in the split of a second. Always one for adventure, that man."

The young man looked uncertain, Ed did not seem himself. "Get me my flask. I've smartened up being Sheriff, been beat up and shot at too many times to not bring me some pain reliever along. Ah, thank you."

After taking several gulps, Ed turned to Joseph, his protégé, "A word of the wise, do not take sides—*ever*. Stick to the law, anyone who breaks it, it's up to us to take care of it."

Joseph looked up the hill and back down, knowing men on both ends of the spectrum.

Ed added solemnly, as if to himself, "Even if they're your friends. Never take sides."

The sun dropped beyond the horizon and campfires lit up in its stead. All was quiet and it seemed to Ed that the only way out of this was the inevitable, a shootout until the end, until one of the prideful men gave up, and this seemed highly unlikely to happen anytime soon. Ed huddled beneath a blanket. It might be near the end of June, but it was going to be one long and chilly night.

<hr>

As the sun rose the next morning, the scent of bacon frying lured Ed from his sleep, and he heard men's voices speaking in low tones. Since they could see now in the fresh morning hour, Joseph began to properly bandage up Ed's shoulder with medical supplies he'd received from Dr. Colvin, being turned down flat by Dr. Grover and his staunch position.

"The boys are getting exactly what they deserve, shooting at each other like Cowboys and Indians . . ." Joseph walked away hearing words such as "uneducated" and "simple people."

This day was dreadfully longer than anyone thought possible. There was to be a stand off, and the Sheriff and his deputy made their own camp. Should they be of use to anybody was the question of the day. It was on the second night that Joseph woke up suddenly to the sound of shouts and gunfire splitting throughout the air. The moon was full and bright, sending down an eerie illuminating wave upon the plains.

"Ian's burning the fence," Ed filled in his sleepy-eyed partner. "I saw the flames start up and so did they." He jerked his chin toward Clyde's camp. They could hear the snapping and whipping sounds of barbed wire being cut and saw torches along the fences moving slowly by those who carried them, lighting piles of torn down fence posts.

"Johnny, you and Jesse go down a ways, keep your distance and use your rifles, they'll shoot a farther distance than your pistols." Of course they already knew that, but nodded in agreement. "Take out those suckers with the danged torches!" Thomas ordered.

Duffy Clarke heard Thomas and brought his boy, shoving him forward, "My son, Brandon, here is a crack shot."

Thomas looked at the boy, "That so?"

He nodded.

"Well, then, go with my men, and don't do anything they don't tell ya' to. Understand?" He answered with another quick bob of his head. Clyde was pacing angrily up and down the line of wagons when he heard rifle shots. He saw torch after torch go down, and then some were being tossed aside, and he knew that the holders of those death traps were scrimmaging and running for cover. He laughed a hearty laugh! "That was a fool thing for Ian to do! He darn well lit up his own boys as targets."

Coincidently, Byron Slate repeated the same sentiment, "I told you, Ian, but you just had to go and burn up his fence in the middle of this godforsaken night!"

"Shut up!"

"I won't shut up, and I recommend you don't tell me to do so!"

Byron could not see Ian's face in the darkness, but guessed it to be flaming with rage. "Now, I say again that we call 'em out tomorrow, one at a time."

Ian turned to him, "It'll be as you say, whatever you want. Just *don't let* him beat me!"

Byron did not spell out the obvious, but Thomas Engel had the advantage over them. He could care less about Ian Zemke and his pride, or the man's land. He wanted Thomas, and he was sure this was his chance to get him.

❧

"Seven dead men and none of them are his!" Ian roared. The sun broke open the day and seven men lay sprawled out along the fence line. Extinguished torches fizzled out at their sides, mimicking the way they died—life is but a vapor.

Ed stood, grimacing in pain, and said to Joseph, "Maybe they're ready to call it a truce."

"Today's our day." Byron Slate walked up and down the small crowd of men, tired, hungry, and sick of sleeping on the cold, hard ground.

"Today's the day we show them that they ain't won! We show 'em what *we're* made of! Ian's a good man, he deserves, as any of you do, to let his cattle roam free, to feed off of this land that no one has a right to cut off from another. It's why we got round-up!"

Men shouted their agreement, slapping one another on the back, their way of encouraging and showing camaraderie. Byron stood back and admired his work as General. Getting the men fired up had been easy, now if only they would stick together and hold out still needed to be determined. "We can't let our boys here have died for nothing!"

"No way!"

"Let's charge 'em!"

Byron allowed them their outburst of emotions for a time and then spoke reality, "That sounds good, except it would be suicide. I propose to call 'em out, get into their heads . . . anyone of you have a grudge against any up the hill there?" Minds stilled in thought.

"Pa and me, we hate the Clarkes," Ronnie said evenly.

"Clyde thinks his daughter's too good for my boy! Wouldn't even consider letting him court her. I can't stand his looking down on us that ain't *big* like him." An older man spoke up, one that hadn't said much the whole time.

Some wondered why he was even there. "That's it. Keep thinking along those lines, I'm going to meet with Ian for a moment."

"Something's going on, Sheriff," Joseph said needlessly.

"Guess we aren't gonna see a truce today."

Clyde Montgomery appeared at the top of the hill and hollered for Ian to come and see him.

"Look at him up there, looking down on us like he was God Himself," Ian mumbled to Byron.

"Give up, Ian. We got two more of your men up here. Nine total, all dead," Clyde stated simply with no concern or sympathy in his voice. "It ain't worth it, be reasonable. Leave my fence alone and we'll go. It's as simple as that."

Ian spit his hatred to the ground. "Ever heard the term, 'when hell freezes over'?"

Clyde shook his head, and before he could respond, Byron and another started shooting at Clyde's feet. "Look at 'im dance! Whew-hee!" Thomas was the first to return fire. Back and forth, crossfire broke out for several minutes. Individual streams of gun smoke filled the air; the fight had to stop eventually for reloads to take place.

"That was a stupid thing for you to do, Slate!" Thomas yelled. Enough of this pettiness and messing around. It was time to get it over with. He walked rapidly toward the front of the wagons, to two pistols fully loaded and a rifle ready to go.

"So, he speaks," Byron murmured to himself, reloading, clicking in one new bullet at a time. He looked at each one insanely, shining them off and naming who would be lucky enough to receive it.

"Thomas."

Lincoln County had long counted on Thomas and his men to protect them. What would they ever do without them?

"Johnny."

What would his place be in town if he were called upon to protect it? He'd learned a lot since coming here . . . a new place would be good for Byron Slate.

"Jesse."

It was time to settle down, maybe not in the traditional way with a nagging wife or bratty kids. But a place in town, where people who would look up to him as they did to Thomas Engel.

By nightfall, Byron had made his way to Thomas while he relieved himself. With gun pointed behind him, Byron hissed, "I only want you, Thomas. I don't care about this land or that land." He aimed to shoot and found himself being spun around by a bullet propelling into his arm—his firing arm. Panicked and spiteful eyes scanned above him, and he saw Ed holding his stance, ready to fire again. Byron picked up the pistol that had been whipped from him, keeping his incoherent eyes on Thomas and the sheriff. His senses were slow in coming back. He knocked at the side of his head a few times, as if to clear it, and retreated cautiously down the hill.

Ed called after him, "Give up, Slate. I'll be arresting you all shortly."

Thomas looked at Ed, "Thanks for watching my back." His words were grateful, yet stingy, and he left.

Joseph appeared next to Ed in surprised confusion, "Thought we weren't suppose to take sides?" Ed did not contemplate one moment, "When a man's about to get back shot, you take sides. Problem is, now we gotta watch our backs." He walked away, leaving Joseph to his troubling thoughts. The sheriff had done it again—used the partnered word "we." Only this time, it didn't sound as though it came with any glory.

A sudden blast lifted an entire wagon off the ground, shredding it and burning it to pieces. Men were confused and looked in horror as more blasts and fires occurred all around them.

"Dynamite!"

Men scurried, grabbing guns, settling horses. Some took off and rode away, yelling that they didn't come to get blown up for nobody. "Got what I wished for!" Thomas yelled at Clyde, who was swiping chunks of wood from his head and shoulders. "Yeah! What's that?"

"I wanted the petty fighting to stop!"

Clyde laughed despite the wild war-like scenario happening before their eyes. "I'd say you got your wish alright. What's your plan?"

"Jesse! Get me a wagon before they blast all of them. Fill it with wood!"

Understanding Thomas's intentions, Clyde nodded his agreement, "Good idea, Thomas Engel. Right good idea." The target was Ian's men huddled around a circle, apparently lighting up dynamite sticks.

"We gotta hit our mark, Jesse; it's our only chance at this point."

Jesse, Brandon Clarke, and Travis Dayton ran alongside the burning wood-filled wagon until they felt they were in firing range. "Let her go!" They stopped, panted from lack of breath, and watched with delight as the wagon veered straight where they wanted it to go. Someone looked up. Unfortunately, for him, he was holding a lit stick and yelled his face off. The burning weapon steered a bit to the right but still had a hefty impact.

A grand explosion happened on the other side of the fence, and anyone holding the black powder went right up with it. "This is crazy!" Joseph screeched.

Ed watched the fireball in deep wonderment, "I reckon it is."

"Should I get the Doc now?"

The sheriff nodded, then changed his mind. "No. Hitch up somebody's buggy, I don't care whose. Start hauling men to that uppity doctor of ours. If they're on his doorstep, he can't rightly turn them away, now can he?"

When the fires died down and neighbors bore witness to the gruesome, dead, or burned up bodies littering the ground at their feet, most called it quits. But not the die-hards; no way was Byron, Ian, or Garrett waving a white flag. They denied defeat.

Each side regrouped and assessed their damages. Ed wiped soot away from his eyes and approached Jesse, "How bad is it?"

Jesse looked at the burn in his thigh. "Not bad. Least nothing my Kimberly can't fix up for me."

Ed grinned; teeth pearly white against his three-day's beard growth and blackened face.

Several of Ian's men charged madly up the hill, "Move on out, Sheriff, no need to lose your life over this. Let's go Jesse," Thomas said grimly. What was left of Clyde's men were poised behind remnants of wagons, aiming and shooting off rounds of bullets at Ian's men. It soon became a one on one fight. When chambers were emptied, punching, kicking, pulling, and choking became their defense. Thomas fought his way to Byron Slate, his hazel eyes burned into Slate's hateful ones as he finished off a man that had just stabbed him in the side. Cupping his bleeding flesh, he staggered over to Byron and pointed his gun; after pulling the trigger, he heard a click. Nothing. Thomas looked confused, knowing he saved a bullet for this man who only wanted him dead; he wasn't even fighting for money or a cause. Byron wanted power, and Thomas needed to be gone before that could happen. A wicked smile spread across Byron's thin lips. Yes, he could shoot Thomas, but instead, he pointed the gun behind his enemy, finding a bull's-eye into a man's back. Thomas's head seemed to slowly reel in the same direction with a sick feeling in his gut. He clenched his eyes tight as he heard and felt a bullet whiz past his head, the tight thud let him know it hit its mark. He saw, through blurred vision, Johnny collapse to the ground. Thomas roared, seized, and pounded. His knuckles ripped open, were broken and bleeding, all he could think about was that this man killed Johnny. Why Johnny?

Suddenly, Thomas's crazed eyes looked away from the unconscious man beneath him and looked around for another gun until he spotted one. He crawled over to it, and from his side view, saw the handle of a rifle swinging up over his head—and then there was blackness. Garrett stood over Thomas's body. No one saw what had transpired, so he fled for his freedom.

Jesse wiped his eyes with the sleeve of his filthy shirt, blinking back the moisture that threatened to come. He savagely stalked his way to Ian, who was not involved in the gun-to-gun, fist-to-fist fighting. The coward! He came to watch, watch men die because of his stupid idea that he should feed his cattle for free!

Ian stared in awe at an over-strung blonde man coming fiercely toward him. "Who do you think . . ." Thinking himself untouchable, he looked around to find only one man at his side.

Without flinching and barely aiming, Jesse shot that man and violently grabbed Ian by his shirt collars, jerking him upright. "This is over! You hear me? Tell them this is over! Now!"

Ian shook his head back and forth in fear. He couldn't talk even if he wanted to.

Ed Randall arrived at that time, "He's right, Ian, it's gone far enough. You've more than proved your stand on the matter; you've refused the law to handle it. If you don't stop it now, I'll arrest *you* for murder." He looked at the rage on Jesse's face. "Unless he just takes care of you for me, it'd save me the trouble."

Ian looked from one face to the other; one was calm and confident, the other, crazed and murderous. He nodded dumbly. Jesse let go of him, pushing his butt to the ground. He threw a cloth, white in color, at Ian and yelled at him, "Now!"

Clyde looked down the hill. "Well I'll be . . ." He turned to the destruction around him and ordered, "That's enough. Look."

Half-conscious, soot-covered men looked warily down the slope to see Ian in utter defeat, holding up a white piece of material in capitulation. They were too tired to be thrilled. The ones who'd fought for Ian helped those who couldn't walk and slowly descended the hill to pack up and go home to life, as they knew it, leaving the dead behind. Most of them had never killed another soul in their lifetime, and their lives would be changed forever because of those three horrible days.

Although the town, conveniently being "ignorant" of the hostile and aggressive acts going on between Mr. Zemke and Mr. Montgomery, decided that since it was now over and men had visibly fallen, suddenly became outraged. Ed Randall received the brunt of this affront and some even began to call for the badge of the incompetent sheriff. Someone was to blame for the deaths of husbands, sons, and fathers, as if people did not know this would happen when they packed up bags of provisions for the confrontation just days before. Sheriff Randall sat alone in his jail, writing up the incident per his memory, being honest and forward in his report. Never before had he reported anything to anyone, but it would be here, in his desk, should any higher authority wish to see it. He considered their angry protests, being reminded of how his tenure as sheriff was not legitimate, at least in the beginning. Thomas's old gang leader put him into office and he'd done his best by the town until now. No arrests were made. Each side had their own consequences and would bear under the guilt of men dying worthlessly for them. Cattle barons—a powerful title—one didn't come upon it lightly and usually needed some sort of abuse in power and authority to obtain it. Some rustled cattle to keep their numbers up, others stole land from unfortunate, dirt-poor farmers. Some, like Clyde, decided to enforce rules after years of what was and put up a fence to divide the range from property to property. But none of this mattered as Reverend Andrew, with his wife beside him, wearing a black dress of mourning, read verses over the dead who fought for those cattle barons. For Mrs. Clarke, suddenly upon seeing Mrs. Appleton, husbandless and sonless . . . dislike, feuding, and even hate did not seem to matter and wondered what purpose it had ever served in her life. Mr. Zemke advertised in the weekly paper that he was going to sell out and move away from the unjust territory. No one was sorry to see him go. The pain of losing Johnny was more painful than his physical wounds; his sister had tried to mother and nurse him, but Thomas would have none of it. All he could see when he closed his eyes was the brutal killing of Johnny. Shot in the back. Never given a chance to die in a real gunfight, as Thomas knew he would have preferred. He and Jesse buried him on the ranch under the great oak tree. Johnny would have never wanted a preacher to read words over his dead body, so he was just buried. A wooden marker carved with Johnny's own knife simply read "Johnny." He never provided anyone with his last name in all the years they'd known him. He was and always would be just Johnny to them.

Sixteen

It was near time for the annual Fourth of July Celebration, and the town buzzed in preparation. Bands needed to be put together for the dance, booths for fundraising needed organized, and banners needed sewing. Lacey volunteered her staff and plunged herself deep into it, anything to keep her mind from her woeful life.

Lacey was trying so hard to fit in, even with church ladies that she deemed hypocritical and nosy. She had demanded to be a part of the quilting circle, which had at first stunned most of the ladies to silence. The first time they met, Lacey arrived in a pink taffeta dress with black lace outlining, accentuating places that made the ladies thankful their husbands were not around. They were quilting again this afternoon, and she hurried to her room to get some material for the gathering. When she realized that everything she had was too fancy, she decided to just buy some plain calico from the mercantile. On her way out, she spotted a vase of lilies on her table beneath the window. Frowning, she went over only to find no note. She would ask Lizette about it later.

He wished he had not seen her just now. Despite his words that seemed so long ago, Ed Randall longed to be with Lacey. Each time he weakened and set himself out to see her, he remembered the pain that being with her caused him. He loved her. Was it too much to ask to be loved back? He watched her come from the mercantile with a bolt of material. She halted upon seeing him too. Feelings arose in her that she could not name. Was it need of his attention? Did she love him? Knowing she cared for him brought her toward him. Ed's face turned from hope to despair, back and forth until his Lacey was before him.

She took in his bandaged arm, "I'm glad you are safe. I was so worried."

"You were worried? I find that hard to believe."

"What you said before was a misunderstanding."

"Was it?"

"I promise. Please believe me. I need you to believe me, Ed."

For a moment, he looked away, as if focusing on something or someone. "What happens if I believe you?" Two steps forward was all it took for Lacey to be just beneath his chin.

She looked up, lips so close to his, "I will be yours."

A Lily Among Thorns   125

❧

Cameron sat with nine others in somewhat of a circle. They occupied the churchyard underneath two maple trees that provided shade from the impending heat. Lacey was late in joining them; the women were silent, unsure of how to welcome her. Cameron saw the rise of her stubborn chin. Lacey longed so to fit in. Once again, the ladies took their cue from the preacher's wife.

"Welcome, Lacey. So glad you were able to join us." Addressing the ladies she said, "Such beautiful fabric she's brought."

The murmured agreements moved properly throughout the circle. Lacey threw Cameron a glance of appreciation. Sarah was passing around fresh lemonade on a tray, while they stitched together a large quilt for the picnic.

"Ouch!" Lacey yelped.

Cameron shook her head in warning as Lacey held her breath before something slipped out of her mouth that might offend the prim ladies around her.

"Lacey, why don't you start folding those other quilts and wrap them in the ribbon there. Sarah can help you."

Lacey glared at her, "Fine!" She sucked on her pricked finger, and with exaggerated elegance, stood, smoothing out her dress. She toned down her attire for the quilting parties, but the dresses she wore still outshone anyone around within miles.

Cameron smiled back at her, which made Lacey more determined and rebellious, but she supposed anything was better than wallowing in drink alone in her room. Which reminded her, "Lizette, do you know where the lilies came from in my room?"

"No."

"Are you certain?"

"I haven't put anything in your room."

She shrugged. "Sarah! We've been assigned to the task of *folding*. Apparently, I'm not good enough to sew."

❧

After a boring afternoon, Lacey arrived at the post office to see Blaine standing amidst a small line of customers. Determined not to be seen avoiding or fleeing from him, for it would only make him feel like he was winning whatever contest she had put between them. She dabbed her brow with her handkerchief and poised herself stubbornly. He stood back, leaned against the wall of the building, and watched, amused by her act of unfamiliarity. "Mr. Otis, have I any mail?"

"Let's see here, no, ma'am, I don't see any for you. Would you mind taking this package to Mrs. Owens though? Been sitting here nigh of a week."

"I would be happy to. She's at the hotel now." She arched her neck proudly. At least her trip to the post office wasn't for nothing. Blaine blocked her path. She could no longer avoid his handsome presence, but she refused to look into his face.

"Let me carry that for you."

"I assure you, there is no need for chivalry." He surprised her by snatching it from her easy grip. "And I assure you, I'm not being chivalrous. I merely wanted to walk with you and used this as an excuse." He began walking and looked back at her, "Although I'm sure some would wonder why."

Lifting her skirts, she bounded up to him, piqued. "And you aim to be cruel why you're at it?"

"If the truth is cruel . . ."

"Huh!"

They walked in silence a while and before reaching the hotel. He said humbly, "Please, have dinner with me tonight."

She shouldn't have, had even warned herself not to, but looked into his eyes anyway. The word she'd planned to say was "yes," but what escaped her lips was, "No." She blinked back sadly, held out her arms to retrieve the package, the tool used in bringing them to speak to one another, and he placed it gently into her soft hands. He tipped his hat as gentlemanly as he could, ignoring the ache in his heart, and opened the door for her. She went, wordlessly, away from him, because the words she'd spoken to Ed just hours ago were still fresh on her tongue. Why did a feeling of regret come then? She knew she'd made the right choice, the safest choice.

Ed was returning from the eastern part of town, and thankfully, missed Blaine speaking with Lacey. He headed to his office where he saw Jake Collins arriving with another soul that was unfortunate enough to be drawn onto a wanted poster with the words "Dead or Alive" in bold print. Ed was finding out more and more that "Dead" was the only one Jake appeared to see.

"Got Dru Dressling here," Jake announced blandly. He looked up in thought toward the pale blue sky, as if calculating, and said, "I believe he was worth three hundred dollars." He swatted dust from his shoulders and pants legs and looked at the sheriff for confirmation. Ed sighed and told him to come in.

Opening the safe, he removed the money for his friend, "Jake, you ever consider bringing in someone *alive* for me?"

"Easier to do it dead."

"I can see that."

When Jake turned to go, Ed asked, "I haven't had myself a good game of cards in a long while. What do you say, partner?"

Hesitating, no longer feeling comfortable in any one place for long, Jake found himself relenting, "I'll meet you over there."

Violet carried plates of food over from Lacey's to the saloon, per the men's request. "Howdy, Jake. It's been a while."

Without looking at her, "Yep, been busy."

"It's just that . . ."

Jake looked up into her painted face, "You got something to say?"

She felt it her cue to be dismissed and left them after supplying their table with roast beef, mashed potatoes, carrots, and cold beer. After putting a forkful of meat into his mouth, Ed said, "I got a feeling she's keen on you."

"Nobody's keen on me, you idiot."

Ed smiled, "Why are you trying to be so mean to everybody? You're a jerk."

"I just don't like being around people."

"What the heck am I?"

"Just shut up about it, will you?"

Lacey came down, as she did most evenings, to check on her guests and make sure their every need was met. Doing so kept the class of patrons she wanted in her restaurant coming time and time again. She saw Ed and smiled wide upon seeing who was in his company. She flitted on past them without a greeting.

"What was that all about?" Jake asked.

"She's still angry with you."

They sat in silence, finishing their supper in haste. Kimberly was quick to sidle up to the "best looking men here," offering their favorite drinks to them while Ed ordered a deck of cards from Liam. Soon, a great game of poker was being ensued by five men, and the bulk of patrons stood watching, biding their time until they had to retire or return home to wives. Bethany Hoffman, as always, appeared aloof and emotionless. Jake drank enough to become bold and ordered Liam not to allow her to go upstairs with anyone. Liam nodded his understanding and continued to wipe down the soiled bar.

She had always intrigued him; she was a hard woman, and Jake believed her to be a perfect match for his mood tonight. He also knew by the way she looked, or he would say, glared at him, that she had no fondness for him whatsoever. Well, in her business, she could not be choosy. He tossed back his final drink and watched her glacial stare toward him as Liam whispered something into her ear. Bethany halted at the base of the stairs, put her hand on her hip, and waited impatiently for Jake to come to her, as if she was more than eager to put "this job" behind her, and the sooner the better. Jake scraped his chair back, keeping his dark eyes on her said, "Well, Sheriff. It was a good idea after all asking me to join you in cards tonight. I'll be taking my leave now." He took a moment to scoop up his winnings, stuffed it into a pocket under his vest, and proceeded toward Bethany. He grinned, the first woman he's ever met that didn't want him stood waiting so coldly, so intolerantly—it only beguiled him. "Shall we?"

Seventeen

Townspeople gossiped and Lincoln County was not immune to it. It gave busybodies something to do, and so a rumor was making its way throughout the holiday flock of people. "Isn't she the most beautiful thing?"

"Richer than the president."

"Heard they came to buy Mr. Zemke's place!"

"Her father came all the way from France!"

Chloe Dupree, American-born, was being escorted, as though she might break, by an older gentleman. Shielding herself as much as possible from the tormenting sun with her teal green, laced parasol, it was hard to confirm the words people whispered. Everyone knew for miles that Lacey Jennings had the best and most favored looks of everyone anybody knew, so to set sights upon another even more so was something to see.

A brother chased a sister around Andrew and Cameron as they strolled in and out of the crowd, seeking a spot to claim for their picnic area. Andrew carried the large basket filled with enough food to feed an army, and Cameron carried a rolled up blanket. They passed tables laden with mason jars of pickled eggs, pickled beets, pickled cucumbers, and anything else Kansas womenfolk conjured up to pickle, waiting to be awarded the winner in the competition. Not one to have ever liked pickled food, and Cameron knowing so, she teased, "I should have had Lacey sign you up as judge, Darling."

Andrew grimaced, "I'd rather eat pig's feet!"

"This is as good a spot as any," she said, and after his approval, laid out their soft quilted blanket. Lacey, as usual, raised the most money for the town by being a recipient in the kissing booth. "I'm off to raise my share of money."

"Lacey, please reconsider." She looked at Cameron, confused and then angry at the suggestion. "Why would I do that? I do this fundraiser every Fourth of July."

"What about Blaine?" Cameron knew it was the wrong thing to say. Andrew pretended to be looking for something in the basket, and Cameron admonished him with a hot look.

A Lily Among Thorns

"Blaine Jennings has no claim on me!"

Cameron apologized to Lacey's retreating; she did not wish to quarrel with her today. "She is getting difficult. Did you find what you were looking for?"

Andrew had the good sense to look embarrassed. "You're just now realizing that my cousin is difficult?"

"Very funny! I will go see her later, make amends."

A small entourage passed by them, and Andrew stood as Reverend and introduced himself and Cameron to the unordinary ensemble before them. A man with a slight French accent said, "Pleased to meet you. This is my daughter, Miss Chloe Dupree. I am Jacques Dupree, III." He bowed and Chloe curtsied. Andrew and Cameron felt plain and clumsy.

The angelic looking creature took that moment to ease the introduction, "Please, call me Chloe." She glanced sideways at her straight-backed father and retorted, "Miss Dupree sounds so old, don't you think?" Her voice was soft and airy, but extremely friendly in its effect.

"Would you show us where we might take our meal?" Jacques Dupree asked.

"We've a nice spot, sir. You are welcome to join us," Andrew invited. Jacques thought on it a moment, deciding if this was the best place and company for him and his daughter, when he heard her southern voice, "We would be delighted!" As Chloe began to adjust her skirts to sit next to Cameron, Jacques looked impatiently upon his servant to lay out his thick blanket.

After settling himself onto the ground, he commented, "I suppose I must again get acquainted with this uncivilized society." A dissatisfied look remained on his face as his servant laid out a fine table for him. Silverware, trays of specially made French food, and even a wine glass, which the servant filled with red wine. He signaled for his croissant to be buttered, and not before taking the spectacles from his nose and placing them into his breast pocket, was he finally able to look up to observe his company.

Chloe hid a teasing grin under her fan and winked at Cameron, who had never thought of themselves a "society" before, and were intrigued by this man and woman from France who would take supper with them.

⁂

Blaine watched the line of men awaiting a kiss from Lacey for about as long as he could. He should not have come to the festivities; he'd told himself that this all morning, but curiosity and the desire to see his wife overruled his rationale.

Righteous anger began to stir inside of him. Before he knew what he was even doing, Blaine was at Lacey's side, furious. Furious at the groveling men in line and at her. Although this tradition was always done in a light and flirtatious way, in his anger, he did not see it as so.

"This booth is closed!" he announced, red faced. Lacey was shocked at his abrupt presence and words; she actually remained speechless. Protests broke out from the line, bringing Lacey back to reality.

She hollered, "It is not closed, my young, handsome admirers. He is only jesting." She turned her body fully toward Blaine, daring him to defy her promise to the murmuring men. She was ready to take on both him and his hilarious challenge.

"Why are you so bent on self-destruction, Lacey?" he asked quietly.

She sneered and laughed mockingly, "I don't know what *you've* been doing the last three years, but this is hardly ruining my life." She proceeded to ignore him and said, "Next!" The farmer who stepped up did so cautiously, what was he to do? He slid forward his coin and waited. Lacey said through a tight-lipped smile to Blaine, "You are hurting my business. Go away!"

Blaine stepped out from behind the booth, as if she never uttered a protest and addressed the men, "I understand that you are all here for a good cause, just leave your money on the counter. I said that *Mrs. Jennings* was done and I meant it." With that, he scooped up his wife and carried her over his shoulder back to her hotel. She beat his backside and screamed for someone to help her. She cursed him and was humiliated beyond measure. He deposited his flushed faced wife in the middle of her foyer, and when she went to make her escape, he blocked the door with his solid, well-built frame.

"How dare you?" she spat out the words, seething.

He began to laugh, which flared her temper. He did not stop, but continued to laugh while she paced angrily in front of him. When he settled down, he looked at her, "I can't believe I actually did that."

"You can't believe . . . do you realize how embarrassing that was for me? What will all of those men think of me now?" Her chest heaved in exasperation.

That does it, he narrowed his eyes at her, she had the grace to blanch. "I know you are only my wife in title, Lacey Jennings, but are you so stupid as to not know that I want more? I want us back!"

"Ha! I don't want us back ever again! We were horrible to each other." Her hair was in disarray, but her breathing was calming down.

He grabbed her shoulders softly, "I didn't mean that I wanted it to be like before . . . before. Let's start over. Let me love you the way you deserve."

She jerked away from him, eyeing him with complete and utter distrust; it broke his heart. "Love hurts too much, Blaine. Especially from you." Her words were not hard, just true.

His voice gentled, "*My* love. Yes. *Anyone's* love, Lacey. Because we are human. I swear to you that I have changed. I have found a love that neither of us knew before. I want to share it with you." He steeled himself for her answer to his next question. "Do you have any feelings for me at all?"

Ed broke his way in the door. What he saw was a passionate couple in a heated discussion. He did not know what to quite make of it.

"Lacey?"

She wanted to hurt Blaine; she wanted to scream at him and tell him that she cared nothing for him, had never loved him—that he needed to go away. But nothing came out of her mouth. She wished she had not seen the torment in his eyes, she wished she had not looked at him at all, because what she saw hit her insides so hard she could barely stand. She reeled away from them both and ran up to her room. But Blaine heard her crying, and that was all the answer he needed. With renewed hope, he stepped out into the blazing sun.

Ed was hot on his heels. "Leave her alone."

"I can't and I won't."

"You're going to be sorry if I see you near her again."

"Don't threaten me. Let her choose."

"She wouldn't have to if you would go away. You're nothing to her! You're a womanizing coward! A dog would treat her better than you ever will. You've more than proved that."

Blaine backed away cautiously, inching toward the livery that held his horse. He could not believe that God would want him to come to physical blows.

Ed stalked him until they were just outside the barn, "I am warning you as Sheriff. I want you out of town by next week."

❧

News spread just as the ants across the picnic blankets did about Lacey's abduction. Andrew gave Cameron an approving look and admired Blaine's actions. Cameron wasn't so convinced that it was the right thing to have done and would see to Lacey's feelings on the matter later. Word also spread that the sheriff had banished Blaine from town. Lincoln County was up in arms and excited about a forthcoming duel. This Fourth of July holiday was all the more fervently celebrated. Bringing the latest sensation to town was the Dupree family. While Mr. Dupree worked out his business dealings with Mr. Zemke, Chloe was left to find her own amusements. Since Lacey's was the finest establishment, she and her father and servants occupied three of the hotel's rooms.

Lacey was not only beside herself with the horrid actions of Blaine, but also the teetering whispers she knew to be about her. *That man will ruin me again, one way or another.* She did not know what was worse, her husband or Miss Dupree. Men from all over came to see the fair Chloe. Today, she sat on the boardwalk in a chair supplied by her servant, as men, young and old, sat around her, ignoring the splinters catching their britches. Lacey might not exist at all since Chloe came. It did keep revenue up at the restaurant, which was the only blessed thing to come from the whole inconvenience. She kept Lizette extra hours to meet the needs of the Dupree's, and with the amount of money the Frenchman had offered her for her best of everything, Lacey did all she could without regret. Lizette brought a tray of refreshments to Miss Dupree and her eager suitors. As the young woman handed out glasses of lemonade and smiled into each face, Lizette saw her beauty. Golden tendrils hung down the sides of her highly defined cheek bones, diamond earrings such as Lizette had never set eyes on, dripped from her lobes. A cameo lie snug against her smooth neck, and her nails were untouched of labor and immaculate. But her smiles and expressions of laughter, concern, whatever the occasion called for were genuine. Her eyes were kind and unmaliced, and despite the things Lacey had to say about her, the twenty-two-year-old woman would be well liked. Among those that came to sit at her feet was Joseph Benton.

Down the street, the owner of the mercantile held open the door for Cameron, "Thank you, Mr. Newberry."

"My pleasure, Mrs. Jackson. Enjoy your day."

"You, too, and tell the missus to do the same." She carried a light wooden crate of supplies for their home and the church and was adjusting it onto her hip. Her buggy, not far away, she declined any help from Mr. Newberry.

"Oh, dear!" Cameron stepped into a split in the wooden boardwalk; her foot twisted and fell through. More embarrassed than hurt, she tried to get out. Jake swore and looked around for someone to help her. No one seemed to notice, for they were so involved with one another. He hesitated, he could just disappear. She appeared to be fine, and then she saw him. Her face flamed seven shades of red; not only her rump had been knocked down, but her pride as well—she was horrified. Throwing down his cigarette, he went to offer his help, which set Cameron Jackson into near hysteria, which made him livid.

She succeeded in scrambling up before he reached her, but distressed that her ankle would not cooperate when she tried to stand. She hopped over to the nearest post, but clumsy as she was, tripped over her skirt and landed face down, catching herself with her hands.

Jake squatted down to her level, "Are you finished?"

There was no teasing smile on his face as there would have been before when she knew him to be gentle and kind. She nodded. He lifted her up as though she was a mere feather and set her upright before him. He knew the reason she was skittish. Many times after that last time they were alone, he'd surprised himself by wanting to apologize. But seeing her here before him right now, he knew he could not, for he was not sorry.

"Thank you, Jake," her voice was ever so soft and uncertain.

Without a word, he brushed passed her, leaving his scent of cigarette smoke, sweat, and leather for her to inhale. She compared that smell to Andrew. He never had those scents about him; he was squeaky clean and always smelled of pine soap. Suddenly, her face scalded and it wasn't from the intense heat of the sun. How dare she compare scents of a man, namely Jake's, to those of her husband? She looked around guiltily as if someone would have caught her in the act and frantically began picking up items—she thanked God that Jake was no longer a gentleman and had not stayed to help her.

She brought herself to Lacey's and sat in a booth. Lacey did not come to Cameron empty-handed; she brought a tray of little cakes and frosted shortbread cookies and tea.

"It's a little hot for tea, but there is no fresh lemonade. Apparently, Miss Dupree and her admirers drank it all. I had to scold Cook for that," she admonished.

"This is just fine, thank you."

"It's nice of you to stop by. What are you out doing in this weather? It's horribly hot. Where is Andrew?"

She held up the palms of her hands and said simply, "I fell."

"Oh, you poor thing. I'll get those out of your hands."

They both laughed as Cameron relayed the story of her incident and Jake. "He's a beast!" said Lacey while she plucked out the slivers.

"I've never been so humiliated!"

Lacey's face became solemn, "I'm afraid you don't know what humiliation is then, after what Blaine did to me!" At the very second it was brought up, both women looked at each other. Unsure of how to respond at first, they suddenly burst into laughter so hard that tears rolled down their faces. "Oh, it's so good to laugh."

Cameron nodded, dabbing the corners of her eyes with her sliver free hands. "It is." In all seriousness, she asked, "How are you doing?" She placed a cube of sugar in her now lukewarm tea and stirred it thoughtfully, her brows creasing in thought. "The truth?"

"Of course."

"I honestly don't know, Cameron. One day I feel so lonely and depressed, I don't know what to do with myself. Then there are days like this, with you here, and I know that I am not lonely. It just doesn't make any sense," her voice held frustration.

"It may not make sense to you, but if you'll remember, it was about this time last year that I seemed to be going through comparably the same thing."

"What happened?"

Cameron was making headway with Lacey trusting her and did not wish to speak unwisely. "I started listening to Andrew and going to church."

Lacey sat back—annoyed.

"I know how you feel about church and God and the Bible, Lacey. You had a terrible experience with your parents growing up, but they were so wrong!"

"I've heard enough."

Cameron bit her lip to close her speaking mouth and then changed her mind. Sometimes she felt older than Lacey, who was sitting across from her stubbornly, defiantly. How would she ever hear it if everyone always played the coward to her extreme moodiness?

"Well, you did ask."

"I'm sorry I did."

"Why?"

"You know why."

"But that's the past; why not give yourself a chance for hope? For happiness? You've said so yourself that I have changed."

"I think you've just matured. Married life will do that to you!"

"How do you think I managed after I lost our baby?"

"You hardly managed. You were a hermit, never let anyone, especially me, come and see you."

"I meant eventually. I have a lot to learn about my life and about God. Now, wait a minute, you can't get upset every time I say *God*... He's my life. If you can't accept that, then I guess you can't accept me."

"Don't be silly! Of course I accept you!"

Shaking her head Cameron continued, "What I am trying to say is that, yes, something terrible happened. I know now that if I didn't have faith, I would have been even more devastated than I was. I might have never come out of it and I would have ruined my life and my marriage. It just took a little longer for me than for some, I suppose. It's what causes us to mature in Him and grow with all of our relationships. Nothing and nobody is perfect."

Lacey sat quietly in contemplation, and Cameron lifted her teacup to her lips and couldn't believe what just spilled out of her. She was trembling inside, but it felt good and it felt right.

Eighteen

Sweat streamed from the men as they heaved planks of wood onto logs cut for the purpose of making tables. It was nearing the end of July and farmers would soon be getting ready for harvest, so this was to be the last official church potluck of the summer. Tables were crammed underneath two maple trees; any shade was welcome if it kept the blazing sun off of their white skin. Chloe followed Cameron from table to table, and after the Reverend's wife floated a red and white-checkered tablecloth over the crude makeshift tables, Chloe placed a tin can of freshly cut wild flowers in the center. Watching children run and play, Cameron sighed, "I don't know how they can run so in this heat!" She wiped the back of her sweating neck. "I suppose we did the same when we were children, it wasn't so long ago."

Chloe squinted her eyes and approved of their work. "I'm thirsty, how about a glass of ice water?" At Cameron's questioning, doubtful look she stated simply, "My father brought some ice."

"Your father has *ice*?"

"Yes, even though I told him it would not last long—he insisted on drinking iced tea today. He ordered it from a railroad car that is refrigerated. Have you ever heard of those refrigerated cars?"

"I have, but this town doesn't have one."

"It does now," Chloe said without boasting.

"Well, I'll be! What I wouldn't give for a cupful of ice!"

"You won't have to give anything, just follow me."

"You have a great husband, Mrs. Jackson."

She blushed easily, and did so now, "I know." Cameron held the cherished glass of ice water to one side of her face, then the other, allowing it to sweat its coolness over her flushed cheeks. "Why haven't you married, Miss Dupree? If you don't mind my asking, it's just that . . . well, to be blunt, you have no shortage of interested suitors."

Her laugh was soft as a hummingbird. "My father moves around, he gets bored easily and came back here to seek adventure. I enjoy amusing him by tagging along." She smiled prettily at Cameron, "And I get to meet wonderful people like you."

"You flatter me as easily as you flatter your many beaux. What do you mean, he came back?"

"He was here years ago. We lived in the south, although I'm sure you've figured that out by my accent. When my mother died, my father sent me away to school and went back home to France. After I graduated, he brought me home to him, got the notion to come back to America. So I came too."

"Well, we are pleased to have you both here, and to know you, as well."

Chloe nodded, but Cameron could see her attention devoted elsewhere. When she followed her gaze, her stomach did a turn around.

"Who's that? I've seen him at church, but he always escapes before I can introduce myself," she said this with disappointment.

Cameron looked straight at her and said lamely, "Blaine Jennings."

"Jennings. Why, that's Lacey's last name. Brother and sister?" She asked all too eagerly and daintily sipped her iced tea.

"Husband and wife."

"But they don't live together." It was a statement, not a question.

"No, I suppose they don't." Without getting herself further into this unwanted conversation, Cameron rose and nodded to someone in the distance who neither wanted her or signaled to her. But she went anyway, as if expected, leaving Chloe alone with wherever her thoughts were taking her where Blaine was concerned. Her thoughts were focused on the sheriff and Lacey as they walked arm in arm around the picnic, greeting acquaintances as though they were the married couple. It was all the same to Ed, it was all he wanted. Appearances were important, and Lacey was faithful in making her position clear on which she'd chosen. Thus so, he did not make good his threat to Blaine, who did not leave town, who never intended to leave town, but the sheriff didn't need to dwell on that.

He turned to the beauty at his side, "Come, I've a surprise for you."

He led Lacey to a secluded place that hosted an intimate picnic lunch." With victory in his eyes, Ed allowed them to roam until they rested upon his defeated rival, and he was thrilled that Blaine witnessed Lacey's grateful, tender kiss upon his neck.

The heat from the Indian summer caused for tired induced lethargy, so the picnic was brief and came to an end. But in Ed's view, it was very successful. He only needed to find a way to break Blaine for good. It was time now for Lacey to present divorce papers once again. Ed did as much as possible with Lacey in public, hardly retreating to her room any more. He wanted his presence with her to mean something. When and why it was that he began to have control over her actions he was not sure. He did not care. Lacey made true her words to be his, thus surrendering her stubborn will. It was as if she, too, went out of her way to show that she was with the sheriff. Improper or not, they kissed soundly in the front entrance of the hotel as people passed them by. Ed did not count her gazed look as lack of joy, but of yielding, of accepting his love for her . . . finally.

He released her after one last, brief kiss. "Good night, my love." Lifting the palm of her hand to him as he walked away, she whispered, "Good night."

She returned to her room to find another bouquet of lilies on her table. She stood and mused, knowing it wasn't her friends, for she was with them all afternoon, she wondered for a moment—why lilies?

Blaine Jennings knew she watched him; he'd made the mistake of catching her eye once and saw what was in them. He'd nodded toward her out of courtesy and good manners, but had since avoided her like the plague. There was no avoiding the entourage headed his way now unless he sidestepped them all and said nothing; later he would wonder if that's exactly what he should have done. Stopping to let them pass, he realized that all had done so except her. Chloe Dupree stood before him in the attire of a queen. If he'd thought Lacey's dress unnecessary and ridiculous, he thought it of hers a thousand times more.

"I'll be along, Father." She turned her large, oval eyes to her maidservant and dismissed her also.

"I won't keep you," Blaine said.

"Nonsense, why else do you think I've stopped?" He looked at her, trying not to frown; she did beat all, even his wife's brash behavior. "May I help you with something?" he asked, knowing full well that everything and anything she might need or want was at her disposal, or at least at her servant's. "I wonder, Mr. Jennings, if you would take supper with us soon? At our home," she had planned to say it, but added it as if it were an afterthought. "You may bring the Jacksons, of course, I'm quite fond of them."

"I don't speak for the Jacksons, but I must decline. Thank you for the kind offer." He would have for anyone else, waited for them to take the first leave but did not think that she would, so he did. She watched shyly after him, but not before declaring to herself that he was the most handsome man she'd ever seen, and in all her journeys, she had seen a lot of men. What made Blaine Jennings even more appealing was that he did not seem interested in her. Chloe Dupree was used to getting what she wanted, and she wanted him. An opportunity of some sort was all she needed to be near him. She'd overheard plans for a harvest dance in the near future and decided that her attentions would do well to be spent on that.

※

As September rounded the corner and coolness finally began to settle upon them, it was rumored that the dance would happen sooner rather than later. No one knew how the rumor started and in the end, no one cared. The dance was suddenly organized, and before anyone knew it, a dance floor had been created and a bandstand formed. Flyers were passed out the day before, and people arrived in the very spot of the party if only to see that it were true. Chloe Dupree sat in her carriage and admired the work of her bright mind. She sat declining offer after offer to dance and fervently hoped her eyes did not betray what they sought, for he was not yet here there. The Jacksons brought with them Lizette and Dr. Colvin, who was frail, but spirited. Lizette mothered him until she was whisked away by a young man. Seeing as how Mack was too busy to attend, she did not deem it necessary to sit alone with Dr. Colvin all evening, and it was hardly her fault her husband did not come. Blaine had no tastes for such activities unless his wife was beside him, and decided to see if she was there. What he would do if he saw her he was not sure, he thought of his behavior the last time he confronted her. He smiled in spite of himself and strolled to the Jackson's blanket.

"Howdy, Blaine."

"Andrew, Cameron. Dr. Colvin, how are you feeling?"

"Poorly." He smiled, "Hard to believe I was taking bullets out of you young folk only months ago."

"Now wait a minute, you never had to take any out of me!" Declared Blaine, and the response he got was the truth, "It's because you were always the trouble maker who'd skeedaddle before things got out of hand."

Andrew laughed at his accurate speculation and portrayal of Blaine's younger days. Blaine's gaze wandered around the perimeter, "Is she here?"

Cameron shook her head, "I haven't seen her yet." They talked idly for some time, Andrew finally heeding to Cameron's plea to dance. Blaine settled in near the doctor, who pretended like he could see the young people dancing, but no but it wasn't before too long he started nodding off. This is how Chloe came upon Blaine, practically alone.

Joseph Benton stepped behind her and she was becoming impatient with the men at the party, as if she was the only female on the premises. "Miss Dupree, would you like to dance?"

She turned and with forced patience said, "Joseph, I'm not at all feeling well. I expect I'll just retire here for the evening."

Joseph looked down to Blaine who, to him, seemed irritated instead of pleased as pie, as he would have been should she have retired to his blanket. He shrugged his shoulders and bid them both good-bye. It wasn't long before he found another idyllic partner to swing around the plank boards. Violins, flutes, and fiddles sounded the night air and she said to Blaine, "There, you see, he's found someone already."

He made no move to invite her to sit, but rather focused his eyes on the couples twirling about, the lanterns hanging on all corners of the dance floor swayed along with them. She looked at the doctor and asked Blaine if he was dead and he said, "No, just sleeping. I suppose old age does that."

She stood awkwardly. Blaine's conduct was grating on her. She had judged him to be courteous, that's how she sees him with everyone else. She breathed an exasperated sigh and sat down anyway.

This was her opportunity and she would not miss out on it. "Are you enjoying yourself?"

He was righteously indignant, but felt to behave in a christianly manner just the same. "It's good to see people enjoying themselves and to get away from grueling farm work." She raised her knees to her collarbones and spread her skirts about her. She looked at him from the side, knowing it was the best view of her face. "And what is it you do, Mr. Jennings?"

"I own two opera houses and four hotels."

This surprised her, for she had taken pains to drive past his homestead when she knew he was not there—despite her maidservant's disapproval, and he did not look like a man of means.

"But there are no opera houses here, and as far as hotels go, I hardly think you own the Half Moon and Lacey . . ." her words faltered; that name was not one she wanted coming out of her mouth tonight. Yet, maybe this mistake would allow her to retrieve this constant consummation of where he stood with Lacey Jennings. She'd found out that the woman was set to divorce him, and even had an affair with the sheriff right under his nose! This information had only enticed her to want to know more about this mysterious man.

He spoke in the uncomfortable silence, "I don't own them here, but in Chicago. I have a good man managing my businesses there."

She rippled with satisfaction and excitement—a man of means indeed. Blaine began to be disconcerted, if for the fact he realized he had not ever shared this with Lacey, not that she'd ever asked him what he did. But the last thing he wanted to do was confide in the French flake before him.

Chloe flounced herself about, "Let's dance, shall we?"

He looked at her—unbelievable! "I thought you weren't feeling well tonight." At her confused look, he reminded, "It's what you told the deputy."

She maintained her graceful appearance and showed not the seething she was truly feeling. This man was irrational! She could have anyone she wanted and this man was just a conceited . . .

"I see I've offended you, Miss. For that I am sorry, but I must go. I didn't find what I came looking for tonight and have a long ride home. Good night."

As he tore his irked eyes from her, he saw Lacey and the sheriff. Following his lead, Chloe looked in the same direction. The fuming anger subsided instantly and she pulled herself closer to Blaine, as if at his request. He did not notice. Ed and Lacey had not seen him yet, but were coming his way. Then Lacey did see. What Miss Dupree saw in Lacey Jennings upright jaw and fiery eyes as she lit upon the couple sitting all lovely and cozy on the blanket shot something akin to glee throughout her. Blaine looked as though he was caught doing something wrong.

Ed was pleased more than anybody; he could not have had Blaine appear worse if he tried, "Lacey, we can dance over yonder, if you'd like. I would understand."

She flashed an, *I told you you haven't changed,* look directly at Blaine and outright hostility renewed throughout her. She replied, "I won't be shamed away."

Blaine hung his head in defeat. Chloe reached for him in comfort. He was panic-stricken as he felt her silky hand brush the side of his face and rose abruptly. He was gone. Chloe fumed and hollered at the maidservant standing very near and snapped, "Take me home!"

⁕

"Not tonight, Ed." Lacey did not look into his wounded eyes when she said this. It would be more guilt than she could handle this evening. "Why not?" He cursed, "It's because of him! Seeing your husband with that beautiful woman has made you . . ."

"No. It means nothing, I assure you."

"You know, Lacey, either come to terms with it or divorce that man.

You don't care about him, you despise him—or so you make me believe."

"That's not true, please don't say that."

"Let me come up tonight, show me it's not true." She could feel his breath upon her neck; she arched in response to his nonexistent touch. His coarse cheek brushed slightly against hers and sense came over her as passersby entered the hotel behind them.

"I'm sorry. Please understand."

His physical stature and emotions tensed, "I think I'm already beginning too." Ed leaped from the boardwalk and stalked off, but not before spitting out his next condemning words, "I hope you don't make another mistake with us, I am not so love stricken as I once was. Sleep tight, Lacey."

Her heart fell, couldn't she do anything right? What was she doing to Ed? She remembered his carefree, boyish smiles that once drew her to him. The innocent love he had carried for her was being warped for sure. Ed was only right about one thing, she did despise Blaine. What she could not explain to her warring self was that if she didn't care, then no then why was the pain so fresh and raw? Lacey knew deep down that Blaine was and always would be a rogue, but somehow, when she looked into his eyes, which she vowed to never do again, she began to believe, or at least hope, that he would truly love her the way she wanted. That has been her downfall—hope. How Blaine could have convinced her thus far was beyond her understanding and control. To see him with that insincere trollop had pierced her heart. It scared her immensely that it should have any affect on her at all. She did not want to care a fig what happened in Blaine's life, she just wanted her part in it to be over with and for good.

Nineteen

Dry dirt blew up with the force of the wind as Ed made his way to the post office.

He pulled up the collar of his long overcoat and held a kerchief over his nose and mouth. "All this blasted dust! Why won't it just rain?" Ed retrieved his mail and the postmaster closed the shutter halfway, "Now why would Mother Nature do something we want?"

Ed looked at the dark sky, "You finish closing up, Miles. Thanks for the letters and telegram."

"You best get back to your cells, Sheriff. Might be a tunnel making its way."

"I'm heading there now. Not many people out today."

Miles teased, "The smart ones are at home."

"Yeah, yeah."

Cameron barely noticed the high wind until it blew up her skirts as she stepped from Dr. Grover's office with both dread and hopeful anticipation. She rushed to her wagon and clucked the unnerved team of horses onward. She was expecting a baby again. She wondered what Andrew's response would be. She had has grown stronger physically and spiritually, both together should account for something—she could now handle whatever was to come of it. She sauntered off to Lacey's. With the sudden turn of the weather, the hotel was by far closer than home. Andrew would be thankful she'd made a wise choice. Blaine was finishing up a late breakfast, and after folding his newspaper, he saw Cameron. Lacey rarely served breakfast anymore. Her absence in the mornings made way for Blaine to get a decent meal without being glared at or ignored for that matter.

"What are you doing out in this storm?" He could have sworn that she blushed.

"Just came to visit Lacey. I didn't think the clouds meant this, although I suppose I should have."

"Well, now you'll just have to have some coffee with me. Unless you can conjure up Mrs. Jennings?"

"I'll do my best. But please don't expect too much."

"I will not go down there, Cameron. You know better than to ask such a thing of me. You should have seen them. Chloe Dupree has gained his attentions. I told him so." Lacey paced and looked to Cameron as if she were a spoiled child.

Cameron turned to leave in defeat, paused, and had a second thought, "Why should it bother you? You've made it clear to the whole town that you're with the Sheriff."

With that, Cameron left. Where her bold audacity came from she did not know, but it sure felt good, and she smiled all the way down to Blaine. He cleared his throat at Cameron coming alone; why she appeared elated was beyond him. She said, "Well, she won't be joining us."

"How is she?"

"Ornery."

"I shouldn't have asked you to go up there, I apologize." Blaine stirred his coffee and took a swig. Off Cameron's look, he said, "What?"

"She's jealous."

"She isn't."

"I know I shouldn't be grateful that someone is jealous, after all . . . it's wrong, but I think this might be alright, just this once," Cameron stated without shame.

"I wish I could agree. I don't want to win her back on that merit." He made an odd sound in his throat, "As if I could win her back at all."

For his sake, she changed the subject. "I hear that Mr. Dupree believes Lincoln County ought to have a mayor. Wouldn't you know, he believes it should be him?"

"It appears that way." Blaine had a few choice words to say on the matter, but did not voice them.

"Why don't you run against him?"

Blaine only laughed and shook his head, "I'm not mayor material. Besides, there isn't any 'running,' as you put it. It's in the rich man's head to be Mayor, I'm sure that's what he will be."

"Not if Andrew has a say in it, which he does." She sipped her coffee with a sly look in her eyes.

"Besides," he continued, "I have to go back to Chicago."

She peered at him, alarmed. "It's not what you think, I'm thinking of selling my businesses and building a home here. I said I wasn't going anywhere when I got here, and that's still my intention." He grinned, "Despite how much Lacey loves me and enjoys my company."

"She is stubborn, isn't she?" Cameron commented.

"Speaking of . . . my goodness, she is beautiful."

Cameron turned and saw Lacey, she agreed. She noticed that she'd freshened up, even changed her clothes since she was with her. Cameron smiled wide. If Lacey wasn't jealous, she wasn't a preacher's wife. It was all the hope to be had for at this point. Lacey entered into a deep conversation with Lizette, and then, of all the people who could come in that morning, Chloe came through the restaurant outshining Lacey with everything about her. Her servant followed her about, fixing her gown, sweeping the outside dust off of her. If Cameron didn't know it before, she recognized that as of late, Chloe seemed to be intentionally disregarding Lacey whenever they were in the same room together. Courtesies were no longer exchanged between the two as they were with anyone else. Chloe's face beamed when she saw Blaine; she did not mind him sitting with Cameron at all. It only seemed to make her scheme easier. Wisely not addressing the man who'd recently snubbed her, Chloe came in an exquisite fashion to their table and said to Cameron, "It's so good to see you, Mrs. Jackson. Why, I was going to make a trip out to your house this very morning, but the weather. Well, I had to stop here you see. How kind of you to have saved me the journey."

"You were coming to visit me?"

"I was wondering if you would like to come for supper at our home on Sunday?" She remained standing graceful, hoping her distress, if Cameron declined, would not show on her face.

Cameron said with regret, "We would love to, but that's the day we have company for supper in our home, it's become routine."

She put a pout on her lips, "I would love an opportunity to get to know you and your husband more, being part of the church community and all."

What could Cameron say to that? "Why don't you come and join us? I can make room for one or two more."

"I'm afraid my father won't be at church on Sunday. You see, getting ready to be mayor and landowner takes up all of his time."

"Yes, of course. So it will just be you?"

"My maidservant will be chaperoning me of course, but she will not eat with us."

"Of course she'll eat with us," Cameron said, appalled at the thought of ignoring her servant while they partook of a meal together.

"She will not." The decisive statement was clear as a bell.

Feeling uneasy for the first time in Miss Dupree's presence, Cameron wished she could take back the invitation, but could not do so. What would be said of the preacher's wife if she did? "We will look forward to having you." Cameron made a gesture toward Blaine, who was like a piece of furniture in their home on Sundays.

"Oh, excuse me, Mr. Jennings, I forgot my manners." Chloe feigned embarrassment. "Do you attend these gatherings at the Jackson's as well?"

"Of course he does, he's family," Cameron answered for him.

"You're sure I shan't be an imposition?"

Cameron saw the discomfort in Blaine's eyes and felt remorse for her part in being so easily taken. "You will be welcome."

"I'm grateful for your kindness and shall leave you two . . . to whatever it is you were doing. I'll see you Sunday, Mrs. Jackson." She looked at Blaine with purpose and without reserve, "And you also, Mr. Jennings, I look forward getting to know." She swept passed Lacey with a full-fledged look of triumph. Lacey was shaking inside with anger and did not know why. Why on earth should she care about Chloe Dupree's interest, and why did she wish she could wipe that tart-laced smirk off of the Frenchwoman's exotic, perfect face?

"Blaine, I . . ."

"Don't bother, Cameron, it isn't your fault. Apparently, I haven't been aggressive enough in my deterring her attentions from me."

"I did not have a clue it was that serious. Why didn't you say something?"

"What? That I'm being hunted like prey?"

She laughed and he said, "It's certainly what it feels like. I have to say it makes me realize how women feel when they don't want a man's attentions but get it anyway."

"I'll ask Andrew what he wants us to do for Sunday."

"Keep the plans. I don't have to come."

"Please come, Blaine. It wouldn't be the same without you. Besides, if you don't, she'll only keep pursuing."

"Suppose you're right. I'll just get it over with. If only . . ."

"If only Lacey acted like your wife you wouldn't be in this situation," Cameron surprised herself by saying.

"I'm sure it's more than I deserve, in her opinion, and more so, maybe to see if I've really changed, a test of some sort."

"Miss Dupree sure is beautiful."

"That's exactly why I need to show Lacey that I'm not the same anymore, I'll tell you this . . . before . . . married or not, I would have fallen for Chloe." He shook his head with shame, "I can't believe now that I was such a lecherous man and husband, but I have a feeling Lacey is just waiting . . . waiting to tell me 'I told you so.'"

Twenty

Cameron took great pains to ease Blaine's comfort on Sunday, seating him in between her and Andrew. Chloe looked disappointed, but determination replaced that feeling quickly, as Chloe was not known for quitting—and as usual, she seized the moment. They talked of the fine things in the South, and Blaine was prompted by all to talk about the opera houses and its shows. The evening went on relatively well and when Chloe's maidservant all of a sudden became ill, it was apparent that Chloe needed an additional escort home, as she needed to take care of her servant and couldn't drive and do that at the same time, now could she? Andrew had no desire to drive "that woman" home and selfishly did not offer, even after a hot look from his wife came his way. Later, when they were alone, he said he was sorry, "Blaine is on his own with this one." Andrew's well-maintained tolerance ran thin; he'd held his tongue at Chloe looking down on his wife throughout the meal, making this comment and that about her cooking, which he thought was fantastic.

"You are the Reverend, Mr. Jackson. You're supposed to tolerate everyone and their behavior," Cameron reminded him and was pleased that she could.

"That woman does beat all. I have run out of tolerance for the day." He changed the subject and grabbed her by the waist. "Now, let's talk about our son."

❧

To Blaine's chagrin, the maidservant seemed to feel well on their drive home, so much so that Chloe had the gall to have her walk a little to "get her strength back."

She sat closer to Blaine than he knew was necessary; his face was set and implacable. Chloe said, "It's such a nice evening, the fresh air will do her good."

After all, she did not wish for Blaine to think her insensitive.

"Maybe you should walk with her?" he proposed. She turned roughly away from him and placed the back of her gloved forefinger in her teeth. "You are so rude to me. What have I done?"

Here it is, the moment he needed to capture and end this attention. "Miss Dupree. I find your attraction out of line. You know that I'm married."

"But she wants a divorce," her tone was unsympathetic and he was on the verge of losing his temper.

"You seem to know a lot."

"Don't you find me attractive at all, Blaine?" He glanced at her sideways, "Yes."

She smiled under her glove. Not willing to push her luck with him, she said, "The moon is beautiful tonight, transcending down like that, it's glorious." Chloe's servant had been allowed back into the carriage, and Blaine turned the horses down the hill toward the Dupree's property, noting how much work Jacques Dupree III had done since he purchased it from Ian Zemke.

He untied his horse from the tail end and bid the two good night after declining Chloe's persistent invitation to join her father for his nightcap. She watched him ride away, her knight under the silvery moonlit sky, and reckoned with herself that the evening was not a total waste. She had learned Blaine's temperance and tolerance, and she knew more than anything how to break a man down. Chloe Dupree congratulated herself on making her acquaintance with Cameron Jackson. She hoped the preacher's wife in all her expected kindness would become her ally.

Thoughts of Blaine and seeking his attentions consumed Chloe over the next few days, and the need to see him overwhelmed her, but bringing herself to linger around town was not something she was used to doing. Chloe Dupree was always the pursued! She was not pleased in the least that she was forced to become the pursuer. However, she would wholeheartedly take the challenge. Blaine was worth having, and Lacey . . . well, she was worth setting down a few notches. She was not by herself this day, of course, but surrounded by Joseph Benton and others seeking her attention, or at best, a beautiful smile. Chloe only wanted a glimpse of Blaine today, to set her sights upon his good looks. She would work on his charms, if only given a chance. She wanted to greet him innocently, her plan was to cease her attentions, to show him that it was neither here nor there to her where he was concerned.

Joseph cut into her thoughts just as a frown escaped from her lips at the scene in front of her. "Miss Dupree? I asked if you would like anything cold to drink?"

"No, Joseph. If you'll excuse me."

Lacey Jennings did not pale today next to Chloe Dupree, due to the extra care she took with her hair, make-up, and clothing. For some insane reason, after Chloe's blatant attitude toward Lacey in her very own restaurant, she became enraged, and that day she looked upon herself in the mirror and was not pleased at what she saw. She had neglected herself, and that would just no longer do. This day, she could walk past Chloe and all of her admirers with her head held high because she knew she looked like a million bars worth of gold. Chloe noticed her competition had risen to the occasion finally. Some of her onlookers had the audacity to look away from her. Their eyes followed Lacey and received warm flirtation as a response. Thinking Lacey much too old for such a showing, Chloe stood abruptly, not planning ahead of time what she would say, "Mrs. Jennings, have some apple cake with us, our cook makes the best."

Lacey mused at the insincerity of the request and said, "Thank you, but no."

Chloe called after her, "Mrs. Jennings." Lacey turned politely. "Have you seen Blaine? I haven't seen him since he brought me home last Sunday. I've been meaning to ask him something."

"I don't keep track of Mr. Jennings comings and goings, Miss Dupree. As I'm sure you're well aware," she said tightly.

Joseph, who liked Lacey Jennings, felt uncomfortable and looked at her apologetically. She smiled kindly at him and left.

Lacey wanted to run. That woman infuriated her and tears stung at her eyes, but she gracefully composed herself back to dignity. Without asking for it, thoughts of Blaine taking Chloe home, sitting together closely in a carriage plagued her from all directions. A renewed sense of anger stirred within her, but with it came for the first time a tugging of affection for her husband and then a sense of loss. What she was to do with these emotions and torment that were beside her? So, she did what she knew to do, and went to Liam's for some cards, entertainment, and company from men who would actually accept her. She remained in the saloon for some time and had to be escorted, once again, to her room for lack of self-constraint in the area of drink. This time, Liam stepped in and Lacey had given him an earful as he half-carried her upstairs. No matter, she would forget the incident by morning.

Blaine braved a trip to see his wife, regretfully, to say good-bye. He felt to do so in case she thought him to be gone for good. *As if she would care*, he thought wryly. It was close to noon. His train left at one fifteen, and Lizette informed him that Lacey had yet to descend the stairs.

"Would you please get her for me?"

Lizette looked flustered, "No one dare disturb her until she calls, Mr. Jennings." He waited twenty minutes before going to her room himself. He prayed to God that she was alone, or else . . . what would he do? He heard her mumble and groan irritably upon hearing a knock. He pictured her stretching, then yawning. So she wasn't yet awake? He knocked again and smiled when he heard her curse the intrusion. Lacey flung open the door—a murderous look pierced the intruder. She rubbed her face and focused on her unwanted guest.

"Blaine?"

"Late night?"

"What are you . . . get out of here this instant!" She suddenly became aware of herself and left him standing there, not knowing if he was leaving or not, she rushed to her mirror and began to brush out her tangles. He walked in and stood watching her. How he would love to once again curl his fingers throughout her hair, black as night. He remembered with longing it being silky, smooth, and soft.

"You are becoming too bold, Mr. Jennings!" She scolded, glaring at him through the round mirror at her vanity.

"I waited for you in the restaurant, but you never came down. I see now that I would have been down there an eternity if I hadn't come up to you."

"Lizette should have spoken to you . . ."

"She did, I insisted. It wasn't her fault."

"We'll see about that."

"I came to say good-bye."

He saw her brushing falter and her eyes sadden just briefly, but it was long enough for him to know for certain that he, indeed, saw it. She lifted her chin, "Why are you telling me? It's nothing I didn't expect." Her method of defense as usual came in a mocking way and she snorted, "Did you think I would be disappointed? Beg for you to stay?" Her guard was letting down and the next question came out softer, as if she hadn't meant to speak it, "Did you think I would miss you?"

Blaine looked at the patterns in her carpet, "Maybe I was hoping for all three." His voice was husky and defeated.

What was she supposed to say? Do? This stranger standing before her, she had to admit, was not her husband. But who on earth was he? Blaine told the truth months ago and has been trying to prove that he'd changed ever since, why couldn't she just let go? Then she saw Chloe's face before her and remembered why. She refused to be hurt again by this man. She tossed down her brush; it rattled her pearl necklace as it bounced.

She stood and faced him, "Why are you telling me, really? Why don't you tell Chloe Dupree, or have you already?" The words were tough and meant to hurt and cut him down.

"Why would I?" He looked at her flabbergasted.

She did not miss his kind eyes. She allowed her gaze to shift over his features. She'd seen him laughing genuinely with townspeople, helping older citizens, serving the community, going to . . . church. Nothing that could identify the old Blaine Jennings of the past. These thoughts flittered about her mind as she took in the handsome sight of him. He stared at her—revelation hit. Maybe not the kind he wanted, but it was there never the less, and he confronted her on it. "Why, you are jealous!" If he wasn't happy about that, he would be lying, but it was written all over her face.

"I am not!"

"Yes. You are, Lacey Jennings." He crept toward her, nearly circling her.

"You can go now. You did say you were leaving?" She backed away.

She sat hard in her chair and he was there suddenly, kneeling before her, her eyes grew wide. He took her hands in his. "I'm only going temporarily. I'll be back well before Christmas, you can count on it."

"I don't care," she said stubbornly.

"Oh, yes you do." He pulled her hands to his breath, "And when I come back, you best be ready, young lady. I'm going to court you like there's no tomorrow."

She was so taken aback, she barely saw him leave her. She had so many questions. Where was he going, what was he doing? It was almost an hour before she gathered her wits about herself and got dressed for the day. As she was leaving her room, Lizette came with a tray of food and a vase with white lilies.

At her questioning look, Lizette smiled knowingly and set down the tray. "I guess it's been Mr. Jennings all along. He told me to bring you up some food and these." She nodded her head toward the note, "He put that on there himself before he left."

Watching Lizette go, she turned slowly to the note. Picking it up cautiously, shaking as she opened it, and then scolding herself out loud for acting so foolish—she read it.

My Dear Lacey,
Like a lily among thorns is my darling among the maidens.
Love always and forever,
Blaine

This mysterious message prompted Lacey to pay an unprecedented visit to Cameron's. All of a sudden, she had an overwhelming desire to learn more about her husband—for better or worse. What would be more rewarding for Lacey than to ask the people he spent most of his time with? Cameron knew something was on her friend's mind, but she also knew Lacey's prideful nature, and she would find out nothing if she prodded. She happily entertained her and set out some left over fried chicken from last night's meal and opened a jar of applesauce. The idle chatter ended and Lacey presented Cameron with the letter from Blaine. Cameron's eyes watered after reading it. "Lacey, that's beautiful."

Andrew came in from working outside and asked, "What's beautiful?"

Lacey looked at Cameron a moment and decided to show Andrew after a fleeting second of hesitation. Andrew smirked after reading it and congratulated his cousin-in-law . . . *that's good, well done, Blaine.*

"It's from the Bible."

Lacey said, "No."

Andrew jested with her, "Believe it or not, dear cousin, there is talk about love and marriage in the Bible."

"I've never seen that statement, Andrew," Cameron said.

"It's in Song of Solomon, maybe you should read that book." His eyes twinkled with mischief, "You might like it."

She gave him a look of consternation before turning to Lacey, "It's very romantic." Lacey looked at the note blankly, "It is."

Andrew sighed dramatically, "Well, it seems as though I should leave you to your womanly conversations." He winked at his wife, causing her to blush, as he knew she would, "I expect you to read that chapter, Mrs. Jackson."

Lacey confessed to Cameron the threat Blaine spoke to her before he left and admitted it frightened her. "I've never been courted before."

"Do you want him to?"

"I don't know. Yes. No! I have Ed." Her answer sounded so very weak. "I will not hurt Ed again. He's been nothing but kind and loving to me. I can't treat him poorly any longer. I will lose him for sure, and then I will have no one."

"That doesn't sound like a very good reason to be with someone. You must ask yourself—are you using Ed because you're afraid to be alone?"

"I care for him, you know I do."

"I know you do. If your heart is speaking that you should be with Ed, then by all means. But if it's not . . ." Cameron dared the statement. She could be confident that Lacey's "heart" wanted Blaine.

"I can't understand why Blaine would still want me. I can't seem to make him give up."

"Maybe you don't want him to give up."

"Of course I do! If he only would, my life would get back to normal."

Cameron refilled their mugs with spiced cider, "Would it?"

"I need to be able to think again. To not feel as though I'm going insane with tormented thoughts about who I should be with. The bottom line is, I will not turn out Ed, no matter, as you say, where my heart is. I don't deserve anything for myself anyway."

"I wish you didn't say things like that. I wish I could take away your pain and your doubt, Lacey." Cameron hesitated, not wishing to break this flow of closeness between them; it was an unusual occurrence for either to be so transparent. She plundered on just the same.

"What about starting fresh?"

"Specifically?"

"Maybe try a different approach to relationships. Maybe come to church."

"I will not. With no offense to you, church is just a room filled with hypocrites." She laughed in spite of Cameron's face, "Even the likes of Blaine Jennings gets through those doors. No thanks." The words hurt, but

Cameron had nothing to lose by pushing. "Tell my why you feel this way, please. I want to understand."

"It's everything about it. You and Andrew say that religion is not what my parents taught me it was. For them, God was a punishing God. If I didn't know certain scriptures, they beat my hands and my backside. They despised my face and said beauty was sinful and took every mirror out of the home, saying it was evil. My hair was cut short all my childhood days, it was horrible." She sneered, "You should have seen them, uppity as could be when people came to visit. They had the gall to read the bible and pray of all things! I grew to hate God," she snorted. Her words were said as fact, not self-pity. "Men noticed my looks before noticing me, and I found out easily enough that I could get away from those spiteful people, giving myself to whoever would want me."

"Is that how you see Andrew and me?"

"You know I don't."

"What about Blaine? He has since found God, and with God in your life, you can't do anything but change for the good, no matter where you've been."

A tear escaped from Lacey's eye. "If that's true, then Blaine surely wouldn't want me now. I've just done too much that he wouldn't appreciate."

"You think he doesn't know that? He hasn't forgotten where he came from, what he did to you. He left you for another woman. If God is so vengeful and punishing, would He have wanted someone like Blaine?"

"Somehow it doesn't hurt anymore, Cameron. The part about the other woman, I guess we are even if you were to look at it that way." She tried to be humorous but cried instead. "I don't know what to think. When I'm around you, or Andrew, or even Blaine for that matter—you just seem so . . ."

"Content."

"I suppose." She searched Cameron's face for hope, "I don't know if I can do it. I'm not strong enough to live like you do."

"I assure you, you might not want to live like me. I'm a floundering fool sometimes, I say what's on the top of my head, think things I shouldn't." Lacey's eyes darted to hers and Cameron said, "Yes, it's true. But I know I'm loved and always will be. It's something you'll need to seek and find for yourself. No one, not even Blaine, can sustain you in the way you need."

"I want to believe you."

"I know. Maybe you'll visit church with me someday and make a new judgment on the matter."

Lacey made a face, "Well, it would certainly give the old biddies something to talk about."

"Indeed, it would. I know I just ate, but I'm starving again! How about some peach cobbler?"

"Absolutely. When is your little girl coming into the world?"

"Our *son* is due to come at the end of spring."

"Nah, I'll bet it's a girl."

"We'll see."

It was out of curiosity that Lacey decided to take Cameron's suggestion and visit church on Sunday, that, and Blaine's absence in doing whatever he was doing assured her he would not be there. It was the perfect opportunity to be somewhat hidden and able to observe. Lacey plucked open her umbrella and stepped into the light rain shower. She wanted to walk and did not tell Cameron she might come today. How could she? The idea had dropped upon her suddenly as she did her routine complaining to Lizette about no business Sunday mornings. As she drew near the white building that represented religion in this county, something akin to nervousness resonated throughout her. She could always turn back; no one would be the wiser. Except, she reasoned, it was harmless enough, wasn't it? It must have been the last hymn sung because the organ's notes drifted and Lacey, as she stood in hesitation and presumption upon these steps and listened to the rustle of shoes and the sound of quiet. Andrew's voice became audible and Lacey waited, she could hear his words, they did not mean anything to her. They did not send her away, nor bring her in. She rather liked it where she was and tuned in to her cousin's passionate voice until he finished talking to those that left their dwellings weekly to hear him speak.

Lacey brought nothing back to the hotel from Andrew's sermon, she realized, though, what she did gain was an absence of disdain. The upbringing she had from her parents was a long time ago, over and done with. Interestingly enough, it did not seem to be the reason, she told herself, any longer why she did not wish to go to her very own cousin's church. Andrew was nothing like her parents, and therefore, she could do no comparison. She did not have to like religion or what it stood for, but could not justify those past reasons for not supporting family. The rain had ceased and the town was beginning to come alive by those not in a Sunday service. When Lacey stepped into her dwellings, she was taken by surprise, and the greeting, if you could call it that, from Ed Randall was less than pleasant. He looked hurt and furious all at once. She should have been humble, she knew she should have been, but it would not be in her nature to do so, and she asked, "Why the scowl?"

He kicked himself from the bedpost his booted foot was upon and actually grabbed her by the shoulders, grief-stricken. "Don't play stupid, Lacey. It's beneath you."

She tore herself away and would not cower, would not let him know he disturbed her. "I really don't know what you mean, Ed." She unpinned her hat, placing it gracefully into its box, trying to remain composed.

He cursed, "Lizette told me you went to church." His laugh was shaky and filled with disbelief at the notion of this conversation.

"What would it matter if I did?" There. She felt her rebellion coming back. "I do what I want."

"And with whom you want? Isn't that what you wanted to say? Was he there?"

She removed her pearl necklace, "Who?"

Ed was raised by decent and loving parents. He respected women and never abused anyone, but right now those convictions were slowly being drained from him.

He made a fist in anger and to his credit, his hand remained at his side. "What are you doing, Lacey? I thought this was all worked out between us."

She turned to him, his manner placated as she stood up to him face to face, mere inches separated them. "I love only you, Ed Randall. I didn't go into the building. Cameron wanted me to come, so I did. I couldn't go through with it, and Mr. Jennings is out of town. So I'll thank you to take back those accusing words."

His eyes held hers to discern honesty, or lack of, then took her quickly into his arms and buried his face into her loose hair. "I'm so sorry. I can't help myself, I want you so badly." He lifted her chin so that she saw his pain and anxiety. His voice was not the same as she has known, "We'll take care of this mess together. That man will sign any paper I give him to sign and then it will just be us. We'll be married. Finally."

As he embraced her, fear came over Lacey. It was suddenly a frightening sense to be in his arms. What was she doing to this man? He was once so thoughtful and kind beyond her wildest dreams. He was changing for the worse, and it was all her fault. She was not going to get off so easily as to where her life was destined to go. Someone would be hurt, and she did not know yet who it would be. Maybe she should just go away, escape all of this madness.

Twenty-One

It was late the next evening and Blaine stepped from the platform of the train station and was met with a crisp and cold wind whipping at his face, his breath came out in a cloud of steam. Exhaustion overcame him. He was tired from sitting for hours and attempted to stretch his legs. He pulled a scarf around his face and wove throughout the small crowd toward the hotel. Too concerned about having a good night's sleep, he gave no thought about whether or not Lacey would want him to stay. There was no way he was riding home with this wind chill, and no way he would step foot into the Half Moon. Blaine shouldered his bag and walked as quickly as his tired old bones would carry him. Lacey's hotel guests were just finishing with their desserts when she heard the bell chime. As was her habit, she smoothed out her skirts and made haste to fix the wisps of hair escaping from her updo. An unexpected site stood doggedly in front of her, he looked weary and she did not know what to say to him.

"Do you have a room?"

He mistook her silence and asked impatiently, "Can I stay here, Lacey?"

She blinked. "Of course you can. Anybody can."

Blaine gave her a wry look. After all, a short while ago *he* had not been welcome to stay here, much less set foot through the front door. She actually looked flushed and uncertain as to what she should do or say. He continued with the one-sided conversation. "May I have a key then?"

"Oh, yes. Here you go, top of the stairs to your left."

He seemed so uninterested in her that she began to wonder if he remembered saying those sweet words of courtship to her before he left. Or if he remembered his note she read daily—she even took time to read the entire book of Song of Solomon from that Bible Cameron gave her. He removed the key gently from her soft hand and made his way to his room, leaving Lacey unusually perplexed.

A short while later he was surprised to hear a knock at his door. He had just removed his shoes and let down his suspenders and loosed his shirt. "Yes?"

"It's me."

He frowned, he was in no mood for Lacey's coolness or reminders and lectures about being hurt by him and intended to let her know this. When he opened the door, he was impressed to see his wife holding a silver tray of tea fixings and shortbread cookies. She shrugged, "I thought you might like refreshments." Forgetting his rough travel and tiredness, Blaine finally looked at her with eyes of love and desire. It was what she wanted, wasn't it? She stammered lamely, "I always bring this to guests . . . on their first night."

Eyebrow raised, he asked, "Really? And do you *join* your guests as well?"

She raised her chin, "Absolutely not, sir."

"Sir, is it?"

"When you act like that it is."

"Like what?" He could see he was losing her to stubbornness, so he said quickly and apologetically, "I am sorry. I am inviting you in to have some of this tea with me." He took the tray from her and walked to deposit it on the table, she was still standing in the doorway when he turned around. She was staring at him and his casual attire, half-dressed he was, and he knew then that she missed him. Lacey resented being caught adoring his features. *Well, who wouldn't?* She justified with anger and indignation.

"Well?" he pressed, "Tea?"

She was lonely, but was she desperate enough to keep Blaine's company? She debated this for a moment until loneliness won out. "I'll be back with a cup for me."

Blaine smiled wide—only when she was gone of course.

<hr />

"Don't you want to know where I've been?" he said when she decided to stop fussing with the tea and food and settle herself down before him. She did not reply.

"I'll tell you anyway. I went back to Chicago to see to business matters." She shrugged and he said, "Don't tell me you haven't given it a thought. I think I know you better than that." He was right. She had given it too much thought, especially at her growing unease around Ed. She shuddered to think of what would happen if he found her in this room.

She sipped her lukewarm tea. "Maybe a little curious."

In recognizing that this coolness was a part of her, he was not threatened by it, but embraced it because he loved her. The only thing Blaine wanted to change in her was the desire for him to come back. He wanted everything else about this woman. She distracted the direction of his thoughts, "What was your business?"

"Opera houses and hotels." He sank back into his chair.

"I see. Like the hotel you started here? You come to take it back?" Her question was entirely unexpected. How could she even think that?

She asked, "It is yours, isn't it? I only took care of it to support myself and, of course, because you abandoned the both of us." The way she said this, so matter of factly, was the very reason he was so shocked. Reality hit him like never before. "I would never take this place away from you. It was your dream that built it."

"But it is in your name."

"I'll change it to yours before tomorrow's over."

Uncomfortable silence filled every corner of the room. She looked away, what was she doing here?

He was out of his seat fast, "No, don't go. Don't run away from me."

"What do you want from me, Blaine? You come back into my life and disrupt everything that I've built in your absence. A fine establishment, notoriety in this community, and yes . . . relationships."

"I expect one last chance."

"You expect too much."

"Don't you think I know that? I have been racked with guilt for so long."

"So this is about you. Absolving your sins?"

"No!"

"Why not? It's another selfish thing you could do."

"Don't push me away any longer, Lacey. I beg you. You're only doing it to prove me wrong and you're wasting your time. I love you more each time I see you. Each morning I wake up, it's you in my thoughts. You're not giving me yourself because you want to punish me. But I know you, you know I've changed and . . ."

She really should make herself go—not yet. "And what?"

"I don't believe you truly care for Ed as much as you are making yourself to believe."

"That's the difference between us, isn't it? You're wrong." What started out pleasantly was not ending in Blaine's favor, far from it. He had to rectify swiftly.

"Remember what I said to you before I left?"

Lacey did not turn or look back at him. She gripped the tray tightly and said just above a whisper, "Yes."

"Good, because I meant every word of it."

Why does this man do this to me? Lacey was a passionate woman and felt uneasy at the stirrings under her corset. She gathered the remaining dishes as if they were hot and went to the door of her husband's room. Regret and sadness consolidated in his stomach.

"You don't have to go."

A sob tore from her, "Yes, I do."

"Please stay."

Uncertainty enveloped her, she no longer felt secure with Ed or with this man. Physical torture would have been easier to bear. Blaine knew he shouldn't, but he did anyway. He touched her shoulders ever so slightly, removed the tray, and turned her into him. Her body lax, her will weakened, and her lonely heart begging to be loved, she allowed it. He held her for several moments, intoxicated by her sweetness. The front of his shirt became moist with her silent tears, no doubt she was maintaining a stoicism of emotions, but feelings could not be held in; her tears were betraying the evocable love she felt. "Blaine . . . even if I tried, I can't just forget what you've done to me."

"Neither can I, and I can't make it up to you."

"No, you couldn't."

He smiled at her candidness. In her state of being she had no discipline, she took in her husband's long eyelashes and felt his body's closeness and memories overwhelmed her senses. He closed his eyes, he must show restraint. She was not in a good frame of mind. *God, how can I let her go tonight?* He set her from him. Regret seemed to be his closest friend. "Let me take you away from here. We'll go to the city, any city, and reconcile without influence. I want you to get to know me again, Lacey."

"No. I mean . . . I can't do that," she said, yet excitement filled her with just the thought.

"You can."

"It's an outrageous suggestion!"

"Do you want to know me the way I am now?"

"It's too much to ask."

"Do you want to know me?"

Seeing Ed's wounded eyes came at her from all directions, seeing his anger and hearing his threats plagued her. She put a hand to her temple.

"It's your decision. I can make you happy, more so than you've ever known."

Before she could stop herself, she said, "Yes, I'll go."

He wanted to leap in his elation but held his eyes to hers. "Don't waver, no matter what anyone says."

"No one can say anything if they don't know." Lacey could not believe this. How could she submit to this scheming? She was going mad, no doubt about it.

But just to let him know once and for all she replied, "This is your last chance, Blaine Jennings, so help me if you . . ."

He put a finger over those lips of accusation; he removed it and planted a kiss onto her forehead. "Thank you. You won't regret this, I promise."

Feeling rather euphoric, Lacey descended the stairs with the empty tray.

Words filled with condemnation stopped her in her tracks. "Going from one man's arms into another? My, what excitement you must have in this hotel." Chloe had been waiting longer than she wanted to, but nevertheless it had paid off.

"Whatever it means to you makes no difference." Lacey was beginning to really hate this woman, leering around corners for heaven's sake!

"We'll see about that." The bells chimed above the hotel's entrance as Chloe departed. All of a sudden, dread filled Lacey. What was she getting herself into? No. She was going to do this. She would not worry about Chloe or anyone else. She had no plans to share this venture with anyone and hoped the conniving twit didn't speak of this incident. The inner turmoil must stop, and seeing Blaine for who he truly was would be sure to lead the way in deciding for herself her own future.

※

Lizette served the couple breakfast, utterly confused as to why her employer was seated with Blaine Jennings. Of course, he was more charming than anyone else she'd ever known, and that could be thought with much justification in her opinion. She had only Mack to compare, and practically everyone was more charming than he.

Blaine poured maple syrup over everything. "And what of Mr. Dupree and his, ah—election."

Lacey giggled, he liked hearing her do so. "The 'election' is to take place in the spring. Since no one is running against him, he's already acting as if he's mayor. Pompous!" It was Blaine's turn to laugh. He had been thrilled when she accepted his invitation to join him not only for breakfast, but for their secret trip as well. He thought to hear the first words from her mouth this morning a decline to go away after all. She never ceased to surprise him.

"When and where should we go?" he asked.

"Shh, we mustn't talk about this here."

He whispered smartly, "Why ever not? We're not children."

Lizette glanced their way and Lacey said, "I just want to do it on my own with no one else's input or thoughts on the matter."

"Fine. But how will we make travel plans if we can't discuss it?"

She toyed with her food a moment in thought, "I'll come to your room tonight."

He raised an eyebrow.

"Very funny, Blaine."

"But I've already checked out, there's no reason for me to stay here. I only stayed last evening because I was weary from travel."

"I guess you're right. Come to my room tomorrow."

He hated to ask, "You're sure?"

"You mean will I be alone?" She couldn't help it, still digging into his heart with words of a dagger. "Yes, I will be."

Blaine was thrilled to say the least of this new change of heart Lacey seemed to have. If he'd known of Ed's guilt-ridden conversations toward her and the pressures he placed upon Lacey, he would know one reason she was coming with him. What he did realize was that she'd lived here for years and wasn't so foolish as to know she might use this "get away" as an excuse for adventure. But she was going with him, and that's all that mattered.

❦

The plans to depart were actually coming to fruition and Lacey was scared beyond imagination. She set up her room to accompany Blaine. Not knowing if he would be hungry or thirsty, she had Lizette bring a little of everything from cold, sliced meat with cheeses to oatmeal cookies. Also gracing the spread was an assortment of tea, fresh coffee, and just in case he would like, his favorite wine. She wasn't trying to please him, but merely setting up an environment to which he could be comfortable and make her way to plan getting out of this place. All of a sudden, the thought of traveling made her giddy, and she wanted to begin packing right then, but a light knock sounded at her door. He was here. Speechless, Blaine entered.

She realized then that she had done too much and quickly amended, "Lizette . . . she . . . has outdone herself, hasn't she?"

"It appears that way."

At her stricken look he said, "It's wonderful, really. I'm famished."

She smiled, "Help yourself."

She's in rare form tonight.

"When are we leaving?"

And she's getting straight to the point.

"I was thinking in two or three days. Will that be enough time?"

"Oh, yes." She was so agreeable, he wondered if he was doing the right thing. He had to be, time alone was the only way to make her see . . .

"Where shall we go?"

He topped his sandwich off with a slice of thick-crusted bread and sat at the table with her. Lacey's eyes lit up. He asked, "What do you say about Wichita?"

"It's not too close and not too far. Sounds perfect."

"Just so I know, you are coming for us?"

"There're many reasons I'm going. One of them is to see what, if anything, can be salvaged between us."

"So there is a chance."

Her skepticism was obvious, "If there is a chance, we'll soon find out."

He took a large bite, "Well, that's all I need to know."

The door burst open and Ed stood there, eyes wide in unbelief. Lacey was on her toes instantly, ashamed, shocked, guilty, everything not good she could feel hit her. Ed made a mad dash toward Blaine and yanked him from his seat.

"Ed, no! You're the sheriff!"

He looked at her incredulously and tore off his silver star.

"Not tonight. Get out of the way, Lacey."

"No."

"Yes," the voice belonged to Blaine.

"Stop it!"

Ed pushed Lacey out of the way, and with full force punched Blaine straight on in the face; blood poured instantly from his nose. He looked up through blurry and burning eyes only to land another in the same place. Lacey came into view and Blaine shouted, "Get out of the way!"

When Ed pushed her aside once more, Blaine charged him. Ed's back slammed into the wall, pictures fell. The wind had been knocked out of him, "I don't want to fight, Ed."

"No?" Ed swung right and clocked his cheekbone, Blaine's skin split. He knew it was fight or be plundered, possibly to death. How long was one supposed to turn the other cheek anyway? He pounded Ed over and over into his ribs until he ran out of steam. Both men, haggard and beaten, gained new strength and went at it again. Lacey had seen and been involved with enough violence to not seem too shaken. For she knew she could only wait until they either killed each other or passed out. Lizette had gone home for the evening, so it was up to her to claim Dr. Grover for the aftermath.

When the two arrived, they found Blaine lying near the foot of the bed, rousing to and from consciousness.

"You fool!" Lacey ran to get clean linen and water for the doctor. Once assured Blaine would be fine, she set out to find Ed, and find him she did in the saloon. His bloody knuckles curved around a bottle of whiskey. His face looked halfway decent, but his body was bent into an awkward position and pain was evident upon his features. She brought a wet cloth and sponged his face. "We weren't doing anything."

"Maybe not at that moment. But you would have, it's not the only time you've been alone up there together."

Chloe!

"We've only talked. I swear it to you."

"You shouldn't be talking with him, you . . ." His eyes pinched closed in pain and he breathed out a crackled, wheezy breath. "You're supposed to hate him."

"I know."

She couldn't stand this tug of war within her any longer. She ought to just go away alone, forget them all and it would serve them all too well if she just never came back again! Her thoughts were big, and although she knew she never could do that, deep down, she knew she must give her husband that one last chance she promised to give. He didn't deserve it, but that's the only thing that would release her, she told herself this.

"You need to lie down, Ed Randall."

"What I need is to be left alone."

"Let me help you, please."

"I want him gone. I don't want to see him in this town again. If you care for me at all, you'll tell him that. And if he cares for *you* at all, he'll pay heed to your words."

Was that an unspoken threat?

The lie slid off her tongue easily, "He's leaving in two days, that's what he came to tell me tonight."

Ed took another swig to ease his pain and dull his mind and looked evenly at her, "If he's so much has ever touched you in a way . . ."

"Please, Ed! He hasn't!"

"I expect he'll be gone then, if you say?"

"It's what he told me."

"And you don't care?"

At her hesitation, he grabbed her chin, "Listen to me. I am sheriff of this town. I've made something of myself, and Lord knows I've kept you clean and out of trouble, don't repay me unkindly. I've been humiliated more than enough from you; it was more than I ever should have had to take. I'm done being your stomping ground." He jerked her face away—her finger touched the abused spot and a tear slid over her hand. This was not her Ed. If she had him back as he once was, she might not even have found herself in this dilemma. She had to believe that, and even worse, because of what he was becoming, she must continue to deceive him.

"Let me take care of you."

He flashed a heated smile toward Kimberly.

"Maybe it's not you who I want to care for me tonight." His eyes closed as the scent of her left him. He'd had no intentions of Kimberly entertaining him, but Lacey needed to feel what he felt on a constant basis.

By the time Dr. Grover was finished treating Blaine, Lacey had her room mostly straightened up. The broken picture frames, the broken lamp and chair she set next to her door, then observed the patient in her bed. Blaine winced in pain as he tried to reassure her with a smile. She thought that humorous and said, "Dr. Grover, you sewed him up nicely."

The self-righteous doctor stood to his full height, "He's going to swell by tomorrow. I did the sutures loosely to allow for that." Dr. Grover looked at Lacey with outright disapproval, knowing her to be the cause of this nonsensical behavior not fit for boys in a schoolyard. "Keep the area clean and bandaged to ward off infection." As he spoke, his eyes roamed her room, as if looking to debase her for something else.

She hid a smile under her hand, feigning eager concern. "I will, and thank you for coming, Dr. Grover."

He grunted and left, leaving the two alone with her husband in her bed.

He tried to sit up, "Don't worry, I'm leaving."

"Really?" She folded her arms. She'd like to see him try and walk out of here. Composing herself to a firm stance, she added in a playful tone, "I'll sleep in an unused room." She handed him a bell. "Ring if you need me for anything, I'll be next door."

She gathered her belongings and thought him sleeping. As she went to douse the one lamp left in her room, Blaine rang the bell and she jumped. When he tried to laugh, an odd sound came from him, bringing Lacey to laugh heartily.

He held up his hand in surrender, "Don't . . . make me laugh."

"You started it. What did you want?" She stood with a pile of clothes in her arms, waiting innocently for his answer.

"To say thank you."

"I hardly think you need to do that. I didn't know he would come tonight and beat you senseless."

His pride wounded, he stated, "I wasn't short of giving him a few good ones."

"I suppose you did," she said sadly.

"Still, thank you for coming back to me." He laid back and put the wet cloth to his aching head. She doused the light. Is that what she did? She came back to him?

Twenty-Two

The guile planning was behind her. Now, Lacey contended with fear, excitement, and wickedness. She felt like a criminal. Blaine was sitting across from her in the coach he managed to procure for just the two of them. She was baffled at his calm and peaceful demeanor. Of course he had nothing to lose at this insane venture! At his look, she smiled halfheartedly and looked away shyly, uncomfortable in his presence. She grabbed the windowsill as the coach hit a rough patch in the road. Earlier in the day, Blaine bribed the driver for extreme secrecy—there was no turning back. They had snuck away from town at two in the morning like thieves.

"You look pale." Blaine eased back comfortably, almost smugly in her opinion.

"I am pale! We are sneaking off in the middle of the night for heaven's sake." Feeling mentally unbalanced, she suddenly laughed hysterically, "Poor Lizette! What will she say? She'll know I've gone mad."

"Why? Because it's out of your character, or because she'll put two and two together and figure you're with me."

She eyed him smartly. "Both reasons I suppose." She took off her kid gloves and laid them on her lap. She pulled her shawl about her shoulders tightly after removing an object from her carpetbag. Lacey had the audacity to bring with her a flask. She brought it to her lips and heard, "Oh no, you don't."

"You've no call to . . ."

"This time I do. On this trip, you'll not drink alcohol." He held out his palm.

"You don't understand, I need a . . ." she finished lamely, "drink."

"What you need is to trust." He pleaded, "Don't turn to that, not now."

She thrust it toward him, "Fine!"

Despite the chilling weather, he opened the door and poured out its contents. He returned the flask; she pouted and did not retrieve it. He watched her. Her emotions always made their way to the surface of her fine, smooth face. Since entering the coach, he's observed expressions from doubt to anxiety and from guilt to curiosity. Sulking was what she was

A Lily Among Thorns

doing now, her pride wounded by the authority he'd exerted and their conversation halted. Tiredness prevailing, she soon began to nod off. She was plenty warm he was sure, but couldn't resist sitting beside her as an excuse to aid comfort during her rest. He took her slouching body into his arms, risking rejection and accusation, and he observed the night sky until the moon descended and the morning awakened with light. Blaine was dosing when Lacey awoke, she slid herself from him and primped. Due to the unorthodox travel they had not stopped for the past six hours, no stagecoach rest stop would've been operating at this time—and it was high time for a rest stop.

The driver must have read her mind and halted the team of horses. She saw tobacco juice stream from overhead and heard a thump on the other side. A man opened her door and she shielded the bright sun from her eyes. Blaine was awake. They breakfasted and stretched out limbs for a short time and were back in route to Wichita. The destination of both dread and anticipation.

"What did you say? She's gone?" Ed raked his fingers through his hair in blatant anger. "When?"

"I only have this note, it says to take care of the place or close it. She said she'd be back, Sheriff."

He looked at Lizette intently, as if daring her to lie. "Did she say where?"

"No, sir. I don't know anything about it."

Dawning realization hit Ed and he stormed out without another word. Lizette was stumped. When Ed came in this morning, she had no thought to conceal what Lacey had done. Why didn't she pose that Lacey was sick in her room—that she did not wish to be disturbed? Better yet, why didn't Lacey just confide in her?

He felt his vein pulsing in his neck as he pounded on Blaine's door. The wood was old and weak and split down the middle, giving the sheriff plain view of his rival's habitat.

Cautiously, Ed stepped inside. "Blaine?"

No answer, nothing. He cursed and threw over a table. He scoured the room for clues, for anything. This place was a pigsty, how could Lacey even consider leaving him for this? But that's exactly what she'd she's done, left him. Something foreign seized Ed Randall and he kicked at the downed table, the fit of rage spiraled and before he knew it, Blaine Jennings' home was thrashed. Ed took in heavy breaths and leaned against the wall near the broken door. He cursed at himself, at his lack of control, at his cursed, dying love for Lacey Jennings. Despite the badge on his vest, he jumped onto his horse and galloped five miles to Jake's home.

※

"Think, man. You're asking me to track Lacey? Let her go." Jake was disheveled; the plundering on his door still reverberated in his head. What a way to wake up.

"Don't worry about that, I will. I have! I just don't like being left without a word. As if I've meant nothing to that woman all this time!" Spittle sprayed from him and he gulped a breath to calm him himself. Ed was a passionate man, as much as Lacey a passionate woman. Not one of them could listen to reason when in their states of being.

Jake said, "Come in, I'll make coffee." He finished pulling his shirt on and left Ed standing in the cold, hoping he would follow.

Ed appeared moments later in the kitchen, "I want to kill him. Blast it! Everything was fine until he came!"

"Was it really?"

"It was good enough for me."

Jake lit a smoke and said, "Have a seat," and he left.

When he returned with five fresh eggs, he glanced at the sheriff. He was sitting with his head in his hands, in grief and frustration, Jake supposed. He completed the coffee and would wait until it brewed. He would go after Lacey, but only to attempt talking sense into her, but he would not bring her back. Why she would go with a man she despised was beyond Jake's understanding, but it wasn't as though he had a good grasp on understanding women himself. He placed an empty mug in front of his unannounced guest and a plate. Ed sat in silence, contemplating a murder, Jake was sure, and soon had a breakfast of fried eggs and coffee steaming in front of him.

"I'll go."

"Bring her back to me."

"What are you going to do to her?"

"I don't know. She shouldn't have done this to me." Ed gripped his coffee cup.

"Lot's of people shouldn't do the things they do to others. It's the way of the world, Ed."

"It's not the way of mine."

By nightfall, the coach pulled up to a grand hotel—The Golden Palace. Lanterns lit up every crevice of town and people were busy about, not upright citizens, of course, but wild cowboys and parlor girls. "It's been a long while since I've been here," Blaine said offhandedly.

"I'll bet."

He looked after her as she walked in to the double door entrance. This is where they were to stay. This is where she was to decide her life. Lacey felt him next to her, "This place is beautiful." She took in the architecture, furnishings, and grandeur.

"It's why I chose it; I want the best for you, for us."

"Don't think you can win me over with riches, Blaine Jennings." She rectified, "Although it doesn't hurt."

They both couldn't deny that they wanted to have a good night's rest. Blaine ordered up baths to be brought up to both rooms. "Make sure the lady's water is extra hot." He tipped the boy and he speedily ran off to the back of the hotel.

They were escorted up the winding staircase to separate rooms. The moment they stood across from each other in front of the doors with numbers on them, Blaine was uncomfortable, and a tightening occurred in his heart. He missed his wife, her feel, her scent, everything about her, and he had to will himself to remembrance of being married all over again in the eyes of God. The thought came that she may not even want him. They stood in the spacious hallway awkwardly. She looked at the greenery and bench all along it and made mental notes for her own hotel.

Blaine cleared his throat, *where do we go from here?* "Well then, have a pleasant sleep."

"I'll try," she said. Always in the past she had commended herself on attracting men to her satisfaction, it fed a need in her, even if it was false security. She was no fool at what she witnessed in her husband's eyes. Although he was careful to conceal it, it was too late. She felt a surge of power and confidence. This was it, no turning back. Lacey was staying in the most elegant place she'd ever seen. Why shouldn't she allow this man who'd once ruined her pay her back with fine things? She deserved to be served and pampered and she would expect nothing less. Lacey determined to press onward and would not think of the outcome of being hurt again.

Her smile became bleak as she entered her suite. She gazed about the elaborateness of every fine thing in the room. A tea service tray sat on an oval table in the corner near a writing desk, rocking chair, and ottoman set up for comfort. The four-poster bed framed the farthest wall and to its right was a large painting of landscape; she guessed it to be European. With delicate fingers, Lacey outlined the fine linen, imported, no doubt. She was going to see that Blaine Jennings spoiled her these few days. Suddenly, and most unladylike, Lacey threw herself onto the colossal soft bed and laughed aloud—feeling free. She stopped herself as a light knock tapped upon her door and two young men placed an iron tub inside her room under the moonlit window. Both gawked at her beauty and one shyly retreated, the other looked at her with open desire, and then she remembered what she was. Beautiful. While her bath was being prepared, her sparsely packed trunk arrived. She peeked inside it as the young men departed—Blaine would need to purchase her a few dresses. Lacey looked upon tomorrow with anticipation, she would not forget who she was again, or the fact that Blaine was a man like any other, an area in which she had much expertise.

Lacey appeared a bit overzealous at being with him. Blaine determined to not be concerned about this. After all, how much did he really know about his wife? Maybe this was her way of caring for him, they ate breakfast together with fine china and crystal and tasty food, and Lacey indulged herself in every bite. She waived the server over to her and he refilled her coffee. She did not acknowledge him in any way and kept her eyes trained on Blaine, who said, "Thank you," to the man after declining his own refill.

"What shall we do today, Blaine?" He studied the embroidered napkin on the table. "I was hoping we would talk."

She shrank back, "I was hoping we could see the town. I'm in need of a few things. We can talk then can't we?" Her eyes brightened and he could not say no.

"Of course we can."

He waited until she was satisfied and full, then offered his arm. "Let's see Wichita."

Her beaming smile was reward enough for him; he would make her see that his heart was to provide for her in all ways. He had her alone, no interruptions, no influence, it was perfect.

Two gowns and three hats later, they returned to the hotel. After perusing the city, Lacey deemed that they were indeed in the finest building and quickly became disinterested in the rest of Wichita. The peace Blaine believed to have felt began to seep away. He did have peace didn't he? He seemed to forget the moment of rashness that drew him to suggest them getting away. He was doing the right thing, what else could he do but get her away from Ed Randall? He neglected to acknowledge a small voice—*trust in me*. He would have his way and they would take the afternoon meal in his room. "I want to be alone, we haven't spent as much time together as I would have liked to this morning."

She balked, "What are you talking about? We've spent the whole day together!"

He wanted to remind her that she was with the seamstress most of the morning being fitted, and he was left to make a worn path up and down the boardwalk outside in the crisp air.

She said, "I'm famished and must rest." Off his look, she amended, "Only until supper, then we'll join each other again."

Without giving him a chance for response, she opened her door. Once inside, she leaned against it and sighed. She did not want to have fun this morning but she had. She did not want to sup with him later, she told herself. But she couldn't wait to look her finest. Blaine looked at the closed door, she was resisting him. He could make no other justification. If he did, it would mean defeat and he could not admit to that. He did not come to Lincoln County and endure an unfaithful wife within his sights or to bring Lacey here to know him as a changed man only to proclaim it useless. He touched her door handle . . . then let it go. He would see her in a few hours.

⁂

She possessed the most beauty in the entire room. Lacey Jennings walked down those spiraling stairs with grace and ease. Blaine's heart drummed to his ears, he waited at the bottom to escort her to supper. Emerald green jewels glittered from her lobes and collarbone, matching the many shades of green in her silk gown. Blaine was both speechless and breathless, if for the fact that she had dressed for no one but him. The crystal teardrop chandelier that lit the foyer enhanced her entrance. Men greeted her in appreciation, some being scorned by the womenfolk at their sides. They tipped their hats to her and said a greeting to Blaine as if they found him a lucky man. And he was.

"You do make a captivating entrance, Mrs. Jennings."

She smiled despite his use of the spousal title. She needn't be riled by something as trivial as that any longer. She was no longer threatened by him. He brought her to the dining hall where they served wine and drinks of the upper class, this was not a place where tawdry women walked about and men drunk themselves senseless. It was a perfect place to court his wife, which was why he had chosen the hotel, chosen to bring her away, now if she would only relax her staunch position where he was concerned and allow it. They ate a creamed soup with fresh asparagus and smoked ham all the while listening to a woman sing solo on a platform with a pianist playing at her side. Operatic songs from the east no doubt, the entertainment was foreign to them both and they took it in. He watched her from time to time, gaining interest in every part of her. *What does she like? What is her favorite food?*

She turned to him and whispered, "What are you thinking about?"

His eyes answered for his voice and she wished she didn't ask. It weakened her defense when she let herself look at him, for looking into him gave away his thoughts and must surely also give away hers. She lifted her chin and feigned focus upon the woman with the voice of an angel. The singer winked at Lacey almost knowingly and her voice rang out sweet words of love and splendor.

※

Lacey welcomed her husband in to her room, almost knowing she could not wisely keep him at arm's length any longer. The day had been grand, and her purpose to use him for gaining fine things began to slip as he took her hands in his. "It seems to me that you are in your realm."

She looked up, "Whatever do you mean?"

"This is you. Extravagant surroundings, being waited upon . . . I can give you this and ten times more."

She turned away as if money meant everything to her, only it didn't; she needed to turn away from him and his warm, soulful brown eyes. "How do you mean? Have you riches somewhere?"

"Maybe not riches, but I'm well off, you could say."

With evident sincerity, she asked, "Why do you live where you live then? It seems to me you don't have much." A horrified look came over her. "Not that it has made a difference in my . . . feelings for you."

"I told you I had business in Chicago?"

She shrugged, not recalling.

"I owned several businesses, I've since sold them all. I plan to live out my days in Lincoln County with you and that is no secret."

"Money doesn't last forever. How will you make due in Lincoln County?"

"It doesn't matter, although I did keep one investment."

Monetary curiosity roused in her, then tamped it down to a mild question, "What is this one investment?"

He replied, "Oh, it's nothing much." Shame on him for wanting to watch her squirm, he smiled enticingly. She stepped closer as if she could intimidate him, "Stop playing with me ... what do you own? Are you going against the law?"

"Wouldn't you like that? Would you put me away, Lacey?" His eyes twinkled with merriment and then he knew not to mess with her temperament any longer. "I own exactly one half of the railroad. The one they call Pacific and will run out west."

She gaped, "No!"

Before she could stop herself, she rambled, "We really could live like this?" He blanched, she said "we." But she also aligned it to living like this. Wouldn't he be enough for her? Frustrated with himself, he'd not planned on telling her this until he had her heart. How would he ever truly know? All of a sudden, anger radiated through Lacey.

"You mean to tell me that I've lived in squalor while my husband has been rich?" She stomped around her room almost in a tantrum, Blaine was stupefied, and something he rarely felt filtered to the surface—anger.

"You've hardly lived in 'squalor,' Lacey Jennings! When are you going to forget about the past? Blast it, woman! I'm here *now*, I'm offering you myself now. What do you want me to do to make up for all I've done? Tell me!" He took her by her tiny shoulders, gripping her in angst. "Tell me and I'll do it!" Tears rolled down her face, confusion etched his. He let her go, "I'm sorry, I didn't mean to hurt you."

"I know." Unstoppable tears poured forth, she covered them with her hands. "I don't know how you can make it up, Blaine. I don't know how I can forget." She looked at him with great sorrow. "I want to forget, I've tried so hard." She sniffed loudly and he took her into his arms.

He said, "The only way I know to forgive is to be forgiven. I believe it's why you can't do it on your own."

"That doesn't make sense, what have I to be forgiven for?"

She looked like a lost child, how could he explain? He buried her head into his chest and cradled her. After a time of standing, he brought her to the bed and they sat in silence until she looked up at him until he bent toward her, until they kissed. Images of caressing her and kneading his hands through her thick hair rose in him. The intense absence of physical passion began to overrule his natural thinking. Her moan and her arms coming across his back almost tore his heart out because he must stop this. How many times had he declared he would not take advantage of her insecurity? She must know forgiveness for herself before he could allow this. He parted his lips from hers with utmost regret. If he was the same, he would continue, she had to see that! He stood, paced, left her sitting there almost numb. Her lips were swollen to the point that he only wanted to kiss them and make them feel better. He hadn't meant to be so rough.

"Lacey," his voice was hoarse.

"Why do you stop? You say you want me, I can see it in your eyes." She braved a deep gaze, "You don't need to stop, Blaine."

He wanted to cry out! She wasn't saying this because he was her husband . . . she wanted to please him, she would only be doing what she knew.

"I want us to be married."

She looked at him as if he were the one mad.

"I mean, under God . . . the right way, as if we were starting over." The mention of God disturbed her and she slapped both hands upon the mattress and rose. "I don't understand. I thought that's why we were here, to start over."

He nodded, "I want you to forgive me. We start from there."

"Even if I say I forgive you, that doesn't mean I can. I said I've tried, all those times I saw you in a different way. I thought I might love you again. But it's always here—the thoughts." She pointed to her temple, "And then I remember and then it hurts all over again." The torment she dealt with daily made him righteously angry. What could he do? Nothing in his own strength. No matter what he did or said, she would never be free from this torrent of unforgiveness until she surrendered it. He would need to trust that that could happen.

He took a step toward her, but not too close, for the physical moment they shared was still too tender and he needed to be wise.

"Do you love me?"

She searched him anew for several minutes it seemed and nodded. "I believe I do."

He could have shouted, "I have longed to hear you say the words, Lacey."

Her lips formed and the searching grew more intense, and what she said was barely audible, "I love you." Fresh tears streamed down her cheeks, "I love you." Blaine held her in the security of his arms never wanting to let her go again. "Will you marry me?"

She laughed and a snort escaped her, "What?"

"Marry me tomorrow."

He began to leave the room as if he had many things to do, but waited with his hand on the doorknob for her forthcoming answer of confirmation.

"I'll marry you tomorrow."

With a smile that stretched his face, he left her.

Twenty-Three

Blaine struck a match on the pewter dish and lit the lamp. The fire sputtered until the darkness had a ray of light. Before Blaine's eyes were focused upon his surroundings, he heard the click of a gun. Jake Collins sat in a chair in the shadowy corner of his room, a look of nonchalance and patience narrowed in on Blaine. Defenseless, he raised his hands. "What's this all about? I've no quarrel with you, Jake."

"Maybe not." Jake studied Blaine should he become an adversary, "Did she come on her own volition?"

"Of course she did! How did you find us?"

Jake uncocked his gun and laid it upon his lap—in position of readiness. "You forget what I do for a living. I've come to bring her home."

Sensing no imminent danger, Blaine walked the distance to Jake, "She's not going with you. She's my wife."

"In more than name?" Jake's cocky insinuation perturbed him.

"That's none of your business! Did Ed hire you to do his bidding?"

"I don't need to be hired to care for a friend." Jake's temper rose and he pointed at himself. "It was *me* who sat by her side day after day and every night when *you* took off with another woman!" Blaine looked away, but Jake was only beginning. "You were a fool to leave her! What I don't understand is this new fondness she has for you. She hates you! What nonsense have you been speaking to her?"

"The truth."

Jake laughed, "What? That you've given up your old ways, that you'll never hurt her again? No way. Tell yourself whatever you want, but you're the same, Blaine. You're still an inconsiderate, womanizing . . ."

"I don't have to listen to this!"

"I can't let you hurt her again."

"Is this you speaking for yourself, or for the sheriff?"

"Suppose for both of us."

"Then talk to her, she'll tell you want she wants. She told me so herself moments ago."

With distrust, Jake scoped Blaine entirely, seeking motive, lies, anything to render excuse to involve himself for the good of Lacey. "What you did was the lowest of all, I can't forget that . . . I don't know how she can."

A Lily Among Thorns 181

Blaine replied, "Maybe you don't give her enough credit. Maybe you should go back to Ed Randall and discern for yourself who is good enough for her."

Jake shrugged, as if to justify Ed's behavior, "She's made him the way he is, I'll admit, she can drive a man crazy. However, before you came she was content."

"Was she?"

The question threw Jake off guard and would never acknowledge otherwise, even if his gut told him opposite. "They were happy, Blaine."

"She's happy now, and that's all I care about."

Jake eased himself from the chair. His attire and features were rough and did not match the exquisite furnishings around him. He went to Blaine, "Consider this a warning then."

The smell of smoke and whiskey wafted beneath Blaine's nose, nausea formed at the remembrance of those scents upon his own flesh once upon a time. "I'll do that."

Jake retreated and replaced his gun as if he'd just paid a cordial visit, and Blaine posed a question, "What about Ed?"

Wondering just that himself, Jake pondered, "I guess he's a big boy. He'll need to get over it. Better Lacey not know I was here." With that, he was gone, and Blaine sat at his table emotionally exhausted. He realized he was indeed pushing things his way and in his own timing, but he couldn't withdraw his offer to Lacey now. She would not understand.

❧

As much as Ed said he despised Lacey, he still wondered how much fault she was in the dilemma before him. No matter how hard he tried, he could not deny the part of him that foresaw Lacey in his future with children running about, and his bride, full of love for him, their father. He devised a way to have Lacey see her husband at his worst, and if it hurt her in the process, well then, she would reap what she sowed. Ed would need to pay a call to Chloe Dupree, knowing full well what she thought of Blaine. Whenever the deceiving couple returned, Ed would be ready for them. Chloe would benefit from a tryst with Blaine, and the veil of deception would finally be lifted from Lacey and she would return to Ed. The relational rules would change. Once his, Lacey would be a true wife and watch over their family, meet his needs. But he would forgive her, it was more than she deserved. The train arriving broke his justifiable thoughts, the snow was heavily pouring down among Lincoln County's inhabitants.

Passersby took notice of the elegant woman detraining, and there were whispers among many. She appeared to be unchaperoned and with child. Her lacking confidence was evident, and she spoke to a man passing by, "Where would I find a place to stay?"

"Straight down that way and to your left, ma'am."

"Thank you kindly and, it's Miss."

Aghast, the man looked on as if he would be spurned just to be near her. One of Nancy Glorfield's delights in life was to shock people. She turned down "that way" and smiled succinctly.

Lizette clamored under the pressure of working alone, and worse, she had no idea when Lacey Jennings was coming back—if ever. She made haste to the entrance in the foyer and welcomed a young lady. Lizette looked behind her, as if waiting for another.

"It's just me. How may I get my trunks delivered here? I took the train."

Lizette wiped her sweaty, work worn palm onto her apron, "I'll send for them. One room then?"

"It's all I need." Nancy rubbed her abdomen, "For now least ways."

Having no other choice but to settle this woman herself, she grasped a set of keys and said, "Follow me, please."

Cursing herself up the stairs, Lizette wondered why she did not close the hotel and restaurant. Then she remembered. What else would she do? Skulk about at home alone? It was her saving grace that she kept so busy. She figured that was better than nothing. Since Lacey was not present to look after patrons during the night hours, the duty fell to Lizette, who did not seem to be missed at home. Once she informed Mack of the temporary arrangement, he had yet to stop by and check upon her status.

She turned her attention to the guest.

"Anything you need, I'm in room eleven."

"Thank you kindly." The young lady stretched out a gloved hand, "My name is Nancy Glorfield. It's a fine place you have."

"It's not mine, the owner is not here at the moment. I'm Lizette."

"Pleasure to meet you just the same." Nancy ventured into her room and turned shyly, "Who, may I ask, is the owner?"

"Lacey Jennings."

"I look forward to making her acquaintance." Nancy closed the door then and a chill ran through Lizette. She looked blankly at the door a moment until her unease passed. She was anxious to lock up and go to bed herself and went downstairs to do just that.

Something wasn't right, but since she'd no place in history for foretelling, she could do nothing about her wayward thoughts.

Who would tell that in a few short days that the whole town would know?

Nancy kept to herself until the third day after her arrival. When she emerged, she looked beaten down and unhappy. Lizette served her morning meal and Nancy asked, "I have some inquisitions for the sheriff or marshal, whatever this town has."

"We have a sheriff. His office is across the street but he comes daily for a meal." Lizette removed the dirty plate, "Is there anything else you would like?"

"Do tell the sheriff for me that I would like to see him." She rose with grace for being burdened in the middle and walked away. Lizette decided that she did not care for the woman's character.

Twenty-Four

"I now pronounce you man and wife." The Reverend closed the Bible in his hands and waited expectantly. Strangers were the witnesses of this union, and Blaine wondered what his bride would do if he kissed her. He needn't wonder for long because she raised her lips in acceptance and he lowered his head. He kept his eyes upon her for the brief contact to see her every feature and emotion. When he was done with the soft and feathery touch, she opened her eyes slowly. Thick lashes splayed in wonderment and she smiled. He was touched by her shyness and then the supporting crowd whooped and hollered—unbeknownst to them this couple was already wed, a harmless deception, in Blaine's point of view.

"Thank you all for being here." He looked around in thought at the ten people in the room with them and the Reverend. "Please, have a meal on us at the Golden Palace."

More cheers went up and he called out over the noise, "I'll make the necessary arrangements." He looked at Lacey, "Let's go."

Her heart shuddered, she was sure. She'd not given much thought to being his in anything but name. It's not as if they were youngsters courting for the first time with coaxing from parents and friends on either part. They were alone, married, with a lot of past between them both. Would they survive this? Was it truly as foolhardy as she felt it to be? He pulled her along the congratulatory and very pleased crowd as her thoughts played mercilessly with her doubt. Lacey decided right then that she would live for the moment, a shiver went through her at the thought of returning home. At the thought of Ed and his anger and hurt, she remembered his threats and recent change of heart. He was an intelligent and caring man. He would see that they were finished and that she had to do this. She chose Blaine because he seemed stable, because he seemed to love her and have patience for her. Time would only tell if this was all a horrible mistake, but she figured that nothing could ever be worse than what she'd already endured with this man. She looked at him strangely, it was interesting that she should risk it all again. Compared to Ed and his dwindling affection for her, Blaine was her only chance of security. Ed would overcome his fondness for her and would realize it as obsession. She would make him see that he was better off without her. She'd she's only ever caused him pain anyway.

⁕

The witnesses from the wedding ate dinner around them, but they felt as if they were alone in the restaurant—just the two of them. He pushed his plate from him and took every inch of her in. "Thank you."

The forkful of herbed chicken was near her lips and she brought it down slowly, nervousness fluttered about her middle. "For what?"

"Having faith in me, in us."

She pierced him with an honest look, "I don't know what I have in us. I know that I've risked everything I have back home for this. I hope I made the right choice."

Her words stung. Would they always? "You did. I promise you."

Privately, Blaine thanked the Lord above for this occurrence and repented for putting things ahead on his own. But he would not dwell on that, he would dwell on his wife before him. He would pray for her daily and wait until he saw full-fledged forgiveness in her eyes. That was his purpose now.

The moment came when the incredible tasting food had disappeared, dessert had been partaken of, and Lacey couldn't eat another bite. The time has come for them to go up those endless spiral stairs and stand before one another as man and wife. The challenge Lacey once relished in dissipated in terms of the power of loving. She'd prided herself the ability to love without feeling, how many times had she been successful in that area? Could she accomplish this outpouring of emotion with Blaine, her husband, as never before? He saw her brief flicker of panic and smiled. He'd won. The seductress in Lacey was past; she would love him because she wanted to. No coy games. He was beginning to gain pieces of her heart, little by little. He took her graceful fingers and led her up those stairs. They entered her room, both wordless. His look upon her was raw and passionate, Lacey suddenly turned reticent. This was the way it's supposed to be. Pure and innocent, they were married now under the eyes of God, and Blaine finally had peace in his heart. Tonight he could love his wife in every way he was meant to.

⁕

Ed stood in front of the door in hesitation. Was Lizette sure this woman wanted to see him? What an odd request to send for a strange man to come to a private room, sheriff or not.

At his knock, the door was opened by Nancy. "Sheriff Ed Randall, do come in."

She smoothed the material of her gown and stepped aside.

He removed his hat, "You wanted to see me?"

"Please, have a seat. I'll have tea brought up."

"I just ate." Remembering his manners, "Thank you just the same."

"Well then, make yourself comfortable."

Not able to help himself, his gaze raked over her as if he'd never seen a woman expecting before, at least not one—unattached. Her hair was light and curly and she had a mischievous spark to her blue eyes. He concluded that she was not beautiful, but very pretty. He gestured for her to sit first, she chose the settee, leaving him the arm chair under the window, where all could see him in the mysterious woman's room if they'd a mind to look up.

Tears formed and sadness overwhelmed her, "I'm so ashamed!" She burst and buried her face in a lace kerchief. Ed's compassion overruled his caution and he moved to sit next to her should she need his comfort.

"I have a delicate matter to discuss with you, sir."

"I'm here to serve . . . Missus?"

"Nancy Glorfield. I'm not a widow."

"Oh."

She shook her head incessantly and took in a long, deep breath, "I'm unmarried, you see. I came to find someone."

He was beginning to see. Someone must have made sweet promises to this deserving young woman, only to leave her upon getting what he wanted. Anger radiated through Ed, if this man was indeed here, he'd make him see his obligations, or the scoundrel would be jailed. He waited for some time until she calmed again.

"Do you know a man by the name of Blaine Jennings?"

A knot formed and tightened, and Ed's pulse raced faster than it should. The room shifted momentarily, and he heard her asking if he was the one alright. His balance restored, "Did you say Blaine Jennings?" Hope restored in her eyes and they brightened, she turned toward him with anticipation and he felt sick. "Yes! Is he here?" Her voice was deep and airy and suddenly full of life.

"Not at the moment," he said.

Nancy looked downcast and she picked at her dress, "Do you expect his return?"

He couldn't think. He rose from his seat from the place that put his emotions in turmoil. He would kill for sure. As soon as he laid his eyes upon Blaine, he would not think twice to shoot.

It would destroy Lacey. He forgot he didn't care what happened to Lacey and saw this poor, innocent girl carrying a baby with no support in the world. Rage toiled and worked up until he realized he must suppress it—for her sake.

"I imagine he should be home soon. I'll let him know you're here."

"Oh, no! Please. Let me, I haven't seen him in well . . . a while now." Shame entered her face again and she turned despondent.

"May I get you something? Maybe have that tea brought up before I go?"

"You're too kind, Sheriff. You have my gratitude."

"I'm sorry that you are going through this, Miss Glorfield. I assure you that this town is behind you with our full support."

"You'll not tell him?"

Ed's stance gave way his frustration, "I'll give you the pleasure."

"Thank you. I believe I will take that tea."

※

It seemed that abandonment followed in the wake of Blaine Jennings no matter where he went or whose lives he touched. Ed's pace was hard and fast to his office. Where was Jake? Why wasn't he back yet? Was the treacherous couple ever to return? They must, Ed needed to avenge his dignity, his honor, and position as a man! Agitation wouldn't leave him and he ordered Deputy Benton out of his way. Joseph went quietly wondering at the man's brooding moods of late. Ed wasn't himself for sure, but he was beginning to change even before Lacey disappeared. Joseph wanted the old Ed back, the spirited, lighthearted man he first knew. Joseph kicked at a pebble in the street and decided to see what joy he could retrieve from either Kimberly or Bethany.

Ed slammed a fist onto his desk, took out a flask from his drawer, "Blast it all!" He walked to the livery and ordered his horse saddled. He must undo what he and Chloe had planned . . .

Chloe took Blaine's actions with Nancy as a personal affront. Where was she to be left in this, what would she gain?

"To think I wanted him!" she ranted to Ed. "How many other women can we expect to come traipsing through this town asking for Blaine Jennings?" She threw him a spiteful, yet conniving look, "One thing can be said about this, those Jennings certainly deserve one another!"

They were in her parlor. Jacques Dupree III was in his library, working on the mayoral speech he would give once finding the opportunity. Ed had a guilty countenance and Chloe lowered her tone so her father could not hear them. "Don't tell me—you are still expecting her to be with you? Why ever would you be such a fool?"

"I'm not a fool to waste three years of my life. Three years, by now I could have formed a family. She'll come back to me once she sees Blaine for what he always was and still is."

Chloe raised a conspiring eyebrow in understanding, "Then you'll have the say in your relationship because she's messed it up. Lacey will feel terribly and come to you like a sickly little dog and pay penance. I've misjudged you, Ed Randall."

"Lacey won't leave her restaurant for too much longer. I know her, she accepts responsibility wholeheartedly, it's why she's with him now. She can't go on with her life until she's exhausted every possibility to make things right. Now, she'll come to terms finally with her husband. I'll have her then."

Interjecting her thoughts, Chloe said, "And this town will not tolerate a man who's done such a terrible thing to Miss Glorfield." She smiled wickedly and poured brandy for them both, "We'll just have to make it known so that he must leave this place—and take that expectant little tart with him."

Ed took the offered drink and tossed it down, "I'm only sorry that you won't come out with what we'd intended."

She toasted him. "No matter, I'll create another method of entertainment for me in the near future. Right now, I'll scheme right alongside you, *Sheriff*. I'm having fun!"

Ed cringed, he wished he didn't have to *scheme*, as she put it so naturally. This may be only entertainment for her, but this was his life. Was it so bad that he wanted things only as before? Chloe lounged on the sofa and her gaze fixated on him from across the room and sent a thrill straight through. They were in this together, once this was over and Lacey and he in a fine house somewhere, he needn't be consumed with this beautiful, enchanting, and bewitching woman any longer.

It was to be the last scheduled Sunday morning service until spring. The Jackson's bade parishioners' farewell—until the snow would let up. It was nearing the holidays and an early winter had most of them spooked, especially after the scarlet fever outbreak and storms of last year. Cameron was hopeful, yet disheartened at the turn in Blaine and Lacey's relationship.

Why did they need to sneak off like that? It had been close to two weeks and they'd not the courtesy to send word on their whereabouts or safety.

Cameron rested her hand on her protruding abdomen, "Andrew, I believe I just felt our son."

He shut the door on the cold wind and turned to her. "That's wonderful." Concern furrowed his brow at times at how his wife was so at rest during this pregnancy.

He placed his hand over hers, "Maybe I'll get to feel him soon."

Cameron smiled with gratefulness, "I'm so happy." He gathered her cloak and placed it around her and they went out into the snowy breeze. "We need to get supplies before we go home." He looked toward the gray skies, "We may be there a while."

Decision-making had been hampered lately for Cameron, the amount of oats and molasses they might need weighed her down without necessity. She stood at the counter with great consternation. Andrew answered the clerk for her. "One pint of molasses and three pounds of oats, and an extra pound of coffee, please."

"Yes, Reverend."

"I'm worried about Lacey," Cameron said.

"I know you are."

"What are they doing? Where did they go?" She looked stricken, "And why didn't she tell me?"

"You're more hurt about that than anything else, I imagine." He retrieved their readied goods from the clerk. "Thank you."

Pride wounded, "What if I am? I'm supposed to be her closest friend."

He added the groceries to an overflowing wooden box, placed an arm around her shoulders, and escorted her outside. "Let's just believe for a good outcome." He thought of the sheriff. "That's about all we do for the time being."

They stopped short of Chloe Dupree. It was as if she'd appeared from nowhere, her highly fashioned buggy was parked nearby with her servant adjusting blankets inside. "How nice it is to see you both." Chloe's insincere greeting irritated Cameron. "I was just paying a visit to that poor woman at Lacey's place."

Not wanting to be hooked into gossip, Andrew said, "I'll load the wagon." Cameron bore a hole into his back, *coward!*

"Who's the woman at Lacey's?" Cameron asked with genuine concern.

Chloe placed a hand over her bosom in shock, "Oh my! You haven't heard?"

Could she never be without aggravation in this woman's presence? "Chloe, I do not know what you are talking about."

"Well, I shouldn't be the one to tell you."

Cameron began to lose interest. "I understand your sensitivity, Chloe. You should head home soon, we're about to receive an abundant amount of snow."

Cameron was several steps away when Chloe's voice made her stomach lurch, "Why, it's Miss Nancy Glorfield. The mother of Mr. Jennings's unborn child is here to find him." She poised herself stoically, "Such a travesty, really. She's such an innocent young thing. Blaine probably doesn't even know, I'm sure if he did, he would have never come back here to reconcile with Lacey—unless he was running, of course . . ."

"Stop it!" Cameron held herself upright on the outside wall of the store, her face paled, and Andrew rushed to her side looking questionably at Chloe.

"I apologize, Mrs. Jackson. It was thoughtless of me to ramble on so." She watched triumphantly as the Reverend brought his wife to their buggy. He'd wrapped her legs in blankets as she shook violently. Confounded, Andrew was taking her to Dr. Glover, he would not risk Cameron's health ever again. The story spilled out before they reached the doctor's and Andrew was torn then to stay and seek the truth about Nancy Glorfield or take Cameron home. After much thought, he took his wife home, her state of being was more important than Blaine's conduct. He drove slowly and meticulously home as Cameron did nothing but cry silently.

Having tucked her into bed, Andrew's fingers slid lovingly over her forehead. "There's an explanation for this, Cameron. We must believe the best of others until proven otherwise."

She nodded, grateful for such a kind, warmhearted man of her own. Still, she could not help but think and be confused for Lacey. Whatever would she do? Does she know? Is that why they disappeared? Somehow, she knew Lacey would never tolerate an expecting woman being left alone, for no for she would not place herself before a woman in need. Lacey was not selfish, no matter her wants or desires.

The days had been blissful and Lacey believed she was falling in love with this gentle and caring man. Whether or not that was forgiveness, she did not know, but she no longer carried a bitter thought about him. In reviewing her own indiscretions, it wasn't hard to say that they came to one another equally. As the stage rolled on, she gazed at the freshly driven snow. Blaine saw that she was cold and offered his body for warmth. They were on their uncertain journey home, what awaited them she was unsure. The thought of Cameron and her blessing would be a welcome sight, and the thought of Lizette, well, Lacey would reward her for her diligence.

It was late when the Jennings's stagecoach arrived in town. Blaine refused to take her home with him no matter how much agony gripped him at dropping her off on her doorstep, as if they were culpable of any wrongdoing. His shack was no place for her, but she pleaded, "I've been to your home, I'm not above staying there."

"I should have thought . . ." He kissed her cheekbone, "I suppose I didn't know this would turn out the way it had, or I would have been more prepared." She longed for him to be beside her, "How little faith you had in me, Mr. Jennings." He laughed at that, "As if you led me to think differently."

"Please take me home with you."

His breath was taken away, how he longed for those words to come from her full lips. "You are not making this easy for me, Lacey."

"That wouldn't be like me."

"And that is the truth. You stay here tonight. I promise it will be our last night apart from each other forever. We'll decide where to live tomorrow and then . . ."

"Then let certain persons know where we stand with one another," she finished his thought. It had been decided on their journey home to talk to Ed, to be civil and adult. Their kiss was memorable and filled with anticipation for the future. She slid ever so slowly away from him—from this man who'd captured her heart with his pursuing passion. Maybe, just maybe she could let go of the past. The feeling was euphoric, and her step was light as she entered her dwelling.

Twenty-Five

Blaine looked at the horrific state of his home. The door busted halfway off its hinges, ransacked and in disorder. At first glance he guessed that nothing was taken. He was grateful he'd not brought Lacey home with him. This was an act of vengeance and he knew Ed to be behind it, even if it was not done by his own hands. Coming home wasn't going to be as pleasant and rewarding as he'd thought. Blaine breathed out deep breaths; the cold reverberated through his bones as he worked on a fire. He went to his bedroom and loaded his pistol—it wouldn't hurt to sleep with protection tonight.

The snow was deep when he awoke, his horse looked pathetic in the lean-to, and Blaine had no sled to attach and bring him to town. Had he been a man to swear he would have had reason to. He warmed the horse with blankets, refilled water from the well, and forked hay next to the trough. He looked upon his home with discouragement; he should have stayed at the hotel last night. For some reason, a sick, gnawing feeling that he could not describe plagued him all day. In the cold, Blaine repaired his door with what scraps of wood he could find. Blast it! He was a man with much money and he was living in these squalid surroundings. He opened a can of beans with the blade of a knife, and with rhetoric complaints, he ate as if he were a disgusting mountain man. The sight of more snow falling only served to squash his hope of seeing his wife tomorrow and increased his melancholy. What was he feeling? Why wouldn't this wave of despondency leave him? Blaine was not used to uncertainty, he was full of life and hope and had faith to claim Lacey, as he knew God intended. Something was not right, the will to see her and prove to himself that it was all-real, not a dream. He'd shared the most excellent of all his days with Lacey during the past two weeks. What was happening to make him feel as if it were all going to tumble down around him?

⁂

He was out of food entirely on the third day. The snow was deep, but packed. Blaine felt he could make it to town. Nausea cut to his core as he rode in, outright stares of disapproval raked him up and down. He tied his horse in front of Lacey's. Why should all these busybodies care whether or not he'd taken his own wife away with him?

When he entered the quiet restaurant, he was perplexed, to say the least. It was as if someone had died, loathing and tension filled the room. He sought Lacey. She sat at a table with Lizette and . . . Ed? His wife's eyes were swollen and she could barely look his way. At the only other occupied table sat Chloe Dupree, of all people, and a woman he vaguely remembered, but his care and concern was spent on Lacey. There was something upon Ed's face that pierced Blaine with defeat.

Nothing less than anger radiated through him, and through clenched teeth, he said, "Lacey, I want to speak to you alone."

She looked at him, it was like she wanted to die, like she had nothing to live for. It tore him apart and he did not know why. He'd done nothing, he'd done everything right. He stepped toward her, hands reaching for a confirming touch. If she could only recall being held and caressed with these hands . . . Why were these people here? Where were the hotel's guests? She stood and he thought he misunderstood the eeriness going on around him.

Her words were barely audible, "Go away. I mean it—I never want to see you again."

He was paralyzed with shock and a fear of loss that he'd never experienced in his life. He willed his body to move after her, and Ed stepped in his path.

"Get out of my way."

Spittle sprayed from the force of Ed's reply, "I will not. I will never allow you near her again. Haven't you done enough?"

What?

"What I've done is offer her a life of security and love and I will not stand here and listen to you or let your badge bully me. I say again, get out of my way!"

Lizette began crying, taking Blaine's attention to her. His jaw twitched—figuring, contemplating what do to, and she said, "Please, Mr. Jennings, this is all too much." Her eyes focused in on Nancy, who looked as though she was the cause of all of this. Blaine caught her eye and he narrowed his in thought, *where do I know her from?*

Chloe rose with righteous dignity by playing confused. "Don't you remember Nancy?"

Blaine looked passed Ed up the stairs to where his hurting wife was and then to Ed's hand firmly grasped onto the handle of his gun and he shook his head in disbelief. Why were they all so concerned about his knowing this woman?

Each and every one of them appeared to be waiting for an explanation. "No. And I really don't care to . . ."

"Think hard," Ed threatened.

Blaine saw murder in his opponent's eyes, "I can't remember where I know her from, if I know her at all. Let me past, Sheriff."

Lizette couldn't hold it any longer, "How could you say that, Mr. Jennings?" As she asked the question, Nancy stood awkwardly and her abdomen was displayed.

"Nancy's carrying your baby!"

He spun around to her. "No!"

Sympathetic tears poured down Nancy's cheekbones, as if she could not withstand rejection one more time. Blaine rushed Ed and pushed him out of the way and ran up the stairs to Lacey's room.

It was locked, of course, and he pounded, veins pulsing in his neck, he cried out in anguish, "I swear to you, Lacey, this is not true. It's a lie! I beg you to open this door." He paced, Ed was coming up the stairs slowly, as if Blaine was making his case for him. As if he were ruining himself in front of all of them, especially Lacey. "So help me, I'll bust this down!"

Ed grunted with open disgust, "Just go, Blaine. No one wants you around."

Appalled at the drama around him, he raised his hands in surrender; he needed to think and to sort this out. Nancy? His mind befuddled, he staggered away and down the stairs, as if her were drunk. Chloe feigned compassion and said, "If you ever want to talk . . ." His eyes widened at the horrified thought of being close to her. The woman named Nancy forgotten, Blaine went home, dejected, confused, and knocked down.

Was this the blessing of God he knew he'd receive when walking in obedience? Where was the reward in risking his pride to humble himself before Lacey one year ago on Christmas day? He ended this afternoon in the very same place he started—at the Half Moon saloon, the easiest place in all the world to find what matched his current emotions and self-worth.

Andrew studied the Half-Moon before entering. An odd sensation went through him as he stepped inside, his eyes had to adjust, and once that happened he scanned his surroundings. "Good Lord!" he said above a whisper.

"What's that? Who's there?" Harry came from a backroom. He eyed the Reverend and tossed a soiled towel over his shoulder. He wiped his hands on his butcher apron and extended one to Andrew.

They shook hands and Harry said, "You're here for Mr. Jennings, I would think." Despite himself, Harry laughed at Andrew, he looked sick and mortified. "Need a chair, Reverend?"

"I think I do."

"I'll fetch ya' a glass of water, and Blaine."

The thought of Blaine here in this filth . . . the thought of anyone here for that matter. Spittoons littered the floor with dirty saliva everywhere but inside of them. The scents—Andrew covered his nose and mouth, there was not one smell he was accustomed to, and he tried not to imagine what went on in this place. A prostitute, half-dressed, came out of a room and looked his way, smiled seductively, and walked down a darkened hallway. He shuddered. Blaine emerged and looked anything but like himself. Andrew stood on shaky legs to greet him. Blaine did not have any fire or shine to his dull-stricken eyes. His black hair stuck up on all sides of his head and he had mostly a full gray-black beard.

"I would have come sooner, but the snow . . ." Andrew's voice faltered. *God, we do have our work cut out for us.*

With despair, Blaine stated plainly, "It's over. I can do nothing more. I thought I was meant to be in her life, I've never been more wrong."

They both stood there, ill at ease. Andrew wasn't sure what to make of anything. He'd been to see Nancy Glorfield, her story lined accurately with Blaine's last trip to Chicago. "Blaine, do you realize how this appears for you?"

"Yes!" He paced about the dirty, rank floor and held his head as though he could knock some sense into this all. He pointed vehemently at Andrew, "I have *never* laid a hand on that woman!"

His tone stunned Andrew and that was all he needed to hear, "Well then, that's that. I'll have a talk with Lacey."

"No."

"What? Come now, don't let this be the end. You've made it this far, I still believe for you to be together. Marriage is a covenant under God, you can't break it."

"I've been doing everything in my power to *not* break it, Andrew." His anguish was so evident, even Andrew's heart ached for them. Suddenly, a revelation hit, "Maybe that's it."

Blaine scowled. "What?"

"You just said so yourself, everything in *your* power."

He shook his head adamantly, "No. That's not what I meant."

"Oh? Let me walk you through this. You committed to Lacey that you would court her, you've stated many times to me anyway, that you had faith and hope and trust in God to bring her heart toward yours, as it should be—as man and wife." He paced right alongside Blaine, who was becoming more agitated by the moment. "Then you sneak her off like a thief in the night. Why? You're already married! You wanted her away from Ed; she's a passionate woman, Blaine! You had to know her vulnerable and worked your way into her life in just that way!"

Blaine stalked away from him. Harry arrived with water and looked curiously at both men. Andrew waived his water away after seeing the cloudy drink, "Thank you though." Several minutes of silence filtered the saloon.

Andrew heard Blaine's agonizing words of defeat as the truth penetrated him, "And now it's too late."

"Blaine, you've fought this long and hard. Don't give up, not now."

His voice was filled with strong conviction, "She will *never* trust me again."

"Let someone else worry about that." Andrew eyes flicked upward and smiled. "Now, we need to figure this Miss Glorfield situation. Why would she lie?" He questioned Blaine sincerely, yet without accusation.

"I don't know. I've seen her before though." Off Andrew's look, he said, "I did not turn to my old ways when I went back to Chicago."

"I think I know that, Blaine. You would not risk Lacey for that, and I know you're different." The disheveled and hopeless man looked upon Andrew, "What do I do now?"

Andrew patted his slumped shoulder, "Clean you up, for starters. Then, we'll need a plan."

❧

She managed to coddle Nancy and elicit unswerving compassion from the townsfolk. "Take care, Dr. Grover, and thank you for seeing us today." Chloe Dupree turned to her charge and said, "Well now, that's a grand report, you are healthy and all looks to be good."

Nancy leaned back and placed the warm tea to her lips, "Indeed. I can't thank you enough for your friendship, Chloe." She stifled a cry, "You don't know what it's like to be so alone. I feel as though everyone is judging me!"

Chloe came to her side, "On the contrary. It's not your fault that Blaine did not stay and see out his obligations, you're the victim here—don't ever forget about that."

She sipped, "I suppose you're right. I didn't know he was married, or else I would have never!"

Chloe stopped herself from saying what she truly wanted, that the woman should have never given herself to a man prior to marriage anyway, Chloe said instead, "And we all know that. He will need to come forward and claim this child, whether or not he divorces Lacey."

Chloe stood before the window and looked onto the whiteness all around; she needed to get home before darkness enveloped them. "You are comfortable then?"

"Yes, and your kindness has been much appreciated and unwarranted. I will be fine, I can only hope that Mr. Jennings sees the error of his ways."

"I will take my leave and be by in a few days." Chloe smiled deliberately, she could care less how this wanton was feeling, she would come only to see where they were all situated in this little play of hers. "Good day, Nancy."

As the door was closing, Nancy stretched leisurely. Having the doctor examine her was not necessary, but she allowed it at Chloe's insistence. She'd only complained of a minor ailment. Why was Chloe so bent on taking care that she was comfortable, why should she take sides against Blaine Jennings, what was she to gain by her situation?

Nancy splayed her hands over her taut tummy, "We'll get you a father yet, my love. In due time, yes, we will."

Twenty-Six

The floor length mirror reflected a shadow. It misrepresented the disconsolate being standing in front of it. Lacey wondered how she could even look the same when her insides were broken pieces of puzzle, the puzzle that had finally been put together and having only to stay connected for a few short days. There was nothing to describe her thoughts and feelings better than hate. *Why?* She looked at her pathetic self, was she never to be happy? She was still young and had a long life ahead of her. Why should she hate men at this tender age? It was not fair. Blaine had ruined her forever; she would be an old spinster and not care. The thought of her so-called husband brought burning to her eyes. *No!*

"Blaine Jennings, you do not deserve one tear." She tore herself away from the image and resolved to never speak that name again. Before she could disconnect her thoughts of hating all mankind, there was a light tap on her door, and she was hoping it would be Lizette, for she told the girl that no one should disturb her.

With a basketful of Lacey's favorite food items, Ed Randall entered her room. He glanced unworriedly over her garments that hung loosely upon her frame and set down the goods.

He smiled warmly, "I brought you some things." Ed took out sticky rolls, tangerines shipped from the docks of California, special imported candies, and wines. She looked gravely at him, how she had wronged him and look at him!

Taking care of her as if she'd not recently neglected him. "Ed . . . please." He held up his hand and made a face that would not agree to being crossed, his tone void of much emotion, "I will tell you this once. We will not talk about what happened, we will go on as before . . . I mean *before* he even came. I have forgiven you your poor choices, they can only be explained as coercion anyway, and it will be left at that." Ed handed her a roll, "Now that's that and I want you to eat."

"I can't . . . you can't just forget."

"I didn't say forget, I said *forgive*—and not another word about it. I have to visit Ingrid's place, she's complaining about somebody stealing her chickens again. Take care of yourself. I want to come back to you in a few days with your chin up and the strong-willed Lacey of last year—back for good." With his bullying absence, there was nothing left for her to do but sit on her bed and cry her eyes out.

❦

Calm yourself. Blaine took every step in his mind to not lash out in the fury of his situation. He called for a meeting with Nancy and wanted to get to the bottom of this. *Lacey* . . . No, he couldn't think of her, not until this was all over. Unfortunately, there was no other place to do this except for the Half Moon. He wouldn't be caught dead with her at his home, and the Jackson's was too far to travel; besides, this was his trouble and he had to make it go away. He waited sitting in a grimy chair until half past two, she was late. Harry went to and fro doing his business, whatever that was. He looked busy enough, but Blaine never could figure out what the man did when he didn't have any customers. The folks that frequented this place came at night, and Blaine couldn't blame them. He would not be ashamed to say that the girls working in those backrooms just couldn't be justified enough to be entertained by in the light of day. Blaine heard the door handle turn and did his best to subdue his anger. He forced himself to rise in mannerly greeting when Nancy walked into the room and his face faltered when he saw that following behind was Chloe. *What in tarnation is she doing here?*

It served her right. Chloe stood against the door practically stuffing a handkerchief down her throat. Her eyes widened at the scum of this place and Blaine suppressed a smile—barely. Nancy, however, looked quite natural here and Blaine had a hunch that it was familiar territory to this girl, this liar who claimed he fathered her baby. He racked his brain in memory; her angelic features did not match the coy gleam in her eyes. One cannot camouflage what is in one's heart so easily.

"Please sit down." He directed them both to a chair at his rickety table. Nancy came with a pouty look to her face, as if putout by his unclaiming behavior. Chloe shook her head at the acerbic offer and stayed mute.

Blaine displayed his hands onto the table in a dealing posture. "Miss Glorfield, let me introduce myself properly."

"I know who you are," her voice was soft, yet deep. He hadn't expected it to be that way.

"And how do you know me?"

She glanced at Chloe, who deemed to be no help after all. She fumbled with something imaginary on the table, "I hardly think I need to explain that to you."

He crossed his leg over and leaned back as if he had all the time in the world, for he could play at a low level, he'd done so not too long ago. "I believe you do. For the accusation you've spread against me warrants just that."

Quietly and with shame, "It's no accusation. You know the truth."

His face burned and he prayed for self-control, "Enlighten me, then, it's not too much to ask?"

"Why won't you just admit?"

"You've got nerve, I'll give you that."

"I only want what's best for our baby!" Tears began to flow. Nancy was overcome with emotion and very convincing. She stood and walked around the room, gaining momentum with each outburst. "How could you have said such things to me if you didn't mean them? We spent time together and then you don't admit to it? How could you? How could anyone do such a terrible thing?" Her eyes cut him with condemnation, "What did I do to make you stop loving me?"

Blaine glanced at Chloe, who seemed mesmerized, the handkerchief still in her grasp but away from her mouth that was filled with gratifying awe. His voice strained and he whispered in distress, "Why are you doing this?"

Nancy turned her back to him, "I should be the one asking you that." She cradled her arms across her breast—hopeless. "We didn't have the standard courtship, Blaine, but you said that you loved me. I see now that I was such a fool."

He stood and walked over to her, "I just need to know when? I won't deny that I don't know you, just . . . when?" Slight compassion eased his features.

Her eyes searched his face, doubting he would believe her anyway, "Late summer, you spent a few weeks in my company. I am quite embarrassed really that I need to remind you." He placed his hands upon her shoulders with ease, he saw Chloe's stance straighten in anxious waiting, "Then it's I who must apologize, I am a scoundrel. I saw many women during that time."

The horrified look upon Nancy was well worth the lie. *There now, what will she do with that?* He heard an outgoing breath of shock from Chloe, but kept his eyes trained on his quandary. "What shall I do then for you, Miss Glorfield?" He let his hands slide down her. "I can't imagine it's been easy, I never knew, of course, and any girl can just arrive in any old town and claim—but, I know now that you speak the truth. For I was in Chicago those very weeks and I am ashamed to say that I hardly saw fit to use discretion since my wife stayed behind."

Her voice came up with a clearing of the throat, "I thank you for at least admitting to our relationship."

"That's just it, Nancy, it was not that to me, and I certainly didn't mean for this to happen." She covered her belly as his eyes rested there in amusement.

"This is not a light matter! I did not know you were married or I would have never! You must know that, and now it's too late."

"I suppose it is, I ask again, what will you have me do?"

Chloe's mouse like French voice found it's way into the situation around her, and she braved a few steps toward them. They both turned to her and her input with curiousness, "From what I understand, your wife is divorcing you, Mr. Jennings."

His palms flexed, opened and closed, checking his temper. "I don't see how that's any of your concern."

"Maybe it's not, but it should be hers." She thrust her chin toward Nancy who climbed back into her victimized shell.

Blaine asked, "Miss Dupree, would you leave us alone?"

"Nancy prefers that I stay to bear witness to the accounts said back and forth."

Blaine looked at Nancy angrily, "You want me to be a father to your child, but you don't trust me? I find that difficult to understand." He conceded, "Maybe you're right after all, you don't know me all that well, do you?" He had her there, for what kind of woman would give herself to a man she barely knew?

She blanched, "I know you well enough, you were once kind to me, and now, you're in a situation that once resolved I'm sure you'll return to that kindness." She stepped away from him, just a few safe steps as he said, "I suppose we'll have to hope so."

He moved to her again, "I'm calm now, you see? I will try and make things right between us. I'll need to get to know you first, and I won't be comfortable in doing so if we have a third person with us all the time."

Chloe tuned in but couldn't hear, his voice had softened and become smooth. But she saw Nancy's alarmed look and knew he was gaining the upper hand. Blaine escorted the "ladies" to the door, "I expect to see more of you . . . alone."

He pulled her hand to his lips and kissed the back of it ever so gently. Nancy's eyes glistened with terror and triumph and they left, Chloe would be speechless for days—if he would only be so lucky.

"What did he say to you?" Chloe demanded.

Nancy tossed her an *I don't need you anymore* look and stated with pride, "He wants to get to know me. I believe he's seen the truth of it all and is willing to claim his responsibility. Of course I'll have to be patient for Mrs. Jennings to comply with the divorce."

Chloe's delicate pace quickened to match Nancy's, "That won't be a problem. She despises him for what he's done and has come to her senses where the sheriff is concerned. About you being alone with him . . ."

"I have every intention of doing just that!" She walked ahead of Chloe as she reached her buggy with servant perched, ready to do as bid. Nancy would walk back to the hotel. It was strange that Lacey should let her stay there in her condition, but figured the sheriff had a lot of say in her life and wondered only briefly, *why?*

※

"She's lying."

Andrew and Cameron both looked at Blaine with surprise and Andrew said, "I thought you already knew that."

He shoveled the last of his food into his mouth, "Oh, I did, but to see it close up in her very eyes helped my cause, you could say."

Confused, Cameron asked, "Cause?"

The two men looked at each other as if they had some big secret and didn't answer. Never mind them! The hormones in Cameron's pregnant body kept her in a testy state and she had no patience for games. If they wanted to deal with this, fine! She was using all of her energy on keeping Lacey sane and in good spirits, for what it was worth. Cameron rose to clear the table and Andrew saw her consternation and was wise to offer help, "I'll take care of this, why don't you lie down or read?"

She eyed him with irritation and followed his advice. "I suppose I've Christmas presents to work on, I'll be in the bedroom. Goodnight, Blaine, Andrew."

"Goodnight."

Blaine smiled at his cousin-in-law. Without coveting, he wished and pictured himself and Lacey having a similar conversation. "This will come to you also, Blaine."

"I keep trusting and hoping that what you say is true."

"That's all we can do. What have you found out about your last visit to Chicago, remember anything?"

"I've wired my business partners; one will not be back until next week. I trust Jacob Pearce. I've told him the whole story, and he will talk with Samuel Porter and get back to me. I hope this all goes away quick, I can't stand another moment with Nancy."

"I can't figure out what she has to gain by seeing you apart from Lacey based on lies?" Andrew poured coffee for them both, neglecting the table and it's dirty plates for the time being.

"And I can't stand being away from Lacey."

Just days ago, the intense feeling of anguish had been miraculously replaced with a strange renewed hope. He wasn't about to try and figure this out on its own merit because it could not be of his own doing. Blaine committed to trust for things to turn out in his favor, after all, good things come to those who seek God, and he was trying so fervently to do so. What she was going through was not fair, it killed him to be the cause once again, even falsely so, but they would have the rest of their lives together to grow, love each other, and gain strength from the past.

"How is she fairing?"

"Cameron's been to see her as much as possible with this weather. Whenever I make rounds or go to town, I bring her with me." Sadness flickered in his eyes briefly, "I bring her to Lacey, of course, but there's always that part of me that cannot leave her alone—not this time." He would not risk another episode of last year with blood on their sheets . . . Cameron, listless and dying. He looked hard at Blaine and asked, "Do you really want to know how she is?"

"Probably not, but go ahead."

"She not only hates you, but every other man on this God-given earth." Blaine flinched at Andrew's matter of fact tone and wished he could partner with his obvious merriment, "I'm sorry, Blaine. She is so extreme."

"It's what I love about her. I guess since she hates men, and since Ed's one, the odds are pretty equal." He barely grinned, then said, "Is there any chance for them during this time?"

Andrew eyed him with warning and Blaine said apathetically, "Never mind. I don't wish to know that after all." It was he who starting to clear the table for Cameron, it was the least he could do. They fed him most evenings now with his inability to eat at Lacey's and his home not meant for much. Come spring, a new built home was second on his list, the first was his wife.

⁂

Feeling like a puppet was new to Lacey, she was not one to do as bid. She did the ordering, the controlling, the scolding. The tables have now turned and her life was in order—Ed saw to that. She pasted smiles on when seeing to her customers, she did not frequent Liam's and was forbidden alcohol, and she spent a lot of time with the sheriff about town. She was his showcase. He'd show everyone that he'd won; the belle of the county had chosen him. He looked to be at his peak in life as the couple walked into the only lawyer's office in town. "Draw up them papers, Mr. Tomlin."

The lawyer looked at Lacey and noted her complacency; he had no reason to go against the sheriff, but didn't care to discuss her private life in front of him. Either way, Ed Randall appeared cocky and that didn't set well with Mr. Tomlin.

He replied, eyes on Lacey, "I am happy to draw them up for Mrs. Jennings, if it is her wish that I do so."

She felt Ed stiffen and the lawyer continued in a placating way, "Sheriff, with all due respect, could you please wait outside?"

As miffed as a spoiled child would be, he departed. Mr. Tomlin looked compassionately upon Lacey, who was ready to cry, "Do you want this, Lacey?"

She nodded numbly, "I do."

"Very well, I will make an appointment with Blaine." He dabbed the quill and made a few notes, it was quiet except the scratchy sounds coming from his writing, and she asked softly as to not disturb him, "When will this all be final?" She wanted to forget that she was ever married to a man named Jennings.

"Not so long that you should worry yourself about it." He continued on with his dabbing and writing, and without looking up, he said, "Our work is done, I'll send this when it's signed and completed in an envelope to you." She was about to speak, and then Ed popped his head in the room. Mr. Tomlin appeared annoyed. Ed's voice was strangely sweet and indisputable. "Lacey, you must want to come back to the hotel with me now."

"Thank you, Mr. Tomlin." Lacey picked up her purse and rose, Mr. Tomlin looked at her forlorn and unhappy face, "If there's nothing else I can do?"

Ed placed his arm around her back and led her away.

⁂

The outlaw traipsed snow into the doorway of the Half Moon Saloon, his eyes scowled through the dense smoky air. He seated himself at a table with two other men,

"You're the only table not playin' cards. Any reason? No? Well alright then, let's get one started." He glanced at his two opponents, *green as grass*.

For good measure and sportsmanship, he said, "A bottle of whiskey on me." The men found themselves caught up with a formidable player. The outlaw, David Beck, called to Harry behind the bar counter, "Whiskey!" He slammed his fists down in impatience.

Harry threw the three shot glasses filled with a tawny drink onto a tray and Lola brought it over to them. When she set them down, David grabbed her roughly and placed her in his lap. Trained to not become alarmed and paid to be nice, she allowed it. Harry kept watch on the stranger; he did a quick visual check to his shotgun under the counter. There was going to be trouble tonight. Clancy sat across from David and wondered what he'd gotten himself into. The man was mean-spirited and a poor loser. He reached to pull his winnings toward him when David nonchalantly rested his pistol onto Clancy's forearm. Whether in jest or warning, he was not sure, and David said, "Been winnin' a lot for your younger years."

Nathan was simpleminded and not a sharp whip like Clancy, who wisely remained quiet, and he spouted, "Clancy? He's one of the best players here!" Nathan looked around the frozen room to gain agreement. "It's why nobody was playing in with us, sir . . . 'cause he's the best. Yesiree! Thank ya' for the whiskey, too, right nice of ya.'"

Clancy's face flamed and David lifted his pistol.

Instead of replacing it into his lap, however, he left it in plain sight, and he said nastily, "Carry on." He pushed Lola off of him and she nearly fell to the floor. One of the patrons, at Harry's nod, headed to the darkened backrooms and lit out. Nathan babbled on much to the annoyance of both David and Clancy, and Clancy desperately wished he would shut up . . . for his own sake!

Nathan asked, "Why is everyone so gloom all of a sudden? Especially you, Mr. Beck. I'm losing worst and you're the one in a mood."

"It's time to hold your tongue now, Nathan." Clancy warned and then wished he could take back his tone at the hurt look in his friend's eyes.

"Let's just play out this hand, then we'd best head on back to the ranch." David interrupted, "I'm just beginning to reclaim my money. I suggest you don't leave yet."

Nathan finally realized that this wasn't fun anymore and agreed with Clancy, "Yeah, boss is gonna make us muck out the pen tomorrow if we don't strike out for home now."

Nathan rose and David said, "Sit down." His hand went to his gun's handle. Nathan looked to his buddy for guidance.

Clancy said, "Look, Mister, Nathan can't play worth spit and we're expected back soon, we're just poor cowpokes. How about we finish another time?"

With an even-tempered, yet dangerous voice, David said, "Let's finish this hand and see where we go from there." He focused on his cards, which happen to be a winning hand, and Nathan lost his balance as he went for his seat and staggered onto David . . . causing his hand to become displayed on the table. Clancy closed his eyes and waited.

"Get off me you fool!" He shoved Nathan off and aimed his gun at him. It all happened so fast, no one was prepared. Clancy raised his arms, signaling the desire for wanting no trouble. Nathan was on the floor, scurrying away inch by inch.

"I had that pot, if you didn't mess it up for me. You two conspiring, is that it? When I win, you become clumsy all of a sudden? Well, I won't stand for no cheaters." He stalked up to Nathan and burrowed his gun into the boy's temple.

Clancy urged, "Please . . . take the money, all of it. Just let him get up. Sure he's clumsy, but we didn't wrong you on purpose." The door burst open and the barrel of David's gun changed aim. He smiled, the sheriff of all people arrived to save the day.

"Fancy you being here, Sheriff. You need to do something about this cheater . . ."

"Only thing I'm gonna do is something about you. Toss over your gun." Ed's gun was aimed at David's midsection and likewise, one would bear out consequences should one decide to pull the death trigger. Clancy took the opportunity to stand slowly, "Sit down, boy!" David tried to watch all three, the other customers in the place had long since moved to the safety of the far wall. David was good, but not confident in taking them all.

Ed said, "I don't want a shootout, but if you shoot me, Clancy will shoot you."

Nathan egged, "He ain't only good at cards, he's a fast draw!" David glanced at the gun in Clancy's hand, and Ed moved in a few steps.

"Your gun. I want it on the floor by the count of three. Then we'll see who fires first and last. One. Two. Thr—"

A gun skidded over to Ed's booted toe.

"Clancy, search him." David's eyes bored into Ed's, his look—lethal. Ed knew his kind, the kind that went out of their way to make trouble. What irritated Ed the most was that he was taken away from Lacey's presence, called out to perform his duty as sheriff. That's what he gets for giving his sheriff the night off.

Lacey was relieved beyond words when Ed was called away. She'd chosen this night to reveal her true feelings for him, but lost her nerve. When there was trouble at the Half Moon, she was thankful to have gained more time. She went to her boudoir and removed her hidden flask; she took several refreshing gulps and replaced it, tucking it safely beneath linen. Anything to numb her feelings was welcome, she'd even accrued some laudanum from Dr. Grover; it didn't come easily though, and she had to be very persuasive about having the pains in her head. But she would save that for later, for when Ed returned and she must heed to his controlling presence—she did not wish for the laudanum to go to waste. How many times had she considered leaving? If Lacey only knew of a place, she would leave everything, finally, behind without a care in the world. What she needed was new people, new surroundings, and a town that was so big she could lose herself in it. She looked at the plans of a house on the table. Ed was building it for them. It was a massive home, how he could afford it on his salary was beyond her. He must not realize that even though Lacey claimed all income from the restaurant, it was in his foe's very name. It was not hers, nothing worth having belonged to her. The darkness required her to light the lanterns in her room. She would sit under the moonlit window and take the laudanum when she saw the sheriff's shadow making nightly rounds on the town before he came to her room. Then she would be clouded with sleep until another day arrived. That's what she would do, but not before envisioning the plans of her future lifeless home engulfed in flames from the lantern.

Twenty-Seven

"I won't sign!"

Blaine strode back and forth in Mr. Tomlin's office. The old man repeated, "It's no use hanging on, Blaine. One way or another, you'll need to settle with this and grant Lacey her wishes. If you don't do it here, then she has every right under the present circumstances to take it to a higher court."

Blaine's body whipped around, "Don't think I don't know that. I just need more time!" He had yet to hear from his business partners. *What is taking them so long? They could vouch for me that I never spent time with Nancy. What's the hold up?*

"I understand." Mr. Tomlin was compassionate. This was the lowest point of his job description, and he hated to see this affect people such as the Jennings.

Before Blaine left, he stated, "For what it's worth to you, I'm not a cheat anymore. I would not do this to Lacey, that's all behind me, and for some reason, it's found its way to creep back into my life. Only this time, I am innocent!" The lawyer has heard many compelling arguments in his day, and he hoped he could believe Blaine. Something in his mannerisms spoke truth.

"Then we have to believe for the truth to be exposed, whatever that truth is."

"That's the day I'm living for, Mr. Tomlin. Good day."

Blaine stepped from the boardwalk. He saw, for the first time in weeks, Lacey across the way and wanted to call out to her so desperately, but he did not. There would be time enough to share his life with her later. He must go on with that faith, it was his driving force. He was glad he'd stayed silent, Ed Randall tucked her under the chin and then and his eyes caught Blaine's. Ed said something to her and she disappeared into the milliners shop, unknowing that the man who loved her truly was just beyond reach. The sheriff made his way to Blaine, who was still in front of the lawyer's office. It was evident he'd just been there. Blaine's stance was defensive and Ed's defiant.

"Finish your business with Mr. Tomlin?"

"I will not satisfy you with an answer; it has nothing to do with you."

Blaine turned to leave, but Ed wouldn't allow it to be so easy and kept on him. "If that's what you think. I've been meaning to have a talk with you Blaine, stop walking!"

Blaine stopped. *Better to just get this over with*, he thought.

Ed continued acidly, "I want you to leave town. Take Nancy Glorfield with you and just go. The sooner, the better."

Blaine forgot all that Andrew had instilled in him the past several weeks and grabbed Ed by the collar and shoved him hard against the rough building. "You don't know nothin' about Miss Glorfield, and you've no right to order me from town."

Ed jerked Blaine's hands from him and straightened up, a cocky laugh came from him, "You're right, I don't know about Nancy. You dug your own grave with that one. It's better than I could have expected, but you've no reason to stay here." He glanced toward the lawyer's door, "Now that you've signed, you're free to go."

Blaine wanted to strangle him, and Nancy and Chloe for that matter, just for good measure, for without them, all life would be so much easier. But for some reason it was not to be this way, and he said with pleasure, "I didn't sign, and you will not be rid of me so easily." He walked away and Ed cursed.

When Blaine was out of sight, he paid a visit to Mr. Tomlin, "Why didn't you make him sign?" The older man set down his papers and looked at the unreasonable man.

"I can't make him do anything, even if it's the sheriff who's doing the ordering."

Ed slammed his fist onto the table, perspiration lined his face. He wanted to be married to Lacey, tied to her forever. It was taking a lot of his time and energy keeping that woman in solitude. "He'll be back. When he comes, you have those papers ready."

"They are ready," he said evenly and was grateful to see the retreating back of the obstinate man.

Distrust was in David Beck's gaze as he accepted a dinner of roast, mashed potatoes, and even pie. Ed held firmly to it in challenge, and David asked, "Is this to be my last meal? I didn't kill no one."

Ed let go of the plate, "At least not in this town."

"Ah, you got me there." David sat on his cot in the jail cell and tore into the biscuit. "What's it all for?"

An almost regretful Ed replied, "I have a deal to offer you."

"A deal that's worth this supper?"

"I will offer you more than that. I'm prepared to let you go and to conveniently lose this arrest in my log book."

"Why would you do that? You're not as legal as I thought, Sheriff. Fact, I might even like ya' after all."

"It ain't your affection I want. I need you to do something for me—with discretion, of course."

Gravy dripped onto David's beard, "Of course."

"I have drawn up a map for you with instructions."

"Pretty confidant I'll do your bidding, ain't ya'?"

Ed gripped the bars, "It's either that or I convict you for murder."

"I haven't murdered no one." Holding up a crude picture with the word "reward" displayed across the top, Ed said, "This paper—says otherwise."

"Well then, you got me there. I'll do it, I get my freedom then?"

A knot formed in Ed's gut, "You'll get your freedom after you do this, after that, you're on your own."

"Which is the way I like it."

Ed left him; he refused to think of what he'd become.

⁂

It was late Saturday—the light in the sky was barely giving Blaine enough to see his chore. The path from his home to the lean-to was nearly cleared, and he hoped the snow would halt and give him easy access to his horse tomorrow. He fed the animal and filled a bucketful of water to take back; hot, steaming coffee would be his reward once leaving the coldness outside. The kettle whistled and Blaine retrieved it from the iron kettle in the fire. When he turned around, his door was wide open and a shadowy figure stood outside. Setting the pot aside, he reached, without taking his eyes from the person, for the gun on the mantle. He felt better once it was in his hands, "Who's there?"

David Beck stepped in, "I came on an errand for one Lacey Jennings. We can do this the easy way, or I could make it very painful and difficult for you."

"Get out of here. Lacey would have nothing to do with the likes of you."

David aimed his gun high, level between his eyes and sneered, "All you have to do is sign these." He thrust an envelope to Blaine. "Why is it so difficult for you to understand? She doesn't want to be married to you." David was at complete ease in the torment and bringing fear upon another. Blaine laughed, "I'm gonna have to disagree with you, see. It's not Lacey who sent you, but our so-called sheriff."

"I don't care who *sent* me. I get a job to do, I do it. That's all." He thrust them again in a weary fashion, "Sign 'em and I'll be out of this stupid place and on my way."

"I don't take to being bullied into this." Apparently, Blaine did not take him seriously, and David decided to show him that it was not an issue to be persuaded. With a flick of the wrist, he pistol-whipped Blaine to the back of the head.

David was enjoying the cup of coffee meant for Blaine when he aroused. Blaine focused on the yellow-white sheets of paper in front of him with a lead pencil when he heard, "It's all ready for you."

Blaine threw it away from him and David's temper was let loose. He kicked and kicked at Blaine until he was in a fetal position.

"You're . . . making . . . this hard . . . for yourself!" Both breathless, David stepped back. Blaine moaned and heard the click of a gun and then he felt cold steel behind his head, "Ya' ready to comply?"

Blaine nodded against the gun and crawled to the papers; he picked up the pencil and poised it to sign. He gripped it tightly, and with great force he plunged it into David's neck, managing to miss an artery. David hollered in agony, he was still pinning Blaine's legs to the floor. He pulled the pencil out. He grabbed Blaine's hand, shoved the paper underneath, and said, "Sign it!" He cursed, when Blaine did not move to do so, and David shot him in the thigh. When Blaine recovered from the shock of it, he rasped through clenched teeth in utter misery, "No."

"I ought to kill you anyway and save everyone the trouble."

"I'm willing to bet that wasn't in your orders to do so. It might look bad for the sheriff." Blaine grimaced in pain, it was so great, the searing, burning sensation made him almost unconscious, and even worse—he'd lost.

"You are right, it was in my orders to keep you alive and well. Apparently, you're leaving town." With that, Blaine Jennings and his broken body were tied up to the leg of the table as blood seeped onto the crude plank floor beneath him.

"You're free to go for the evening," Ed said and turned back to the papers on his desk. It was obvious by his vacant look that he wasn't reading them. Deputy Joseph Benton was put out. He'd been dismissed so many times this week he wondered why Ed even needed him. He mounted his horse and would head back to Jake's, thankful he had a place to go, thankful Jake had him take care of it when he was gone on his bounty hunting sprees.

Ed began to pace and wrung his hands together. He shouldn't have done this, what was he thinking? It all seemed so right and easy at the time; he shouldn't have trusted the outlaw to do this. Where was he? The man was scum and Ed was no better, he'd let a murderer free on account of his selfishness. He would go to Blaine's himself and put a stop to it. Blast it, all he wanted was the freedom to have Lacey.

Ed crept toward Blaine's. Smoke spiraled from the chimney, a lantern was in the window. It all seemed so quiet, Ed wondered if David came after all. Of course, if he didn't do this task, Ed was bound to report an escape and David would be hunted down. Maybe that was what he had chosen. Ed was relieved until he heard his voice come from the house. "We're gonna be here all night, Jennings, see. I got nothing to lose by sitting here all night in a comfy, warm place. It's awful cold out there, but as soon as you sign, I'm free to go my own way. It's your choice."

"I think you're gonna kill me either way." Blaine coughed; blood came from his mouth and nose.

"Well, we won't know that for sure until we're done here, 'course I owe ya' for stabbing me in the neck." He rubbed the puncture wound and bent down to Blaine and held out the paper mockingly, "Shall we see?"

Blaine kicked him, the table lurched, and he cried out in pain. When focused again he saw that he'd knocked his tormentor to the floor. David scrambled up and lunged at Blaine, his hands came loose, and he fought back. Both men were fighting like dogs on the floor, and when David got hold of his gun, Ed yelled, "Enough!"

Breathless, David said, "It ain't enough 'til I say it is. You told me this would be easy." He wiped his bleeding nose with his shirtsleeve and Ed looked in horror at Blaine—he'd done this to him. "He hasn't signed yet."

David aimed his gun and Blaine saw that he would make good his threat. Ed did nothing but wait, victory capitalized his rationality, and Blaine saw it in his eyes. He winced in pain and made his way to the chair and pulled himself up.

"Give me that blasted piece of paper." David thrust it before him and he took up the bloody writing tool and signed with a shaking hand. As Blaine signed, David cocked his pistol. Ed was not ready for that and saw that David was going to kill Blaine regardless. He should have known, but he did nothing to stop him. It was almost—almost a wish come true that he might be disposed of. Just as Blaine folded the paper and turned to give it to Ed, he saw David's gun in his face. A shot was fired. In the stillness, David's eyes bulged as he fell to the floor. Ed spun to the open door and Jake stood there, poised to shoot again if necessary. Jake announced, "You have some explaining to do, Ed."

Ed's face paled, "I didn't mean for this . . . I never meant for . . ." Jake's eyes raked over Blaine in his deplorable state, and to Ed he said, "I've been trailing David Beck for three weeks, and I track him all the way to my hometown in your very jail. How'd he end up here?"

"Jake, I've made a terrible mistake."

Blaine's eyes closed, he'd finally succumbed to blackness. As he was sliding from the chair, Jake stated, "I can see that. Let's get him to the doctor. You'll have time enough to explain what the heck happened to me later."

❦

It was summer and Lacey sat gracefully in a field of flowers. A young child of four or five walked his way and said, "Father, come play with us." Blaine left his place on the blanket, and after kissing the babe in his wife's arms, he ran to join his daughter. He twirled her around and around in the flowers and she laughed joyfully, her hair as black as a raven's, as black as Lacey's. He glanced back at his wife and her eyes were so filled with love for him and their family . . . and then he woke up. It was not Lacey's face before him as he'd hoped so earnestly for, but Jake and the woman called Nancy. She took away the cool, wet cloth from his forehead and looked ill.

"You've been dreaming again." His body protested to being awake, his view cloudy, where was he?

"What are you doing here?" He panicked; he did not want her near him.

"My, aren't you ungrateful. Someone needed to care for you and I volunteered, it's a wonder why!" He realized he was in his own home, that Nancy was in it taking caring of him as if she was . . . his.

"Nancy, leave us," Jake ordered. She snatched the bowl of dirtied water and left them alone. "I want to explain some things to you, Blaine, and then I'll let you decide."

Blaine looked at Jake warily. He'd never had a reason to dislike him and felt as though he was a fair man. He held a hand to his aching head and waited.

"Ed lost his reasoning."

"He wanted me dead."

"No, he went out there to stop it. He wanted David Beck to threaten you into signing. He came to his senses."

"So much so that he watched until I was seconds away from losing my life? I suppose he came to his senses so much that he's with my wife this very minute? Oh, wait . . . she's no longer my wife!"

It was beneath Jake Collins to get involved with relationships. The very thing he was worst at, but he found himself there nevertheless, due to his brotherly affection toward Lacey and friendship to Ed, "I'm here to ask that we keep this to ourselves."

The gall this man had, "Why should I do that?"

"For Lacey."

"That's good, Jake. Real good."

"Ed messed up, I've spoken with him, and he's going to leave you alone. Trust me. But I don't want his life ruined over this. I can't see that you would be of a vengeful sort."

"I only wanted a fair chance at Lacey and that was taken away from me when Nancy showed up with her claim." Blaine sat higher in the bed and reached for his aching leg. "This is what your sheriff let happen to me, and the thought of that man being let out of jail for this confirms my opinion of him. You know what? I'm just going to let Lacey find out for herself what kind of man he is. I'll not stoop to fill her in on it."

"That's a good plan, Blaine."

With amusement, Blaine said, "You say that to me, but you would have killed him if he did this to you." Jake rose to leave, his work was done.

"Yep, I reckon I would have. That's the difference between you and me, and it's all the proof I need that if it's at all possible for a man to change his ways, I'll be the first to admit that just maybe you have." Nancy must have had a keen sense on when to come into a room, because she chose just the moment they were done talking to see to Blaine. Instantly fussing over him, he said, "I imagine I'll be alright now."

She laughed, "Imagine all you want. Who's gonna take care of your horse, your home? You are without use of a leg for some time, if I leave you here, you'll starve and die, and then I won't have a father for my baby!" Jake's eyebrows rose at her misuse of words. Blaine caught it as well, "Your baby? I thought it was ours."

"I . . . it is. You know what I mean." She looked concerned for him, "I'm here for you. Just as you'll be for us." She glanced around his home, surprised at it. "We have a lot of work to do on this place. Why is it so rundown?"

"Wasn't planning on living here forever." He tested her, "I was planning on moving into a new one with Lacey." Jake smiled and made his way out of the room, Blaine was on his own. Nancy stiffened and looked at him stubbornly, "I suppose that's out of the question with you and she being no longer married." He held up his hand to shush her and she looked annoyed, but he said, "Someone's here."

"It's just Jake leaving." She heard a sleigh outside and rose to see. Her face fell when she saw the Reverend and Mrs. Jackson. She sat next to Blaine and waited for them to come and then go as soon as possible.

The sight of Jake caused Cameron to become flustered and she was angry at herself for this. In their brief encounter, her heart fell at how much he had changed. So cold, not a kind look about him. His unkempt hair and stained buckskin coat reminded her that he was alone with no one to care for him. Her thoughts were interrupted as she listened to her husband's quick greeting and farewell to Jake. They used to be so close. Life dealt such unexpecting blows and this very thought was with her when she walked in to see Nancy Glorfield bent over Blaine, adjusting the man's pillow, for heaven's sake! Cameron did not so much as glance her way as she made herself to Blaine. "We've been so worried about you. We only found out this morning what's happened. I'm here for you now."

Her tone would have dismissed Nancy if she was of normal mind, but she stubbornly remained possessively to his side, leaning against the bed as if to guard off Cameron.

"I have been here since yesterday. He's been fine in my company and well taken care of."

Cameron looked at Andrew in demand for action and he was quick to say, "It was very selfless of you, Miss Glorfield, to stay with Blaine. We are grateful to you for this, but it's hardly appropriate to have you stay here alone together."

She answered the charge impetuously, "It isn't as though it's out of the ordinary, Reverend." She lifted her defiant chin, "I'm going to have his baby in a few short months." Cameron began to pack some items for

Blaine, throwing them into her own carpetbag. She was shaking and seething inside.

Nancy asked, "What are you doing? Put those things away."

Cameron got into her face, "You have no claim on this man! I am sorry for your condition, but I will not tolerate his reputation to be on the line with you making for yourself a home where you are not welcome."

"Well!"

"You should go back to Lacey's or wherever you want to, Miss, but Blaine is coming home with us." Cameron clutched Blaine's belongings and walked to their wagon only to see that departing figure of Jake. A tear escaped her and she took in a deep breath, having shed much emotion this morning. Andrew wondered a moment in front of Nancy. His wife grew testier every day, this day, however, she was in the right, and he could not have said it better. Blaine looked at Andrew in surprise, the two women were fighting over him as if he were not in the room just now, and when he smiled about it, it hurt.

✦

The absence of Ed, for some reason raised concern. Not that she wasn't happy to be out of his presence for a few short days, but it was just out of his character to be gone so long without a word. Lacey couldn't help but wonder why he had not come to see her. The answer to that question might have something to do with the envelope Lizette just delivered. After much deliberation, Lizette asked shyly, "Did you know Blaine had an accident?" Lacey's heart fell, "What do you mean? Is he alright?"

"I heard he's doing just fine, the man who escaped from jail attacked him in his home." Just in case Lacey did not ask, Lizette volunteered, "He was beaten and shot in the leg."

Lacey looked appalled. Lizette tried not to show her satisfaction in seeing her employer's concern and said, "He's a hard man to keep down. You, of all people, should know that he'll recover nicely."

Lacey looked bewildered as Lizette left her. *Shot?* She pictured him last year helping the children with scarlet fever in this very hotel. *Blaine is in the prime of his life.* She assured herself, *It's as Lizette says, he'll be just fine.* She opened the contents of the envelope. Lacey stifled a cry, he'd done it. Blaine signed the papers. Why should it have affected her so? It was to be expected. She supposed it was truly over now. She was free—finally. As she looked around her room, she realized that it would take a lot more than singleness to be free; all she'd done was allow herself to be prisoner to someone else.

Cameron spoiled her guest, tearing herself between Blaine and Lacey—Lacey and Blaine. It was exhausting work and she was disheartened by the fact that Blaine and her truest friend were now divorced. She'd given up talking sense into either one and would just love them for who they were, for where they were.

"There now," she watched Blaine as he eased himself onto a crutch and began to take strides with it. He bumped into everything and she giggled, "I'm afraid our home is too small for this."

He looked at her, "It's also too small for me. I'll be going home shortly. Thank you for taking such good care of me, really, Cameron, you needn't have coddled me so."

Her baby kicked her and she said, "I'll need to get used to it sooner or later." He grinned and she said, "Andrew's home." She welcomed her husband at the door and retrieved his coat and packages. "It came!" It was the first she'd ever ordered a store-bought Christmas gift. She was off to the bedroom, adding it to her collection of homemade presents.

"You're looking good, Blaine."

"I feel wonderful. I will be out of your hair by tomorrow."

"Nonsense, that's not what I meant."

"I know it."

"I have something for you. The postmaster asked me to see that you get it."

Blaine tore open the letter from Jacob Pearce, his friend and business partner. He scanned his scrawled writing, "I knew it!"

"Good news?"

"The best. I remember now how I know Nancy. I met her once over a year ago, we sat together at a dinner party. I rebuffed her attentions toward me; she was sort of a loose cannon, very clingy. If it wasn't to me, she easily found herself another man to hold on to. I can't believe I didn't remember that."

"Well that doesn't make sense. She's only a few months with child."

"She must have known that I was back in the summer, I never saw her that trip."

"Then how would she know where you lived, where to find you? Why would she accuse you of such a thing?"

"There's one thing you don't know about me, Andrew. I am in partnership with the Pacific Railroad." Andrew was surprised, but his questions were still unanswered.

"Where does Nancy fit into all of this?"

"One of my business partners happens to be her uncle. Apparently, she believed I would be roped into this and she would gain some respect—and wealth."

"What are you going to do?"

"Have no worries about that, this will all being taken care of before month's end."

Andrew sat near the fire and gestured for Blaine to do the same. "Now, I expect you to tell me what really happened the night you were shot. I haven't been able to ask you with my wife clucking about you like a mother hen."

"What makes you think something happened?" Blaine shifted uneasily.

"You're telling me you were actually assaulted by a stranger and that Jake just happened to be there when it happened?"

"Jake had a bounty on him, you know that?"

"Yes, but I also know that David Beck was in jail, and no one escapes from Ed's jail."

"Alright, you got me." Blaine looked toward the bedroom, "I stake my life on this secret, Andrew. I can't ask you to hide something from Cameron."

"If it's something that doesn't benefit her knowing at this time, I'll allow it."

"Very well."

Twenty-Eight

Deputy Benton arrived at work and sighed heavily at the state of his boss. "Ed... wake up." Joseph removed the empty bottle of tequila from his grasp and sat him up. Ed did not wake up until Joseph tossed some water onto his face. He sputtered and swore.

"Sheriff, why don't you go home and lie down. I'll come and get you if I need to."

Ed shook his head adamantly. "No."

"But you are not well."

"Don't tell me what I am!" His voice slurred and he pointed at Joseph. "I'll tell you what I am... a good for nothing disgrace for the law, that's what!" He staggered to his full height, "Yes, I'm a miserable cuss and I'm retirin' my badge." He looked at Joseph's stunned face through bloodshot eyes, "I's just waitin' for you to come in is all."

"You're drunk, with all due respect. Come on now, sleep it off." Joseph led him through the back door that connected his one-room cabin, and Ed said, "I let 'im go that night, Joseph. I let that thievin,' murderin,' lyin' outlaw out of my jail! Yes. It's what I did, I'm a disgrace."

He fell into bed, Joseph nearly toppled over him. Befuddled, he wouldn't believe him, he couldn't. He idolized Ed Randall and everything he stood for; but he remembered his variant behavior over the last few months. *But the sheriff would never...*

"Just sleep it off." Joseph returned through the office to brew some strong and sobering coffee and ran into Jake.

"Where's Ed?"

Joseph grunted, "In bed."

"I see."

It dawned on Joseph that something was going on, and he glared at Jake, "What's goin' on? If something's going down, I need to know about it, don't ya' think?"

"Nothing's going down, as you so put it." Jake sat in Ed's chair and reclined his feet to the desk.

"Ed said some things just now. Mumbling that he let David Beck out. Why would he do that?"

"He wouldn't, Joseph."

"But he said he did . . ."

"He didn't."

That was the end of that and Jake waited around, drinking coffee, smoking cigarettes the whole day long until his pathetic friend awoke.

He was in his face when he did, "Geez, Jake!"

Ed scrambled up and held his head tightly. Jake thrust a tin cup of coffee his way, both irritated and amused. "I hear you're flapping your jaw."

"Not now, I just want to sleep."

"Oh, no you don't. You want to ruin yourself, do ya'? Then do it on your own, don't drag me into it."

"What are you talking about?"

"I'm a bounty hunter, bound to the law in some measure, you could say. I covered up a crime for you, fool! Now, get over it and stop drinking yourself into a stupor. I'm going to advise you to get over Lacey. You're a grown man, Ed. Can't you see she doesn't love you? She'll never love anybody again. You and that dolt husband of hers have ruined her. You've both done enough. I've a mind to take her away from the both of ya.'" When Jake saw regret in Ed's eyes from his scolding, he said, "Don't worry, I won't, but you leave her alone for a while, would you?"

Ed nodded, "Yes, I'll take some time to myself." Then he smiled shrewdly, "I don't need to worry about Blaine anymore anyway. Nancy has seen to that."

Jake swore, "You never give up, man."

"If she were yours once, would you?"

Pain flickered from Jake and Ed wanted to take it back. He'd had someone good in his life once upon a time and he let her go without a fight. Jake closed his eyes and blocked Cameron from his mind. When he opened them again, he said, "No, I wouldn't."

Joseph eased himself from the door, hearing every word. He was sick to his stomach. *Ed Randall? Corrupted?* No, he would get to the bottom of this.

When the deputy arrived at the Jackson's, he found that Blaine was no longer staying there. He rode back into town to see Lacey; at least he could tell someone what he heard and make right this story that didn't make sense. He knocked on Lacey's door and was shocked at her appearance. *What is this town coming to?*

"Joseph." She was confused.

"Mrs. Jennings, I need to talk to you."

Blaine entered the foyer of the hotel and looked around, he leaned onto his crutch impatiently. It was eerily quiet and that feeling sank in his gut as he remembered the last time it felt like this. Well, he had the upper hand this time, and all he needed to do was conspire—he looked around for Lizette, the ever faithful employee of this place. She met with him and was elated at what he had to share. Finally, something was going to happen to shake up the inhabitants of this place, and she was going to be a part of it. Lizette hugged Blaine furiously and clung to his neck.

"Whoa now." He took her from him with a teasing smile.

"I apologize, Mr. Jennings, it's just that I've always liked you, ya' see. I always thought you were best for our Lacey."

His hopeful eyes sparkled, "Well, you think that, and I think that, we just need to make her see it." He glanced up the stairs to her dwelling place.

Lizette volunteered, "She's a real big mess, Mr. Jennings. Never comes down from her room unless it's with the sheriff, otherwise, I'm the only one to see her." She looked at him accusingly, as if just remembering,

"But then, you went ahead and signed those dreadful papers, sir."

He contemplated a moment, "Don't you worry about that, Lizette. Just remember what we talked about and do your part." Allegation forgotten, she nodded wildly, "I will. You can count on me."

"I do count on you. Now, you best get back to work. I'll see you tomorrow."

As he made his way down the crooked steps, Blaine wanted to tear apart his crutches as inconvenient as they were. He stopped by the mercantile for some food before venturing home in the buggy he borrowed from the Jacksons.

Lacey strode briskly over to the jail. No one was there. No matter, Joseph told her where the sheriff was. She stormed into his room. From somewhere deep within her, a rush of strength and defiance was pulled to the surface. Ed looked at her with his aching head and knew by her fierce look it would not go away any time soon. As she spoke, the pain was so evident in her. She was beside herself with agony.

"Ed Randall, what have I done to you?"

Her grievous question surprised him. "Everything, and . . . nothing."

"How could you have done this to Blaine?"

"So that's what this is about?" He swung over to sit on the edge of his bed. "It's about him? The man who can't stay faithful for someone as precious and as wonderful and as beautiful as you?"

"No. I'm not talking about that, what's done is done with Blaine and me; I'm concerned for you. For the choices you are making. For what you've done to us."

"You've got nerve, Lacey. I'm trying to make a life for us."

"You're willing to hurt someone physically! Even if you weren't the sheriff, Ed, you would have never done this before. This is not like you. As for me, I've allowed you to make me into something I'm not."

"What? An obedient, loving mate?"

"Do you really believe that? Do you really want me as I am? Unhappy? Walking around as if led with strings by you? You've got to want someone to love you for who you are, Ed."

"You did once upon a time."

She shook her head. "We thought that was love . . . I'm not sure I even know what it is." Yet, she did, she'd experienced it recently, only to have it taken away from her, to be blindsided by hurt and pain once again. She looked at him through sorrowful and sincere eyes, "I don't love you, Ed. I loved the idea of us long ago."

He gripped her shoulders hard and brought her to him, as if it would be the last chance to hold onto her forever. Her arms stayed lax at his sides, she couldn't love him back,—she must let go, now and forever. It would be the only way she could save herself from further heartache and the only way to save Ed from disgracing himself. What she would do about Blaine and his injuries were beside her, she was just thankful she'd not laid eyes on him since finding out the ordeal with Nancy. Ed let her go. He was angry when he did it—but he let her go. Anguish tore at his features and his jaw ground back and forth as if to hold back tears.

"I can't live here in the same place as you. I can't bear to see you day in and day out, knowing how you feel, what we once were to each other."

She thought instantly of Jake and Cameron. Then she realized it was when Jake took up bounty hunting in the extreme to avoid her and Andrew. To avoid life. She did not want this for Ed, "I don't want you to go anywhere, I care for you. As a person, and a sheriff, and a special friend. You know me better than most."

He held up his hand to stop her, "You don't get it, do you? I can't live without you!"

"But you can! Give it time."

His only consolation and future hope was Nancy Glorfield. Maybe she would take Blaine away from this place, and he would wait and see what would become of Lacey and her need to be with a man.

"I could never stay if you chose another."

She looked down, "Then you'll stay, for I shall never care for anyone again."

"So this is it. You don't hate me for what I did?"

"I wish you didn't do it." At his look, she finished, "Even if it wasn't Blaine, I would never want to be the cause of someone suffering, you, of all people, know that."

He looked ashamed, "I know, it's why I went to his place, I came to myself, I couldn't let it happen."

"But it did."

He didn't want to tell her that Blaine almost lost his life; that would be better left unsaid. "Thankfully, it didn't." His eyes searched for her lips, he bent toward them, and she gave him her forehead.

"Good-bye, Ed Randall, don't be a stranger at the restaurant . . . a sheriff's gotta eat." She half smiled and left him.

Supper was carefully planned. Blaine escorted Nancy to her seat, her face smug and her attitude adamant. She felt her time has finally come to be acknowledged publicly and was thrilled that Blaine Jennings saw this as well. It would only benefit the man to show some respect for her, for she was growing bigger every day. Blaine hoped fervently that Lizette was correct in that Lacey stayed in her room. She assured him as he walked in, foregoing his crutch for the first time, that Lacey had been upstairs all day long.

Nancy said appreciatively, "Blaine, this is an extraordinary gesture." He shifted his attentions to the companion at his side.

"Only for you. I feel as though I am responsible for the first time in my life. Thank you for making me realize my duty."

Lizette served them each a bowl of French onion soup complete with a basket of crusty bread. Blaine poured the wine and hid his smile at Nancy's obvious anticipation of a glass and he said, "Maybe not for you, dear, probably not good for the youngin.'"

She flinched, "Of course."

They sipped their soup and the conversation erred on the side of caution, each wanting to say the right thing, set the right mood and tone—

even if each had a vastly different motive. Blaine wondered if he misunderstood the wire from Jacob Pearce, he began to sweat beneath his clothes. This night had to work; if it didn't . . . he did not care to think about that. His smiles became forced toward Nancy, he disliked her more and more. She was a spoiled, self-centered girl and he couldn't wait to be rid of her. He felt for her baby and prayed that the child would be properly cared for in the future.

Lizette served to them dessert and Blaine saw panic in her eyes. It was not going to work. Where was he? Then he saw Lizette's face relax and she left them. As she left them, everyone around heard an outcry.

"Uncle!" Nancy sprang from her seat and froze. "Whatever are you doing here?"

Samuel Porter was not a man to be reckoned with. Blaine had partnered with him because of that very reason. His intensity and cleverness at seeing fraud or uncanny behavior from those they worked with made him unpopular at times. His eyes narrowed in on his niece, who found her way to Blaine's side. She gripped him by the arm, "Blaine, take me out of here, my uncle . . . he's a terrible man!"

Blaine shook her arm from his, "This terrible man is my partner, as you well know."

Samuel put his breath very near hers and her proud face lurched from his. "I've been all over this side of the country for you. Well, for my sister, really. It appears you are making trouble wherever you go." He looked pointedly at her abdomen. "And you have the audacity to place blame wherever you deem necessary? Did you really think it would work, Niece?" He was so livid and talking deeply and into her face that spittle left his lips.

She wiped it away in disgust. She swung her body toward Blaine, "It was working! He wanted me. He got a divorce for me!"

Blaine's eyes widened, as did Samuel's, who asked, "You did that for this little chippy?"

"I did not do it for her. I did it for my wife. I'd do anything to make Lacey happy." Blaine looked around at the audience that seemed to grow in number. They had all stopped eating and gawked. Violet and Kimberly left their company in the saloon and listened to the intriguing dilemma. Chloe Dupree would sure be put out to not be witness to this. Samuel pulled Nancy out of everyone's view of entertainment and into a corner.

"You will make a public apology to both Mr. Jennings and his Lacey. You will come home with me, and I will gladly turn you over to your mother. Wait until she sees you! She'll send you off to a nunnery for sure, and that would be more than you deserve." He pushed her from him and roared, "Now, go pack your things!"

To Blaine, he said, "There are no words for the apology due to you. I'm terribly sorry that you ever met her, and I'm thankful you wired Jacob like you did. Her mother, only God knows why, was sick about her disappearance. Well, this time her running away has affected more than just family. I hope this won't interfere with . . ."

"Don't even finish that, Samuel. It all turned out for the good. Now maybe you can return home and do some good for our company."

"I can't wait to be home, so help me if she ever pulls this again, she's on her own. Disinherited she will be!"

Blaine didn't know he had it in him, but he laughed heartily, it felt good to do so. As he brought his face back to say more to Samuel, he saw Lacey briefly. She turned away slowly and walked back up those stairs that kept her far from everyone. Lizette had a conniving smile to her; she'd done her part. She'd brought Lacey down to fix the emergency in the restaurant only to find that she was captive to the happenings unfolding before her very eyes. Blaine would wait to go after her, he'd waited this long. He owed it to her and to Samuel, who'd come miles to save him from further destruction.

✦

It was late, but he went anyway. He tapped lightly onto Lacey's door, and when there was no answer, he was not surprised. Blaine withdrew the key Lizette supplied him with and entered. Lacey turned; she was sitting in a ghostly fashion under the window. It was cold and dreary and the moon shone across her hair and cheeks. "Are you satisfied?" she asked.

"Satisfied?" He was confused.

"That you've proven me wrong, that you've proven the horrible person I can be."

"How could you even say that? I only wanted you to hear the truth. I didn't believe you would accept it from my own mouth, so I chose this way to let you know. It was not meant to be malicious."

She looked at her hands, "I am so awful. I believed the worst about you, especially after what we shared together." Uncontrollable shaking and sobbing tore loose from her. She was exhausted, how much more could she take? Blaine knelt beside her feet, cradling her hands into his, and she asked once she calmed herself to do so, "You can't forgive me?"

Blaine looked away, "I can't say that it didn't hurt, Lacey. But I've tried to understand that it was with merit."

"That's what I've been trying to tell you. We cannot seem to put the past behind us, ever! It won't work, Blaine. I've told you once before, it hurts too much to love. I've given all I can give and taken all I will take."

Silence fell.

"Lacey."

"No, I don't want to talk anymore."

"It's too late for that." He looked at her and said with conviction, "I was so wrong to hurt you. When I left, I ruined my life and yours. I know you see me different, or you would never even remotely allowed yourself to be put in a position to be hurt again."

She looked at him with pain, "Am I going to be hurt again?"

He looked down. She'd pegged him with an unfair question. He refused to lie, "Probably." She expected him to say, "No, never again by me." Lacey smirked callously, as if to prove her point.

"Have you been hurt while I was gone?"

"Of course I have!"

"Was it my fault?"

"Yes!"

He sat there in the humbled silence. A voice of reason came to Lacey. Knowing she couldn't continue blaming him for everything bad that'd happened to her, she said resolutely, "Of course not."

"I only said probably because I want to be honest. I could wake up every morning and hurt you in some way. I'm merely a man and far from perfect. One thing I know without a doubt is that I will *never* leave you again!" His voice held such certainty she almost believed him. Withdrawing her hand, she folded them into her lap.

"Don't do this. Don't stop talking to me, I can see the wall going up as we speak. I need you, Lacey, I want you, and I love you more than I can handle."

"I don't want this wall to go up, as you say, but I can't help it or do anything about it, it's just there. I'm so afraid it always will be." He wanted to wipe away her tears and decided that moment he would. He crouched up to her, he listened to her breath catch, and watched her body stiffen.

She's afraid for me touch her.

He wiped the wetness from her cheek with his finger and stood so very near her. She looked up at him, almost as if granting permission, and he gathered her up into his arms and held her while she cried tears of uncertainty and confusion. Several minutes passed them by and both were depleted of whatever emotional restoration was taking place. He left her then, but this leaving was different—it wasn't done until she felt comforted and loved. "I will give you time, Lacey, but you must believe that I love you still."

Twenty-Nine

"How can he still love me?" Lacey cried. Cameron fidgeted with Lacey's clothing; she was making her come with them to the special holiday service at the church.

"Some people can love when there is something bigger in them besides themselves." She clucked her tongue, "These clothes are simply hanging on you!" Lacey spun at Cameron's guidance and snipped, "Well, I didn't ask you to take me, let alone get me dressed!" Cameron had enough of her friend's sympathetic solitude and strung tight the corset.

"Ouch!"

"Then hold still."

"What did you mean by something bigger inside beside yourself? That makes no sense what so ever. I suppose you're talking God or some such thing. I'll never understand." Cameron eyed her in the mirror, "You'll understand one day, Lacey Jennings, you haven't gone through all of this for nothing." She pulled up Lacey's locks and said, "Now then, what shall we do with this mess?"

⁂

Andrew pulled the sleigh bringing the three of them into the churchyard. Lanterns were all around and the snow falling added to the celebratory atmosphere.

"There's more people here than I thought possible." Andrew said and Cameron responded, "I didn't know we had so many families interested."

Not one to leave out an opinion, Lacey chimed in, "Maybe some are not interested, but simply made to come."

Andrew rolled his eyes behind her back and Cameron said, "Come on, Lacey, it's Christmas, forget about your troubles and let's see what Mary and the children have come up with."

As Lacey meandered up the steps, Cameron heard her murmur, "As if I had a choice."

The pews were filled and Andrew stared in awe. If it would only be like on Sunday mornings. Lacey was relieved to not see Blaine there, but then was disappointed that she had not. Cameron was backstage with the children, so Lacey sat with her cousin. Just as the lanterns were toned down in the audience and lit only upon the makeshift stage did Blaine arrive by her side and asked Andrew if he could join them.

Andrew scooted over, but not toward Lacey, away from her—leaving a nice gap between them just for Blaine. Andrew smiled annoyingly and wondered what she would do. Blaine removed his hat and sat next to her, and Lacey looked straight ahead. His nearness made her heart race. If she did look at Blaine, she would have read his amusing and mischievous look. She slid over more than was necessary. He whispered something into her ear, which sent shivers down her spine. She did not know from his hot breath or from his closeness, his clean smell wafted beneath her nose, flooding her mind with alluring memories. Whatever the reason, he'd unnerved her, and Blaine grinned victoriously.

Lacey watched the dozen or so children and something she had not felt for a time rose in her—affection. She smiled at the chubby little girl playing Mary, with her lisp she spoke to the baby Jesus. The three Wiseman, boys, sang words for away in a manger. Lacey felt herself immersed in the story. She'd heard it plenty of times as a child, but it never touched her as it did now. *You're being silly and too emotional.* She scolded herself and looked around as if anyone could read her poignant thoughts. As the little production ended, all present stood and clapped, encouraging further bows from the young ones.

Mary Keiser stated loudly, "Thank you all for coming. The children have provided baked goods and cider for all to share, please stay and visit." Her face was beaming at the successful evening and sent a smile to Cameron.

Blaine excused himself and her heart sank; he can't stand to be near her. But what about what he said in her ear? How beautiful she was tonight. She'd done a horrible thing to him, taking everyone else's words for his character, and she did not blame him one bit for his disinterest. It's all for the best, he could do better than her, and now he was able—he'd been wise to free himself.

"Would you like some cider?" She looked up to him and reddened, he sat down beside her.

"Thank you." She did not miss the fact that Andrew had long since departed her company and she was left alone. Now Blaine shared a pew with her.

"May I give you a ride home, tonight?" His voice held the anticipation he hoped it wouldn't but he could not change his auspicious tone.

"Why would you want to do that?" She sipped on the lukewarm drink.

"I am going to say to you that that is a stupid question." His eyes twinkled at her wide and surprised gaze.

"I'm serious, Blaine. You simply cannot forget what we've been through the last few months." She looked around conspicuously and there was silence.

He then stated, "Pray tell."

Fine! I'll play his game.

"Alright. You took me away with you. We remarried. We came home and a horrible thing happened. It was I who hurt you. I can't live with myself for that, not after I fell in lo . . ." She let out a gasp and looked like she was going to bolt for the door. "Excuse me."

He put down his drink and grasped her wrist, "No more running, Lacey. Why are you so hard on yourself? Why does every wrong in your world need to be punish, punish, punish? I am not upset with you, my goodness, woman, you need to learn about forgiveness!" His temper flared. What on earth was it going to take to get through her thick head?

"I forgive you. You forgive me, it's simple." Her eyes watered and she looked away.

"It's not so easy. I'm not like Andrew and Cameron or you. I don't know how to make that something in me love unconditionally—as Cameron puts it."

"You just need to believe to be forgiven, before you can let go of your entire past, just believe. Make yourself available to God, Lacey. There it is, simply put. It's up to you now." He grabbed her hands and pulled her up, "Get your coat. I'm taking you home tonight."

The ride in Blaine's sleigh was silent, but pleasantly so. Lacey pondered his words and he dwelt on his love for her. He walked her to the foyer and lit the outside lantern for her. She actually looked nervous to be with him.

"Good night, Lacey."

He left her, knowing he would see her tomorrow, for it would be Christmas day. Lacey turned into her bedroom door, back against it, contemplating, sorting her thoughts, or at least hoping so. She wanted whatever she was feeling now, for the feelings of her husband to grow and be nurtured. How was one supposed to diffuse these misgivings and be at peace? Lacey walked to the window of comfort and watched townsfolk come home from the program. Some of her guests even went to the church tonight and she heard them come in with the chime above the door sounding. They crept up the stairs with heady whispers and made way into their own rooms for the evening. Was she the only one affected so by the childhood story of tonight? It was just a story, a fairytale of some sort—wasn't it? She remembered the Bible Cameron gave to her and then she blushed. She'd long forgotten the poetic voice her then husband transcribed from it the summer. Lacey read Song of Solomon again and wondered if Blaine truly felt that way about her still. She thumbed through its crisp pages and her eyes rested upon the play acted tonight—the Christmas Story. For many hours after, she read and read until she couldn't get enough, until the dawn broke through her window, until she fell asleep on Christmas morning.

It was her turn to host the dinner party. She insisted as much before Thanksgiving, before her life took that extra downward turn. Lacey awoke with a start and at her rustled appearance . . .

"Oh, there's not much time!" She set aside the Bible in her lap and minutes later she entered the kitchen. Besides a bit of darkness under her eyes, Lacey looked as elegant as ever. She tried to shoo away the thought of Blaine coming for dinner, she wondered if he really would? She did not forget that it was on this night last year her wayward husband showed himself at her very door. She mused about it all day as she and Cook prepared the fanciful meal and decorated every inch of the restaurant. Lacey was all a flutter and eventually became edgy, and Cook, as always, took her moodiness in stride.

Cameron arrived with a radiant glimmer to her face, the results of a healthy pregnancy, Dr. Grover had told her. Andrew unloaded the gifts they had brought for their friends to open that evening, they had coveted their Christmas morning alone.

"I miss Thomas," Cameron complained to Lacey, who made her sit down after warning her to not lift a finger.

"Of course you do. Your brother will be home soon, you know how he likes adventure. He's not a man to stay put." Lacey absently encouraged, not really listening in her agitation and preparation.

"Why does he have to be gone on Christmas? He's so stubborn," Cameron continued and Andrew heard this, walked over to her, and tucked her under the chin with adoration, "Just as you used to be, darling." Cameron put on a stern look and commented to Lacey how beautiful everything was, "You've outdone yourself, Lacey."

"Hmm?"

"Never mind." The fragrances in the room made Cameron hungry and she watched as entrée after entrée was brought out to the tables.

Joseph ventured in, followed by Mack and Lizette, who whispered into Lacey's ear, "I told him if he wanted a nice supper, then he better bring me here!" Lacey laughed with her and Lizette added, "I couldn't bear stay home all day long knowing my friends were together without me."

With the Owens family and Joseph having arrived, and knowing Jake would not come, they were only left to wait for Blaine. When the last of the chimes went off, Lacey became alert to the fact that he was here. Blaine entered the dining area after shaking snow from his hat and coat. He had eyes only for Lacey, which amused Andrew. Cameron was just glad he was there so they could eat. Lizette took Blaine's coat for him, since Lacey had yet to pay him any attention, and hung it on the coat rack.

Blaine smiled boyishly at his wife's backside, *so she is going to play hard to get tonight?* He was undaunted.

Andrew said at dinner to Lacey, "This is quite a spread." He generously poured gravy over his mashed potatoes. Everyone else made their comments to the beaming hostess about the wonderful meal. Lacey had planned to spoil her friends and family, but for some reason, she really wanted to impress one person in particular.

"It's too bad we couldn't have a dance this year," she said after replenishing the empty plate of rolls with hot ones, fresh from the oven. Two years ago, the gathering was large, and Dr. Colvin had been there to play the fiddle. Andrew taught them a variety of dances from back east; no one mentioned Ed as having shared the evening with them that night, but Blaine assumed. As Blaine heard them recite that Christmas dinner, he couldn't suppress thoughts of loss and regret. He prayed for renewed strength.

Before long, Lacey dispersed from the kitchen with a large white cake with dark red roses decorating white frosting, declaring, "No, I did not make it, Cook did of course."

Out of habit, Lizette began clearing plates and gave everyone who wanted a freshly brewed cup of coffee with cream and sugar aplenty. Cameron wandered to the saloon and began to play the piano, others followed. It was the least she could do for not being allowed to help attend to dinner or clean up. She was limited to the few Christmas songs she knew from years ago, but that was all they needed.

The snow was not too deep and it was tolerable enough for travel, so Lacey did not understand why Blaine lingered on when she said good-bye to family after family.

Lacey said, "Well, it's getting late."

Blaine did not move. Too much enjoyment came from her discomfort—much to his shame. He finally produced a small package and held it out to her. Lacey looked more than surprised. "Blaine, I . . ."

"Just take it."

She did so, reluctantly and with embarrassment.

"I'll go now," he said, and she was relieved. "Don't open it until you are upstairs."

She looked at him blankly, so he queried, "Alright?"

Lacey nodded, "Alright."

After putting on his coat and making ready to leave, he said, "I would have brought you lilies, but there aren't any in December."

He tipped his hat to her and smiled as if he had just won something and left her gawking behind his back. Shutting the door after him, she wasted no time blowing out lamps and rushing to her room, tearing open the small package. A note fell out, and she read it before opening the box.

When you wear this, I'll know it's because
you want to be my wife and my lover.
Forever and always, 'til death do us part.

Crying, she lifted the tiny lid and gingerly pulled out of the velvety cushioned case, a gold-banded wedding ring.

"Oh, Blaine, what are you doing to me?"

Thirty

He heard the accent of the Frenchman, Jacques Dupree III making a speech from underneath the roof of the post office. Red, white, and blue banners surrounded him and Jake shook his head as he saw people gathering in the cold to listen to the arrogant man talk as if he knew anything about this town or its people. He continued onward and out of town with his packhorse in tow. It would be a long while before anyone saw Jake Collins again.

It was a busy and bustling day. Mid March brought confirmation of the coming spring and families were out frolicking in the sunshiny weather, even if it still gave them pink noses and ruddy cheeks. Andrew silently congratulated Mr. Dupree on choosing today of all others to make his speech, he talked elaborately, bringing hope and vision for the town to anyone who would listen. Andrew whispered something into Cameron's ear and, after nodding her agreement, went to find Blaine, who she knew was getting a haircut after passing him by earlier that morning. Andrew waited with the crowd and clapped alongside them to be of good manners when Mr. Dupree finally finished his speech quoting great politicians. He smiled and bowed to the people as if he were royalty. His daughter shone elegantly beside him, smiling beautifully, and she set her eyes on Blaine, who had just arrived by Cameron's request. When he did not return her smile, but rather looked at her as if she were a common, spoiled girl, she remembered she despised him.

Insolent, horrible man!

Reverend Andrew Jackson took the platform, much to Mr. and Miss Dupree's aggravation.

"May I have your attention?"

Conversations ceased and people turned with respect to Andrew. He clasped his hands together, and in his preacher voice, which proved successful to attain one's attention, he said, "I propose a nomination for Mayor."

Mr. Dupree, who had not left the stage, said in a tight voice, "But that's impossible, Reverend." He swept open his arms to the curious crowd, "We are voting today." Andrew did his best to ignore him politely and continued, "We all know that Blaine Jennings is a kind and honest man."

A Lily Among Thorns

Murmurs went up amidst the people. Those who knew him now either for the first time or had known him before he left four years ago could plainly see that he was now a churchgoing, changed person. There were those who hadn't made his acquaintance at all, but heard about his past sins against their beloved Lacey and took it upon themselves to judge and dislike him.

Blaine, the subject of all the upheaval, looked at Andrew. He was both baffled and honored at the outrageous suggestion.

"But he left his wife!"

"He's been trying to get her back, Moron!"

"I don't trust him."

"He's a God-fearing man now."

"Hold it!" Andrew interrupted, and Mr. Dupree was clearly piqued and stepped back into his rightful spot, seeing his advantage, and certainly not one to waste such an opportunity.

"The Reverend is correct, people."

Andrew, Blaine, Cameron, and Chloe all looked at him astonished.

"Father!"

"I do believe it only fair to have Mr. Jennings run against me. I would have it be a legitimate vote. I will not take office by the way of self-appointment." He bore his eyes into the sheriff's. Ed Randall's face heated and he glared back at the audacious man.

Mr. Dupree turned toward Andrew, "I trust that you will make a way for ballot boxes?"

"Certainly, as soon as Blaine Jennings has a chance to speak."

Jacques Dupree did not expect this, but managed to step aside as graciously as a stiff corpse could. Blaine was at a loss for words, but an overwhelming desire to have this town be all it could be and reach its potential for godliness, growth, and community gave Andrew a bright smile.

Blaine began by citing examples of past community-oriented events and plans for this and for that. He honestly didn't know he'd had it in him, but he shared his heart. When he spoke, it was genuine, and he looked into people's faces, not above them. Mr. Dupree shuffled his feet during the speech, and Chloe bore holes into Blaine with her spiteful eyes. When he was finished, and people were left to make up their own minds, there were still talk and questions brought forth on Blaine's commitment and trustworthiness. Blaine was about to answer the questions addressed to him when Lacey stood beside him.

A hush fell over the crowd. Not many had even seen them together before, and a nervous chuckle escaped from Cameron and she clamped her gloved hands over her mouth. Blaine looked ready to fall over as he heard his wife's words, but could not fathom for the life of him that they were actually coming from her.

"Ladies and Gentlemen, must I remind you of who took care of your children when they had scarlet fever! It was this man alone who labored beside the doctor. He has taken it upon himself to be involved with this community, never asking for anything or expecting praise for his actions. He's the only one that I know of that visits with and spends time with Dr. Colvin. Does this sound like a selfish man to you? I have seen him with my own eyes help Widow Hampton load food stores in her buggy when others have walked on by. Blaine helped me, when I was my wicked self, get unstuck from mud and saved me from being struck by lightening. He is a man of . . . a man of compassion and a man of action." Her words suddenly caught in her throat; she held her chest with the palm of her hand and backed away. Ed stalked off, stunned, and feeling as though his world had finally been turned upside down, never to be righted again. Lacey proceeded from the boardwalk, grabbing whoever's hand it was that was extended to aide her, and she ran back to her hotel. Blaine started after her, but was mobbed by the crowd, who were cheering and agreeing, pleased by his wife's sticking up for him.

After being reminded of his selfless acts, they seemed to forget quite easily what they had been holding against him only moments before. Jacques Dupree and Chloe were seething under tight smiles and tried in vain to gain back the stage. Andrew announced for all the men to go and vote, then looked into his wife's eyes and smiled a smile of supreme hope.

Ed went to the telegraph office and removed from the breast of his coat the letter he'd recently received.

"I need to send a telegram."

Blaine Jennings, the Mayor of Lincoln County, ate at Lacey's whenever he possibly could. He was kept busy, but not busy enough. He hoped and assumed that his duties would increase when winter was over for good and traveling and decisions could be made for the town. For weeks, Lacey resisted seeing him after speaking up for him the way she did. He knew it was her pride, but that day, hope came to him and he clung on to those moments like never before. He refused to give her the allowance to be the way she was. She was too precious and no more walls were going to erect. As those weeks turned into a month, Lacey was no longer discomfited when Blaine ate there. She actually seemed to enjoy his company, and he even became so bold to think that she missed him if he didn't show. Best of all, he thanked the Lord, was her attendance and curiosity at church. She came sporadically, and Blaine knew even that was extremely hard for her to do. He was thrilled to see Lacey listening attentively without mock or disdain to her cousin's preaching. It made for some great conversations between them when she chose to sit with him and join him for coffee or dessert. Those times made his day and he walked with a lighter step.

Being mayor, Blaine had to swallow his dislike and past jealousy and work with Ed Randall on occasion. Both men were stiff with each other and never said more than they needed to or stayed longer than necessary. So when the sheriff left a message with Blaine saying that he required a meeting with him, it naturally brought on a dreaded feeling upon his day. He went to the jail to find both Ed and Joseph there, waiting for him.

"What can I do for you, gentlemen?"

Without any infliction of welcome or kindness in his voice, Ed said, "Have a seat, if you'd like." Neither had ever addressed the other by name; to do so would be admitting the other's existence. Ed continued to lead the meeting once Blaine took his seat. "I'm leaving Lincoln County."

The statement was short and simple and left many thoughts going through Blaine's mind. *Why? Is this temporary? Forever?* No more would he have to look over his shoulder when Ed was in the same area or a short distance from Lacey. He looked from one man to another, "What do we do with you being gone?"

Ed tapped a pencil on his desk, clearly wanting the discussion over. "I'm leaving for good. Joseph will take my place, if it's all the same to you, or you could have yourself another *election*."

"No need for an election, Joseph has more than proven himself capable." Blaine tried to stop himself from asking, but curiosity and hope for finality pressed him too much to not, "Where are you going? If you don't mind my asking."

A full minute must have passed before Ed replied, "I'll be working for the Pinkerton's."

"An Agent," Blaine said, more so to himself than to them.

"Yep."

Blaine rose, etiquette would tell them to shake hands, but that would never happen, not with Lacey between them.

"Well, good luck to you . . . and to you, Joseph. I look forward to working with you."

Ed shook his head smartly with a crooked smile, as if to say he wouldn't receive anything from Blaine Jennings, not even the wish of luck. With this new news circulating about town, Lacey wanted out of guilt to say good-bye to Ed Randall. But it would never do, there was nothing to say except good-bye, and she reckoned that had been done long ago. Ed spent his last night in Lincoln County with a full night of cards, drink, and women in his honor. He left Lincoln County on the first day of April. Other than the few who missed him, life went on as usual.

Thirty-One

The coming of April meant to Cameron that spring was soon to follow. One wouldn't know it, however, with the snow still glistening under the sun's glare. But never the less, it's when Cameron started the countdown for when she could plant her garden, pick flowers, hear bird's singing, and this year . . . meet her son. Andrew came up from behind her as she looked out the window, wishing for her favorite season. "Look at you, so round and so beautiful." He rubbed her blossoming belly, she felt him smile against the back of her neck, giving her pleasant shivers.

"Are you ready to go?" he asked.

She nodded. He brought the thick woolen cloak from the coat hook and placed it about her figure, then helped her down their wooden patio steps to the waiting buggy that would take them to church.

Hymns were sung and Andrew took his place behind the pulpit. Cameron touched her abdomen as her son wiggled and elbowed her; she smiled at the beloved man in her life. The reverend's message and words were about relationship, covenant with one another. Without looking around, Cameron knew where everyone was sitting, knowing exactly who had attended this morning because she'd greeted them at the door alongside Andrew.

She was truly blessed by the people in her life, daring herself to imagine what circumstance and destitution would have awaited for her had she chosen another path. When Andrew dismissed the congregation, people readied to leave and go to the warmth of their homes, to enjoy a day of rest and sup with family. Cameron went to discuss their dinner plans with Lacey, who had insisted on bringing the major portion of it today, explaining to Cameron that she needed her rest. As she spotted Lacey in the pew she knew her to be in, she saw her friend hurriedly wipe tears from her cheeks, clearly not wanting anyone to witness that she had been touched or moved by the sermon. Cameron looked away lest she be caught noticing her pride and gave her a moment. Blaine was off shaking hands with fellows and left along with them to claim horses and buggies. Cameron stepped alongside Lacey and silently helped her with her coat.

"Thank you," Lacey said and sniffed.

"I look forward to your company tonight, Lacey."

For some reason odd to Lacey but not to Cameron, the simple words broke her. She sat on the pew and wept softly. The small sanctuary was empty now and the two were alone. Cameron sat next to her and gently rubbed her upper back in comfort, as a mother would a daughter, and waited.

"I can't do it!"

Cameron searched for words of encouragement and faith. "What exactly is it that you cannot think you can do, Lacey?"

Lacey took her hands from her wet eyes and looked around, "This! Church . . . family . . . relationship. All of it!"

"I suppose you're right."

Lacey looked sideways at Cameron, not expecting that for an answer, "What did you say?"

Cameron shifted so she could sit somewhat comfortably on the cold, hard pew and said, "In ourselves, we cannot do much of anything. Did you hear Andrew when he said that we need each other? We can be accountable to one another to walk in faith, and when we waver, which we will, we have one another to help build us up again. I believe that's what a church family does."

Lacey merely nodded at Cameron, who continued, "It most likely doesn't make sense right now, but it will if you continue to seek the only One who is able to fill all of the emptiness in your heart, every lonely thought. Every rejection you have ever experienced can be taken away."

"I don't want to go back to Blaine until I'm like you. Until I'm right for him."

"So, you do want him in your life?" Cameron asked hopefully.

"Yes."

"It's not as if you cannot go back to him until you feel you are ready. He wants to be your helper. He would do anything for you. He's not exactly where he would like to be either. None of us are. It is a daily process, Lacey, not an overnight one."

Lacey righted herself, "Well! I certainly didn't expect to feel this or anything else at church!" She smiled imperviously and Cameron knew she was finished with the discussion at hand, but she had something else to add, "One thing that would be the biggest and greatest start for you, Lacey, is to forgive."

She watched her friend's face closely and her eyes darkened. "You will never be able to give yourself fully to Blaine if you don't forgive him. Trust might have to come again, I understand that, but please, don't live in unforgiveness. Your parents, forgive them, Lacey, what's done is done and you can only go forward in good things if you let that anger and bitterness go."

Lacey smoothed out her satin skirts. Blaine popped his head in the door and asked if they were coming. Cameron said they were. After he left, Lacey's gaze lingered on where his presence had just been. She gave Cameron an affirming nod and asked, "When did you get so smart, Cameron Jackson?"

Cameron smiled, "As I said, it's *day to day*, and I do have my bad ones. Today happens to be a good one where I could share my heart with my dearest friend. I love you, Lacey Jennings."

Lacey opened her arms to receive Cameron's love and embrace and they discussed food for supper, and to Cameron, she said, "I have made ample amount of chicken pot pie to ensure some for the rest of us."

Both women laughed and Lacey patted Cameron's tummy, "How's the little girl doing?"

Cameron cocked an eyebrow at her and replied, "Like me, *he* is getting bigger everyday, and is bruising my insides with the heels of his tiny feet."

❦

There was a curious knock at the door during supper and Andrew wiped his mouth with a cloth napkin and rose to answer it.

"Thomas!"

He'd prepared himself for his sister's mushy welcome and scolding for being away for so long, her never knowing when she'd see him again or if he was ever coming back. She held him tight.

"Cameron, let the poor man in."

"Poor man indeed! He should not leave like this, he needs to settle down and have a family!" she said with implication, as if he weren't in the room.

"I can hear you." His boots scraped across the floor as she ushered him gently toward the table. He said a gruff greeting to Blaine and Lacey, then stated, "I just came by to tell you I was home, didn't plan to stay." Cameron gave him a warning look, "Well, that just won't do!"

Blaine teased, "Better do what she says, Thomas. She's pretty fierce and bossy with that little babe in her tummy."

Others nodded their agreement and murmured warnings. They feigned fright when she glared at them all; she stood stubbornly and adamantly behind a vacant seat. Thomas took in Cameron's bulging middle and said, "I almost forgot about . . . that."

Cameron smiled, "*That* is your nephew. Now come and sit before their warnings to you are proved true."

The dinner guests scrunched closer to one another and made room for Thomas, who was clearly uncomfortable and wished for the life of himself that he did not come to visit his sister on this day. Cameron never asked her brother what he did in his long absences; she did not want to know. But she sensed something different about him during his brief and wordless time and was only left to wonder.

※

The following week, Blaine arrived at Lacey's and waited to be served by her. He watched her move from table to table with her visiting and welcoming smile to those who frequented her hotel and provided her livelihood, the livelihood that was meant for him to provide. She was beautiful and elegant everyday, but today he noticed her eyes were softer, her smile for him was of comfort and not just one of appeasement. Today was the day the town began building him a new house. A mayor should not be living in the shanty of a home, according to certain upstanding citizens, and he did not argue with them. Lacey looked at him shyly, and it was not a look that he was used to seeing on his wife. She would hardly be described as a demure woman by anyone. As usual with or without her presence, stirrings of love and longing began in him and he smiled when she came toward him finally with a pot of coffee and a fanciful china cup. He visited with her while she poured and she him, it was pleasant and she told him, "I will return soon with your meal." Her face reddened as if she was blushing.
  The feeling he felt was not one he could describe with words when he saw as she departed from him something sparkle on the finger of her left hand. Blaine shook with emotions of shock, awe, joy, and love. When Lacey delivered a meal to another table, Blaine grabbed her hand as she passed his table, as if to never let her go again. He said nothing, but pressed her hand with his ring on her finger into his and stared hard into her porcelain face, wanting to be sure he read what he thought he did. Her soft eyes lingered on him and she smiled brightly. He stood and she said, "What about your lunch?"
  He said, "I have everything I need right here."
  Lacey looked around the restaurant full of people and, knowing her husband to be unpredictable, said in a low tone, "Blaine, please . . ."
  He shook his head slowly and his eyes lit with a fiery passion that unnerved her and shuttered the core of her being. He smiled wide and announced, to her horror, "Stay and finish your meal, everyone. Lizette is

more than capable of taking care of you." He was still holding Lacey's hand and people looked upon him curiously, as did Lizette. Blaine looked at Lacey, his lily among the thorns, "I am taking my wife home now."

As they stepped into the spring air, she had a terrible thought, "But I'm no longer your . . . wife."

He silenced her with a kiss, his breath lingered upon her. "Did you really think I would let you go so easily? Mr. Tomlin left out a minor, but necessary portion on those appalling papers. Convenient, huh?" He kissed her once more, "You are my wife in every way."

Love for her husband rose up in her, as did chills of awaiting contentment. Lacey Jennings allowed herself to be taken away from her work and set in her husband's carriage—knowing full well he meant what he said, "We're going home."

Tate Publishing & *Enterprises*

Tate Publishing is committed to excellence in the publishing industry. Our staff of highly trained professionals, including editors, graphic designers, and marketing personnel, work together to produce the very finest books available. The company reflects the philosophy established by the founders, based on Psalms 68:11,

"THE LORD GAVE THE WORD AND GREAT WAS THE COMPANY OF THOSE WHO PUBLISHED IT."

If you would like further information, please call
1.888.361.9473
or visit our website
www.tatepublishing.com

Tate Publishing & *Enterprises*, LLC
127 E. Trade Center Terrace
Mustang, Oklahoma 73064 USA